# L OST
# A MONG
# U TTERLY
# G ORGEOUS
# H UMANS

## LAURIAN TALER

GONG PUBLISHING TORONTO

L OST
A MONG
U TTERLY
G ORGEOUS
H UMANS

BY LAURIAN TALER

© GONG PUBLISHING, 2015
ALL RIGHTS RESERVED

www.gongnog.com

ISBN 978-0-9919867-7-4

Dedicated

To all those who discovered
that the sole seat of the soul
is in the mind.

Actually, in the minds.


To the main adults in my life:

Minodora, Viorica, Hari,

Xenia, Laura Sophia.

## CHAPTER 1

That's right, I'm a monkey. Actually, more than that: an ape. Or, if you prefer a scientific description, which in my case is warranted, because confusion is not a good thing in the many legal and other connotations of today's life, I am a Simian, a Primate, an Anthropoid, and my species is named Pan troglodytes, if you really want to know. What you call in common parlance, a chimpanzee. Clear now? Not quite? Well, then what about knowing that I am classified as part of the family Hominidae, which sounds awfully close to the word humans, something definitely related to you humans. And if you want to go even further, guess what? Our DNA, that is, yours and mine, differ only by about 1.5 %, which is to say, just by a fickle. Which is to say, not by a lot. Some of your brethren even wanted to put my species in another category altogether, not as a Pan, but as a Homo. Do you see the implication? If I were a Homo like you, and you were a Homo like me, why the heck all these lifestyle differences between us, as if we didn't have the same everything? OK, OK, not exactly the same everything. I can't speak. I don't have a voice like you have. I had to wait for the advent of the more powerful computers in order to be able to communicate more fully with you, my so-called more evolved cousins. You might know what was said some years ago about the act of creation. Not the cosmic one. Not the one by Koestler, implying anything and everything in the world of art. Just the literary one: given enough, but really enough time, a typing monkey could write all of Shakespeare's works and then some...

Well, who said that didn't know two things: how powerful the modern computers have become on one hand, and how smart I look, when I stand on both my hands, or hang by one other member. Should I elaborate? Now that I have introduced myself very shortly, because indeed, I am rather short, except, of course, in my hair, I will swing directly to the branch of contention: I am lost! Utterly lost! Or, to return to the copious title with which I provided you, I am lost among utterly gorgeous humans. Wait, wait, don't start yet to presume that I am a reversal or continuation of Tarzan, or that I might be some pigmy King-Kong, because I'm not. I am simply Onkey the monkey, an unusual primate in that I cannot separate myself for too long from the keyboard, and now you may understand where my name is coming from. How I got here from where I came is also unusual, and it is a good way to spend your time for a while, if you want to find out. You will see that it is worthwhile to spend this time over my story, because you will be able to learn everything that there is to learn from a monkey like me. I will answer the main questions of who, what, when, where and why even without repeating myself, which is not exactly the way most writers, especially journalists, are concocting their stories. You may understand that, even if I am monkeying around from time to time, I tend to go straight to the subject. That's how I am and although my main features come from copying other behaviours here and there, I am still known to be myself in all respects. So, who am I? I am Onkey. What am I? I am a monkey. A chimp. A champion chimp. OK, a chimpanzee. When... when what? It's hard to answer a when what question. Let's adjust it a bit. When did I become ... Onkey the monkey? That 's harder to say in a short sentence, so stay with me and I'll tell you. I might even answer where. But for why, you'll have to be really patient.

It all started in a zoo. At least that's what I remember, after waking up from a rather heavy sleep. Somebody somewhere might have darted me with a too strong tranquilizer, because I don't remember anything about before. You and maybe other beings around me might have thought that I either came from a tropical or equatorial forest, or was incubated artificially on the zoo premises, but I doubt that you know the rules of the game. Game, like in playing by the rules, not game that you shoot. Recently it has been decided that wilderness monkeys, which are shot sometimes, are not supposed to be used for experiments. Not in a lab, or a zoo, that is. From this, you smart-ass reader might have figured out already that I am not wild. And how could I be?

I am exposing myself to you so completely, I show through this writing such a naked truth that everybody would realize it doesn't matter that I am in front of everybody just like that, stark naked. Well, not as naked as you when you shower, 'cause I have my, hmm, excessive hair. Not that I mind that, but you, you are SO NAKED, I sometimes have to cover my eyes seeing you. So, what is the opposite of wild? Yep, civilized. I am a civilized monkey, and I'll prove that to you in no time at all.

The blurry view in front of my eyes dissipated after a few days and I became soon accustomed to my oikos, that is, my location, a large, almost comfortable cage with a few leafless trees, some ropes and other accoutrements for dangling and swinging like a real monkey. There was a rather older, gentle monkey in a tree beside mine, but there was no Jane. I mean when Tarzan got lost, he sooner or later found a Jane around, for whom he had to show not only all his manly physical features, but actually save her from the dangers of the wilderness. In my case, niente. Nada. Gar nix. Rien. Nicevo. Nothing. What the heck, am I going to spend the rest of my time on this planet without a Jane? After all, what else counts in life, if not this? Even a monkey can realize that life without love, romance, or at least a little mating, is not worth living. I was having a smattering of pity on the old, gentle monkey beside me, but I thought that at least his time has passed. And again, I told you that I am as straight as a beam of light, when not bent on its way by some gravitational force. (I did not put this last sentence in without reason; I thought it might give you a glimpse to the fact that something really unusual happened with me while I was asleep). Anyway, not for any attempt at some form of discrimination, but the old one, in my aesthetic sense, had his hair much too long, growing in clumps in some parts and rather unevenly gnawed in others. However, it was his eyes' depth that bothered me, as if the old chimp appeared to have stored not only a long litany of complaints against the world, but also some authentic wisdom. Of course, I couldn't easily accept that: although I had just woke up, I had a genuine feeling of superiority over everything and everyone. To be honest, which I don't know where it was coming from, because actually honesty and superiority don't much go together, I was in a way preoccupied about my feeling of superiority, wondering whether it stemmed from the fact that, indeed, my position on my tree was about two feet higher than that of the old pal on his tree. He might have tried to prevent hurting himself too badly if he were to fall off his branch. You never know who and when happens to shake the tree against your own pleasure. The Spartans seemed to have a predilection for shaking trees with old ones in them over a ravine or glen. As for my superiority for everything else around, it must have been provoked by the fact that there was nothing, really nothing complicated enough for me while looking around with my curious, vivid gaze. Except, maybe, the tablet. It was dangling eerily from a branch close to me, and I was able to notice that it slowly changed images on its screen, as if inviting me to study it. The strange thing is that I never saw a tablet before, or at least I don't remember, as my memory must have been thoroughly cleaned and re-loaded. However, a tablet it was and I didn't feel at all unfamiliar with it, as if it expected me to do something with it. I believe the feeling of "complicated" came from the change of the images, some not at all shocking to me, as they were just places and parts of a forest with all kinds of animals in them, that probably being also part of my instinctual heritage, but there were other images, of small, geometric constructs with drawings on them, which seemed to intrigue me. I felt an urge to put my hands, my fingers actually, on them, and press. I looked around, slightly delaying my decision to grab the thing. The old or maybe just older chimp was making himself look busy with a sort of shirt that he kept putting on top of his head and taking it off again and again. Some current of fresh air, that I found later was coming from an air conditioning unit, continued to maintain the dangling of the tablet while turning its screen away from me from time to time, which made my urge to grab it even more ... what? Urgent! But I needed to also be careful. Prudent. Yes, prudent was the word. Because, I don't know, while gnawing at the bark of a branch with my teeth, I had a strong feeling that some eyes, other than my neighbour's, were following me from somewhere.

It took me a while to temper my sensible desire to show off my canines to whomever was spying on me, even to turn my butt unceremoniously, only I wasn't able to ascertain where was the presumed gaze coming from. So, no direction, no butt turning, not even canines and incisors displaying. I scratched my armpit with a mixed feeling of confusion and indignation. Although I couldn't say that I am afflicted with it, still, a matter of privacy must be somehow respected. Even if my private parts are, well uncovered. I guess that that is a matter of expediency, not privacy, if you know what I mean. I genuflected several times on the branch where I was supposed to feel comfortable and I even brought out a number of light screeches, sign that I was really frustrated. But then, I thought to myself, what the heck? Let them spy on me; I have no secrets for them anyhow. Well, well, well, that was not quite true. I felt there were some secrets about me that I must not share; only I was unable to determine what were those secrets. Know thyself, the ancients among you were saying, and maybe then you'd know if and what secrets are inside of you. Well, I did have some secrets; all champions have them. But now I had this urge. If I could grab that damn tablet and start figuring out what to do with it, this urge would certainly be diminished. Except the urge for a Jane. So, why more waiting? Jane or no Jane, I just had to stretch my hand and grab the tablet. We'll see then who is complicated, the tablet or me?

So I did stretch my hand. The tablet reacted to my grab by stopping its change of screen images. Instead, a small rectangle appeared, grew very slowly as if trying not to scare me, and within the rectangle a growing, longish head with greyish hair on its top but not on its face was benevolently smiling to me, making eye contact with an inquisitive look, after which I saw the slim lips parting, a row of rather small, equally ordered teeth showing up, and heard a warm, velvety voice greeting me with

"Hi, Onkey! Welcome to the club. I'm Jane. Jane

Lost Among ...

Doogirl."

Should I tell you that my jaw fell off toward my knees? I consider myself rather macho, but this was too much even for me! You might want to know why, and I'll tell you, if you are patient. First, this is how I found out that my name was Onkey, because she was obviously talking to me, wasn't she? Secondly, she said her name was Jane, which was exactly the name I had on my mind since I woke up. It's true, this Jane was DIFFERENT of what I had in mind, but she seemed to ape me pretty well, and although she looked a bit over her prime age, she was still a primate nevertheless. And to tell you the truth, which truth is always imprinted heavily on my front lobes, what I had in mind with Jane was just that: to prime mate! What was on her mind is a bit harder to guess, although I found out that in her prime time, she had a humongous capacity for other primates, or prime mates. And I was a primate, after all.

I gave out a large smile, not much different than the one Fernandel used to give in all his films (and I might perfectly explain to you later how a French comedy actor got to be one of my main imitators, or vice-versa). Jane reciprocated, as if she were behind the plastic material of the screen, which seemed incredible even to my so-called limited chimp mind. I passed my tongue over my excited lips. I pushed them forward and smacked them together, making a soft, kissing-like sound, and I even made some short movements with my tongue the way I might have seen a serpent do, but then I realized it was too early in the game. I had to show some gentleman-ship, not that I really knew what that meant, but I do have an instinctual way with good manners. After all, I'm a champ chimp, or at least that's what I think about myself. And what you think about yourself counts. Not earls. Counts. Seeing that she reciprocated to my Fernandel-esc smile brought me back to my cautious senses. How come she is aping me? She cannot be in the tablet, can she?

The feeling of being spied returned all of a sudden. It was like her eyes were watching me not only from the screen of the tablet, but from somewhere else too. Too. Two, two. Eureka! I put two and two together, and also I still counted only to three, that is, me first, Jane on the screen second, and a hidden Jane somewhere else as third. I remained with the impression that it could have been a fourth somebody, at least to let me feel fulfilled to four with my two-two count. Boo, there was a fourth, the old one with the shirt on his head.

Now don't get me wrong again, apart from the fact that I tried to convince you so far that I am not an ordinary chimp, it is well known by those who keep on looking into the strangeness of some beasts that the horses counting in the circus are simply tricks perpetrated by their masters, but a raven can count to seven. S-E-V-E-N. (That seems to be a fraud too, because, mind you, seven is made up of only five letters. Don't blame me if I'm suspicious by nature. I am part of it, ain't I? And then, it's a matter of survival in the jungle.) So, was Jane hidden somewhere close by and real, not just an image on a

13

screen? Really, what does it mean to be real? After all, I am real, although there seems to be something unreal about me, about my capacity to have all these thoughts and desires and questions, especially the last one, about what is real. What the heck is reality? I certainly did not want to mate with just an image, maybe that is something others are interested in. I want a real Jane, be it a hairless chimp or what she actually seems to be, an utterly gorgeous human. I understand that this statement might make you ask, how come do I have this developed sense of aesthetics, not to say anything about the fact that I appear to discriminate between so called cousin species by calling one a hairless chimp and another one an utterly gorgeous something else. Maybe Jane knows something that I don't. Maybe she wants to tell me more than welcoming me to the club. What club? How should I answer her? In the excitement following her greeting, I forgot to react reasonably. What should I do? She communicated with me. I should try to communicate back. It's true I moved my lips in a certain way, but that didn't seem to be enough. The sounds that I uttered were nothing close to saying something meaningful, although I felt I myself was ripe with meaning. Since her greeting, just a fraction of time might have passed, but I was at the end of my wits with what should I do, when the Jane of the screen turned her head to the left slowly as not to startle me and showed her fine profile, then raised her left hand, in which she had a tablet like the one I was holding. A tablet in a tablet, that might confuse even the bravest of you. But not me. Maybe only if the tablet in her hand would have shown a woman holding a tablet in her hand, in which case... You got my drift. I sensed that an important moment was coming. I was all eyes and ears, I wanted to start dancing on my branch, but I realized that I needed to focus for what was coming. Jane brought that tablet closer to her face, pressed a button, I forget where because her profile still mesmerized me, and the screen lit up with a full set of keys. To make it short for you, it became a keyboard. Jane said, slightly smiling, but with enough importance for me to understand the gravity of all of what was coming:

"Onkey dear, you will be able to tell me lots of things by using this keyboard as a means to communicate with me."
After a small pause, to let everything sink in really well, she added, with the same fabulous, velvety voice that made me wish I had her neck, her vocal chords, and especially her tongue in my mouth:
"Don't worry, your mind is super-capable of the task. You'll type in with over eighty characters per minute from the beginning, the XMON chip implanted in your skull will take care of that."
Holy mackerel! Now she tells me! I'm not a chimp any more, I'm a chipmunk! Nah, that's something else. A chip monkey. A monkey with a chip in my head. Should I be glad or what? I pushed my right hand toward the screen, intent on getting the keyboard, but as soon as I touched it, Jane 's face appeared again magnified. In an insane moment of libidinous attraction, I started licking her face,

but it was just the screen that my tongue was touching. Jane smiled more openly, but her image diminished from the screen as if her head was moving away from me. I tried to be faster than her, sticking out my tongue between her separated lips. Again, just plastic. Heck, this was a plastic female! Where was my flesh and blood Jane? What should I do to make her show up as non-virtual? My virtuosity with fast reactions was not helping me here.

I started to sense directly, with my lips, the difference between real and its opposite. I didn't need an encyclopedia of philosophy to give me the definition of what real is. For the moment, the Jane of the tablet, the Jane in the tablet was definitely not real enough. Frustrated as I was, I still thought that behind the image on the tablet, there must be another entity, the real one. I started to laugh. I realized that I wasn't quite so lost, after all. I had a chip to make me super. With it, I'll find a way to get to her, to the real one. She deserved me, as I deserved her. Ah, the real one. An utterly gorgeous human. And on top of that, an utterly gorgeous woman. What a delight! Turkish? Nah, that's locum. I didn't feel so much out of place any more. Lost among...? I bet I'll have to change the title to "Lust among..." How would it sound? I don't know, I can't pronounce this word, lust. I just feel it in my bones. OK, not in all the bones, just in one. Hey, don't laugh at me, it's not funny! If you want to know, that's actually my bone of contention: what is the difference between lust and love? As if you knew. Here you are lost too. But I'll go further and make sure to find out before Jane is coming back with some restrictions about my feelings. Not for anything else, but I like a little rubbing there where it counts, that is where love and lust meet with meat and befriend each other, until there is no more bone of contention. Speaking of which, out of all these synonyms for what a bone of contention is, the best way to put it for an antagonism is screw loose or at variance. Nowhere will I be in agreement with the saying, all is fair in love and war, because nothing is fair there. Everything is in antagonism in love and war. Not because I am antagonistic by nature. On the contrary. I always, or almost always, agree with nature because I am part of it. I am nature. I am natural. Agree, disagree, antagonism, at variance, screw loose, bone of contention. It all brings together two bodies and then depart them from one another to bring them back again. Isn't this the yin and yang, or to sound better, the yang and yin of everything? So, if Jane will disagree, I will pursue the matter in a totally gentlemanly way and make her agree. Yin that becomes yang, that turns into yin. Dialectics of nature. Don't they say, the pen is mightier than the sword? Or, if you are still of the sceptical type, at least its scabbard? And you know how accepting a scabbard can be. Don't you believe me? Just wait and see.

Lost Among ...

CHAPTER 2


So you know by now that Jane wants me to get "in touch" with her by keying in my thoughts, not much different from what Facebook is asking everybody when insisting on their website to fill in at the question, "What's on your mind?" I don't know what Face book would do knowing what is on my mind, maybe sell it to the highest bidder, or to multiple bidders, but they won't find out anything from me. Not because there is nothing on my mind. There is plenty, just why should I tell them when I am so shy? Nobody is supposed to know that I am obsessed with the other gender, or should I call it the other sex? Not for any pathological abnormality: it just happens to be my natural way of being, together with eating, drinking, and sleeping. Oh yes, also swinging. However, it looks like Jane knows that on my mind, or more exactly, in my skull, there is an XMON chip implanted recently. No, you can't eat that chip; so far it doesn't go with fish, only with monkeys, that is, with me. That's why they, and I'm yet to find out more precisely who they are, call me Onkey the monkey: with the help of the chip I am supposed to know lots of things that the utterly gorgeous humans know, and use a virtual keyboard on the screen of a tablet to communicate with them. My deep feeling is that these gorgeous humans (and I don't even know if all of them are that gorgeous, but Jane definitely is), probably know much less than I know, because their brains lack this wonderful chip. Call it intuition, call it old grandma's superstition, it must be that there is something missing in these humans' capacity to understand themselves and understand their brethren, or, well, cousins from the jungle of Africa where we all split from a trunk.

So far, 'they' appeared to be only Jane, but not the real one, not the needed one. Jane is just an image on the tablet that introduced herself as Jane Doogirl. I know who Jane Doogirl is, who doesn't? She is nice. At the beginning, she tricked me. I fell for her. When I tried to lick her face, look for some bugs in her hair and embrace her, it didn't happen. But then I figured out that she was not real. My hunch is that there must be a real one too, possibly the one who is spying on me from some hidden place. I am only guessing, but it goes with reason that there must be a device that follows me. I didn't figure that out yet, although I am supposed to know a lot of things about human technology by way of my implanted chip, which seems to have deposited in it a humongous amount of human memory. As for my own memory, so far is zilch! Tabula rasa! Scraped, clean slate! Clean tablet! They must have had to brainwash me to allow for an easier connection between my brain and the chip. And then they gave me, guess what? A hanging tablet in a tree! Isn't that a duh? But some faint instincts remained, and this is where my urge for Jane, or a Jane, of whatever origin, seems to be sourced. Ah, my instincts! I vaguely feel like going back to them sometimes, but the chip doesn't let me fall into that nostalgic trap. Since I came to this thing with the nostalgia, I do have the impression that if I am careful, I might use this strong feeling in my favour in my relations with Jane, real or not. It's just a matter of how masterfully I may approach her in my writing to her. It looks like the dumb humans who got me the chip were incapable of doing anything good about my vocal chords and their control, so I am limited to punching the tablet keys in my frenzy of conveying what I want. I started with demands. I typed, as Jane has shown me through a short and effective video:

"Banaaaaa. Banana. I want aaaa – a banana."

"Be careful with pressing repeatedly the keys. Oh, you learn fast."

"Heck, where is the banana I asked for?"

"Look, it is coming."

Indeed, a banana appeared on the screen. I jumped up.

" Stop the rubbish! That's a virtual banana. *You* eat that!"

"You didn't specify that you wanted to eat it."

"Am I a monkey or what? I eat bananas."

"What else do you want?"

"Please, don' tease me. Banana first."

"It is coming, be patient. "

A slightly mechanical noise followed soon, and a drawer appeared through a gap in the wall at the back of my cage. There were two bananas in the drawer. I abandoned the tablet, which had a hook for letting it rest pending on a branch. With a few swings and jumps, I descended to the level of the drawer, close to the floor. I stretched my hand to grab the bananas, but I encountered a larger, more hairy hand trying to do the same thing. Par bleu! I have forgotten that I was not alone. Oldey, my comrade-in-cage, had longer arms than mine, and was not as sleepy as he appeared at the beginning. His arm showing up in front of my arm stunned me. He was the first with his hand at the drawer. He grabbed both bananas, flicked them in the air over my head, and caught one straight in his open mouth. The other banana landed in his left hand. I turned to see what else was going to happen, but obviously annoyed at the fact that I was so clumsy. To my astonishment, Oldey turned his back at me, and while departing, flicked again the remaining banana over his shoulder with a short movement from his wrist. It landed this time, due to the masterful throw, right in my hand. Oh, yes. Oldey was giving me a lesson. He was not only older, he was faster, stronger, and, lo and behold, he was also altruistic. It made me wonder if I was prepared to do the same thing in case I were the first to grab the bananas. With the banana once engorged, my thoughts went back to Jane. I took up again the conversation through my typing:

"Why did you send me two bananas?"

"I sent you one banana only. The second one wasn't for you."

"But what if I grabbed both of them?"

"Would you have eaten both of them?"

"I really don't know. Maybe. But what if Oldey ate

both bananas?"

"I know Oldey. He wouldn't do that. He has class."

"I thought we have a classless society here. Don't bring it in now."

"So you try to be funny? You know what class I am referring to."

"Oldey class? Maybe a lot of brass. Gosh, he scared me."

" Even after you have seen how your neighbour had reacted?"

"Big deal, he wanted to show off. But jeez, he was fast."

"So, would you have given him one of the bananas?"

"I guess it would be a matter of how hungry I was."

"Are you still hungry?"

It was at this moment that I realized I could turn the conversation in the direction I wanted. I took a deep breath, I made a sweet face, pushing my lips in the form of a circle, and bent my head backward a few times, closing my eyes. A soft, squeegee sound came out of my mouth. Did I look convincing enough? I typed:

"I am hungry for you, Jane!"

"What, do you want to eat me too?"

"Oh, no, Jane, I want to mate with you."

"Silly Onkey, you are a monkey!"

"So what? Monkeys mate, don't they?"

"Yes, but I am no monkey. I am a human."

"And?"

Lost Among ...

"Humans mate among themselves, but they first love each other."

"I can love you, can't I? And you can love me."

"It's not that simple. But yes, I do love you. You are my cousin."

"I'll prove you that I can love you. I'll write you a love letter."

I heard Jane laugh softly, and then the word PAUSE appeared large on the screen. I thought Jane felt tired or needed time to consider my cheeky proposal. But I felt elated. I scratched my right cheek with high expectation. As far as I could realize, the chip in my head was a marvellous thing, transforming me in a miraculously capable creature. I was not only strong, I was smart too. I knew how to communicate with the humans. I could recall even tiny details from their history, which wasn't a big deal, just a lot of killings around, using some terrifying tools for that purpose. After all, apart from being utterly gorgeous, able to speak and have some technological prowess, these humans were kind of plastic-like, were weak, maybe shy, because they were hiding somewhere, and tired fast, not to say anything about not being able to swing through trees. Well, it's true, there was a Tarzan once, using the vines hanging everywhere for swinging about the forest in search for his Jane. I felt superior, looking down to whomever was below my branch. Not that there was anyone else in the cage, except Oldey. Well, he might be stronger than me, but obviously, he didn't have a tablet, and that made me suppose that he didn't have a chip either. Just a funny shirt that he kept putting on top of his head, maybe that being a sign of depression. Poor Oldey. I'll have to approach him and show him some consideration, before he decides to tear me to pieces. The humans call this diplomacy, although I don't think I need a diploma for doing that. But now I have to focus on my love letter. Cousin Jane, because she claims that we are cousins, needs to be wooed properly. It looks like mating between cousins isn't such a great idea, too much similar genetic matter floating around in the kiddies. Only we are cousins in some other way, aren't we? My other relatives, the simians, were first branching out somewhere on the evolution tree, the humans branched out later. Maybe that's why the humans were left down on the ground. For them, no more branches. They must have fallen off. No wonder, with such short and weak arms! How about telling Jane that with my long arms I could reach her and embrace her even while sitting on one of the tree's branches? Nah, that would be an exaggeration and she wouldn't fall for that. What about saying, "I'll pick you up from anywhere and carry you to the highest branch?" Not a good idea, some branches might not support her. I don't even know how heavy she really is since I never saw her "face to face". What if she is over-dimensioned and I cannot handle her? I don't even have a nest up here in the tree. Since she is ground-bound, should I just invite her into my cage? Firstly, it's not only my cage, I share it with Oldey. Ménage à trois? Nah, she might be strictly monogamous. Heck, I forgot to ask her if she is involved with somebody. Not that it would count much for me.

Lost Among ...

What it counts is that she already said that she loves me, and after step 1 comes step 2, that is, mating. Secondly, her perspective from my side of the cage's bars might be quite different than from the other side. It has something to do with freedom. How is this correct, freedom, free-doom, free-dumb? There must be several possibilities. Is someone with free-dumb free from being dumb, which is not my case since I cannot speak, I can only type, or just plain stupid for being free, which again is not my case, because I am obviously not stupid and not too free, since I am in a cage. Then there is free-dome, like a huge cover over freedom, which obviously would limit freedom, and freedom itself, like a kingdom where everything and everybody must be free. Free, but submitting to a king. Then, freedom is like being submitted to... freedom. Is that OK? How free? Free from the tree - is not good! Free from the green stuff I mostly munch and like, not good at all. Free from Oldey? He just gave me a banana, and even if he still sticks to that shirt of his, he seems rather like me, only older - and a bit stronger, I believe. It's good to feel that you are not quite the only one in this world, that there are similar entities like you, simian or not. As for free-doom, I don't want to go there, whatever goes with doom gives me the creeps. It totally ruins my appetite for life. It sounds like a free - for all Last Judgement, which is too anticlimactic for me. Oh, heck, I must return to my letter writing to Jane. I'll start typing and see what comes out:

"Dear Jane, my head is full of you, for you and by you. Since you appeared in front of me (on the tablet), I

26

could hardly sleep. Actually, I dream of you with my open eyes. This lack of sleep has given me hallucinations.
I saw you between bars, thin and tiny and trying to come toward me. I saw you on the ceiling, floating like an angel, trying to cover me with your large, white wings, protecting me from a lot of garbage that was falling from the sky. Of course, there was no garbage falling, just some memory fragment must have slid out from my chip about how kids are acting when visiting the monkeys at the zoo. I even saw you hanging from the other tree, and, shock of shockers, you were looking like Oldey, my neighbour. See what is the lack of sleep doing with my visions? I see you everywhere, eyes closed or wide open. I even hear from time to time your velvety voice, only that it sometimes sounds like a bell. Not ringing. Banging. Bang, bang, bang. It makes me feel like being in a sanctuary where somebody officiates a ceremony. A marriage ceremony. We are holding hands and stepping slowly, naked, toward a pulpit, but a huge banana separates us and then we cannot hold hands, and then I try to look over the banana and I don't see you any more, because the banana has grown so humongous that I cannot reach beyond it to see you. Then some unknown force peels the banana and drops it right under my step and you know what happens next. Terrible, terrible, it's like re-living all those banana farces ever concocted in the Hollywood. This XMON chip might be marvellous, but I experience too much slippage from my memory. I cannot focus enough at you, maybe from the lack of sleep, maybe because this is how infatuated with you I am. Oh, Jane, I feel like a Tarzan

Lost Among ...

that lost all his powers. I cannot swing any more, I cannot jump from branch to branch, and I cannot even hang happily head down from anywhere. I used to look good hanging. I look miserable. Les Miserables looked good by contrast. When you told me that your name was Jane Doogirl, I was taken even farther. First, it was clear that you were good in all respects, but then my memory clicked in and I realized who you really imitate, even if just on the screen. The famous Jane who grew up with a monkey doll and fell in love with chimps. That's when I realized that you are for me and I am for you, even before you declared that we first have to love each other. You said something about complications, I quote you saying, 'not that simple', which I understand if there are other chimps in your heart, or even utterly gorgeous humans, as Tarzan was, but then you recognized that you love me, and effectively declared me to be your cousin. I know that cousins shouldn't hanky - panky, what with not enough diverse genetic material, but I didn't want to go that far. I mean, if you don't want babies, that 's fine with me. I'm not interested in starting a Humanzee or a Chimp-man branch, even if we could overcome the great barrier, although that might be considered progress in some eyes or fickle minds. We could adopt, or we could be baby-less, and enjoy ourselves even more or longer. I'd be prepared to build for you a love nest here. I am concerned with not knowing your weight and my material resistance calculations are a bit rusty for the moment. As for Oldey, who is my neighbour, he has shown a definite level of altruism in flicking me the second banana, so

28

maybe we could be both nice to him for a while, till he grows even older and then I could take over completely. If you have any difficulties with this arrangement or there are any other problems, let me know and I will think them over with the help of my chip. There is nothing a chip chimp like me cannot solve. Oh, I forgot. I don't know your religious disorientation or b-affiliation, but I hope that in the age of the implanted chip you might have overcome a child-age brainwashing and are now displaced from religious brouhaha. If not, I am convinced that life with me will prove totally liberating in this respect too. Oh, my Jane, you made me insane, I can't wait with you to mate... Isn't that poetic? My romantic feelings have no barriers, notwithstanding that I am waiting for your acceptance answer in a cage.

Your totally infatuated for ever,
Onkey."

I had to wait for a long time to get an answer. In the meantime, life seemed to become unbearable, if not for the daily parade of humongous crowds of utterly gorgeous humans, utterly interested in my swinging on the ropes, on my balancing acts in the tree, and in my visits to show my best behaviour to my neighbour, the perennially depressed Oldey, who continued to set his red and green shirt on top of his head with the same amount of disdain for the visitors. I think Jane needed to carefully plan her answer, and maybe she even thought that if I saw more humans in front of me, I could forget her. But finally, a sound from the tablet advised me of her

Lost Among ...

arriving email, which I read with trembling hands on top of my tree. This is what it said, in rather plain English:

## CHAPTER 3

Just in case you forgot or jumped directly to this part, I shouldn't leave you in the dark: I had been expecting a response to my love letter from Jane. I've fallen in love with her since she appeared to me on the screen of a tablet hanging from my tree. The fact that I am also hanging most of the time from a tree shouldn't surprise you too much. You see, I'm a monkey, a chimp, to be more precise. The zoo, which is my residence, took the liberty to operate onto my brain and implanted in it a very advanced chip, the XMON. I shouldn't complain, because this chip makes me more than super-smart. It makes me a wunderkind of the Hominid family. It's all in the memory of the chip, loaded with everything that humans know up to this point, which is not much. I mean, they know practically nothing about my ilk, or about me and that's exactly why they made the implant. They try to dig into my personality, into my soul. They also want to know, on my account, if they could do similar implants into their own brains, so that they would become smarter. Smarter than themselves. Does that make sense? How can you be smarter than yourself? Maybe if you consider that we are all stupid most of the time, and smart only from time to time. So, you get smarter than when you are stupid. That way it does make sense. Anyway, the terrible thing that happened with this operation is that my own memory got erased, which is bad, because now I am still physically a chimpanzee, but with an encyclopedia in my head. I only know about monkeys what the humans gathered so far. It's true, my intuition, or something with this name, hits me from time to time, as if some ancestral remnants of what has been bred in my bones slip into the chip's memory to remind me that I am what I am. Still, since my encounter with Jane of the tablet on the tablet, and since she taught me how to communicate with her by using the tablet's keyboard, I feel a desire, a call, a crave. It's a hunger, a longing provoked by Jane. She is so attractive, so utterly gorgeous; she has that 'Je ne sais pas quoi' which follows me everywhere since I saw her on the tablet. So I wrote her a love letter, trying to convince her to be mine. Not that I didn't try some more persuasive action, like kissing her and putting my tongue between her thin lips. It didn't work out, and you shouldn't be shocked, as it all ended on the surface of the tablet. I mean, the screen. So far she seems to be just a plastic figure, but I know, I really believe deeply that behind that image there is a real Jane. After all, she presented herself as Jane Doogirl. And Jane Doogirl is a famous chimp researcher. She loves chimps, and I being one of them, implicitly she loves me. Not only that, but she actually has recognized it in our conversation. So why shouldn't I have her? I told you that it took her some time to respond. Finally, I can put it to you. If you are like an impartial judge, what I really don't quite expect from a human, even an utterly gorgeous one, because even judges aren't totally impartial, you may see why I am so stressed out at reading her letter. Here it is:

"Dear Adam Onkey,

(that's the name she gave me, since I can only communicate with her, so far, by keyboard)

I try to understand your large effusion of sentiments toward me. It is not the first time that I had feelings like this come my way. Most of the chimps that I encountered had been so nice to me in every way, and I am proof of it, because I have none of the accidental mutilations that others who came in contact with chimps have suffered.
I don't know if this is just a huge dose of luck or that my charisma has something to do with it. Anyway, to inform you completely in this regard, I need to add that it is not only from the contacts with you, the chimps, that we, the women, are so many times abused and even mutilated, if not directly killed. It seems to be in the blood of the beast, and when I say beast, I include those that you so naively call utterly gorgeous humans. With a rather thick layer of aggressive misogyny, the human males, as well as males in other species, behave as if everything is acceptable in their quest for reproduction and power. In our case, that quest translates in some level of romance and its other misnomer, love. Without trying to generalize, and also

knowing that your understanding is very high because the multiple interpretations coming your way on the basis of whatever is included in your memory chip, I can say that love, and more specifically, falling in love, is something that confuses the mind and makes many act as if blind.
I mean to say that it is a very difficult transformation suffered by the participants. It mostly needs the right perspective to allow those who fall in love to retain a level of balance and not fall into... making big mistakes. This is why I hesitated to respond immediately to your lovely letter. Even I, with my experience coming from the many years of diverse relationships, have a hard time expressing precisely how to show you that there are limits to our relations. Well, for one, the barriers that you know exist between species, even those that are very close genetically, can hardly be traversed. You may be of the opinion that those barriers are not that rigid, and indeed, there are several examples of such crossing over. But those are mostly exceptions to the rule. On top of that, we humans have a rigid moral code that excludes intimacy that goes beyond the pale with other animals. What means beyond the pale? Of course, it means different things to different people, but in a short way, it means to stay within the fences of your own home, of your own turf. That does not mean that we do not have a large capacity to maintain and develop strong feelings for animals in general and for our closest relatives in particular. Only it is not the love that you believe to have toward me. That is, it is not sexual; it is not related to reproduction. The same way that you may feel toward your group, we feel

toward our own group, and do not accept inter-species mixing. At least not yet. Who knows what is going to happen in the future, with all the legal and less legal experiments going on in the labs of the world, trying to modify genetically both plant and animal species? What is the size of a barrier described as just 1.6% difference between your genes and mine? Is there something definitely not passable in that 1.6%? We are still scratching our collective heads at this question. I, for one, with my life experience, am inclined to keep myself a defender of your species as it is, without the mixing that you and Oliver, the chimp that walked, have tried in our regard. Oh, yes, you are not the only one to attempt sex with the gorgeous. In his case, it was a Janet, not a Jane that he approached cupidinously. I will have to help you change your mind in this area by offering you to continue the conversation from now on with Janice, my niece. Not only is she closer to your generation, she is a brain surgeon and an established scientist in the domains of artificial intelligence and ethical experimentation, so she probably would be much more capable to make you understand what are the complications derived from such 'encounters'. I really hope that you will develop the proper attitude and relationship with her. As for me, I have retired from the world of 'encounters', believing that other generations of gorgeous humans will help you and your species survive while trying to understand both you and us better. Adios, my cousin, adios, my friend and purported lover."

Lost Among ...

With this last words, Jane 's face appeared for the last time on my tablet, smiling sadly and making a good-bye sign with her hand, after which a much younger woman's face appeared, also smiling, and saying softly:

"Hello, Onkey, I am Janice. We'll talk about many things from now on. I actually know you quite well, since I participated both at the creation of the XMON implanted in your head, and at the operation itself. I am a doctor of medicine, a doctor of computation in artificial intelligence, and a doctor of philosophy. Still, I know just a small part of what you know, because XMON is such a wonderful chip, having much more in its memory than I could gather in my studies. Are you ready to accept me as your companion in this process of better knowing each other?"

To tell you the truth, I was a bit shocked. After reading Jane 's letter, at which I didn't even have enough time to digest the content, and after her abrupt departure, to be thrown so directly in a new and certainly unexpected from my part contact with a younger and so sophisticated woman, it was, well, disconcerting in some way. Maybe my rebirth as a wearer of the XMON made me have an imprint upon my mind from Jane 's image, as Lorenz's ducklings upon their minds from their mom's image, following her everywhere. Maybe Jane, with her charm and charisma would have mesmerized me anyway, even without a rebirth. I don't know. Fact is, I had a tear somewhere in my heart, or so it felt at least, at the thought of not seeing Jane any more. And it wasn't a mother-son rupture. I turned on my branch a few times, disconsolate. I didn't know how to react. An urge to weep seemed to be coming my way. I turned again, this time the other way around. Oldey, my neighbourly chimp, had stopped his movements and was following me with an increased level of interest. It was like his animal instincts were telling him that I was in real distress. And indeed I was. Janice looked good, was much younger than Jane, and it certainly could arouse a level of attention in anyone like me. But she had nowhere Jane 's charm, although her lips were certainly fuller and more inviting. She was wearing glasses. That reminded me of the fable 'The Monkey and the Spectacles' by the great Russian fabulist Krilov. Of course, I'm no monkey, and neither is Janice, but isn't it strange how memory works sometimes? Especially a leaking memory, because that's what I think I have in my head, unless there is another, better explanation. You don't know the fable, you say?

I wonder if Janice, with her three doctorates, has any idea about it. So, not to be insulting or superior, but I got this other urge, and I decided to ask her:

"Hello, Janice, nice to have your company. It looks that Jane has made a great selection in having you follow my tribulations. Have you read anything written by Krilov?"

"Oh my goodness, you mean the fabulist? What on Earth made you ask that?"

"Well, I was a bit overwhelmed by your high level of knowledge from your presentation, and the first thing that came through my mind at seeing you was, and I hope you don't take it as an offence, whether the glasses you are wearing are for reading or just for looking ... well, interesting."

"What's the matter with you, Onkey, are we starting on the wrong footing in our relationship? And why Krilov?"

"You may remember that he wrote 'The Monkey And The Spectacles'. It's about a monkey who was getting old, and having weak-sight, has heard and saw humans using spectacles, and when he got his hands on several pairs, he tried them everywhere but not on his eyes. In the end, he decided to break them all, saying that humans told him nothing else but lies, as there is no good use of those spectacles."

"So, who's the monkey, am I the monkey now? Did I tell you lies? "

"Oh, no, Janice, it's a matter of interpretation. With everything that's going on nowadays, my chip tells me that many folks are using the spectacles just to look different, or to show off, and the more expensive the frames, the better the feeling... It appears that like in the fable, where the monkey didn't know how to use the spectacles, some people are putting them on for the wrong reason. Not to say anything about those who pretend to protect their eyes against the power of the sun, but in fact hide their shifty eyes that hide even shiftier thoughts. And after a while, they do again what the monkey did in the fable, they throw them away. Isn't that... fabulous?"

"I see that you have a green mind, metaphorically speaking, even with regard to consumables like spectacles, which are much more rarely consumed than others. But aren't you a bit aggressive on my account? I wear glasses because I need them for reading and seeing things better, not for looking better. Looking and seeing are, you know, two different things."

"Ah, come on, Janice, I certainly know that, and I imagine that you look marvellous both with and without glasses. I also know that people have some difficulty kissing one another if they have glasses on, so I was wondering ..."

" Wondering what? You saw me for a few minutes and you already forgot your infatuation with Jane? Don't tell me that now you are similarly excited about me as you were about her!"

" Well, first things first. I was wondering if I could kiss you better with your glasses on or with them off. But not as it happened with Jane. Really."

" Hah, you tried to kiss Jane? She told me nothing about it!"

" It was a kiss between two worlds, because we were thoroughly separated, she somewhere else, and me touching the screen with my lips. Total failure. Maybe she didn't even figure out what had happened. She might have thought that I just wanted to look closer at her; or that I mishandled the tablet."

" You are a naughty boy, do you know that? Jane could be your grand-grand-mother!"

" What does this have to do with age? Don't you love your grand- mother, or your aunt?"

" Yeah, but that's something else, naughty boy! You

are smart enough to distinguish between these kinds of feelings."

"But you and Jane are so gorgeous! I am at a loss trying to resist the attraction both you and your aunt have upon me."

"I'm glad that I'm attractive to you, and if you understand me correctly, I'll tell you that I am also attracted to you, but only for the level of the intelligence that you exhibit. This form of attraction is common between humans, and can be considered a higher form of feeling. So you should be glad too."

"I am glad, Janice, but you are thinking of me as if I am only a brain with a chip. I don't know how you are seeing yourself in this world, but since you made me so smart, I kind of see myself as a totum, having all the properties and needs of a person, not just those of a brain."

"I see that you are using a Latin term now, are you actually fluent in that mostly dead language too?"

"I think you want to change the subject, but since you asked, I have trouble wondering what do you know about how much memory is crammed into your XMON and how was that data deposited so densely. Yeah, totum means all in Latin, and I have more than I can handle in my memory, except I know little on how this memory thing works."

"Percy, my colleague, might be able to answer a few of your questions related to memory. Although I have extensive studies on artificial intelligence, the part about memory I left in Percy's hands, so to speak. Mainly he used the nano-densities available for downloading the majority of databases created in the last period of time. Our preoccupation was to make the chip plastic enough in order to allow for connectivity with your neural network."

"Where is this Percy guy, how come I haven't seen him at all?"

" Oh, you have seen him before the operation, but that's the part of your memory that was erased in order not to interfere with the new one. Percy was so exhausted after the whole preparation of the XMON and the implantation that he decided to take a few weeks of vacation."

"You mean to say that he was not even interested to find out what was the result of his work?"

"Well, we kept him up to date with most things through some emails. He is happy that you came out so smart. Although he is very smart too, he's not the jealous type."

"Why should he be jealous? Jealous on me?"

"There is nobody in this world with the capacity that you have, at least as far as we know. I'm a bit jealous on you, so maybe he could be too, but as I said, he's not the type, as far as I know him."

"You peppered my interest with what you just said. Actually, how well do you know him?"

"You learn a lot about somebody if you work with him as closely as I did. Still, a person has too many attributes to be characterized easily in a few words. I just mentioned that he is very smart and not a jealous type.

Lost Among ...

I cannot tell you more right now because that would mean..."

"What, what, what? It would mean something that you do not want to say about yourself, or about his relationships, of which you want that I should know nothing."

"Discretion is the better part of valour, says the proverb."

"And silence is golden, that's why I cannot talk!"

"You can communicate, that's what's important!"

"Yeah, this tablet is a marvel, but I wish I could do what you guys are doing, talking directly to one another. My limited way of making sounds doesn't go too far. How would you feel of knowing that there is such a great instrument like the voice, but you couldn't use it?"

"You know quite well that among us there are so many speechless people, some deaf too."

"Oh, since you brought this up, you gorgeous people have this tendency to describe people in rather negative terms, with certain connotations that have nothing close to reality. I am referring to the 'deaf and dumb' pejorative, as if a person who is deaf and dumb is actually stupid or an idiot. You know quite well that this is not the case."

"You are right this time too, however, there are influences on the mind development of people who, for a reason or another, cannot hear language. That may have a huge negative influence on their mental aptitudes."

"But you still refer to them as idiots, dumb-wits and so many other things, when they just have hearing and speech problems, at least initially."

"Well, Onkey, we are not as perfect as you believe us to be, but maybe we could improve too with the help of a device like the one you have."

"You refer to the chip in my head? Why, you want to become... trans-human?"

"It's not such a bad thing to want to improve, even by way of the chip. I guess that we started to become trans-humans as soon as we started thinking seriously about that."

"Well, if I'm correct, humans wanted to become something else even since the writing of the Epic of Gilgamesh about 38 centuries ago in Mesopotamia. Immortality, everlasting youth and regeneration from ageing were imagined a long time ago."

"Enhancing human life is a day-to-day occurrence now. Medicine and technology allow us to replace worn or missing parts of our body, even make them more functional than before. The brain is just one more complex part for which there is more work to do. We might get to the time when we will continue to be human, but better than before in many respects. We'll be ... trans-humans and post-humans."

"And I am a pawn in your quest. A cog in your ample machine."

"You are extremely important!"

"Oh, yes, 'L'important, c'est la rose, l'important!' At least, that's what the song says."

"You really amaze me, it's like you have everything working well up there in your mind, if you know what I mean".

Lost Among ...

"Why shouldn't it work well, it was your job to make it work well, wasn't it?"

"Yeah, but perfection is hard to attain, and it seems that you have it!"

"Number one, nobody's perfect, especially me, a slightly improved ape with a humongous human memory, but without anything else to pertain to my own species, to my own individual experience. Number two, if I could speak, I might tell you a few things about perfection, word by word."

"You are so attached to this idea about speaking. Why is that?"

"You do realize that too many technologies interposed between us make reality a bit too... artificial."

"So, what's wrong with that?"

"It's, well, unnatural!"

"Not everything natural is good or perfect."

"But you see, here you are kind of wrong, Janice. The natural forms perfected themselves naturally, through evolution, and reached a certain level of independence..."

"Which actually, doesn't exist, since all the species are interdependent in their ecosystems... Take out a species of its ecosystem and it dies!"

"I agree with you on that, but I am also aware that the artificial implements that I am using now can easily malfunction, simply by dissipation of their energy source."

"A natural form without feeding itself would go through the same situation. Nothing different here."

"That's true too, but when you depend on a multitude of technologies that have, let's put it this way, a

44

short history of development, and maybe even a shorter lifespan, you are bound to think that something could go easily wrong. Then what?"

"Then you get repaired again. Maybe even improved further."

"Yeah, sure, get my head open again to fix my chip. Marvellous, what can I say?"

"Onkey, you are a very smart ape! I wish I had an app like yours in my head, maybe then we'd be on the same... sapling?"

"Sapling you say, eh? Pretty close to sap... and to sapiens. Thank you for reminding me that I am an ape! I was about to forget that, since we discuss literature and literary critique. So, where do you think you actually are, if not on the same tree, evolutionary speaking? I hope you don't get me into the mambo-jumbo thing on Creation and all that. After all, you are a scientist, aren't you?"

"Of course I am a scientist. However, you should know that there are lots of scientists who can perfectly confuse the problems in this area. It's more like an acceptance of the cornerstone in your thinking. If the cornerstone starts with belief in the supernatural, almost nothing can correct its architecture of thinking. And most people grow within families that, one way or other way, convey the traditional concept, no matter whether it is right or wrong."

"Why do you say, right or wrong? Aren't you sure of what is right and what is wrong?"

"Maybe I shouldn't have said right or wrong. Maybe real or unreal would be more appropriate. You see, it 's easy to confuse what is real with what is not. We imagine things that are not real, but our dreams exist in our minds during the sleep. The dreams are real, but not necessarily what we dream. We have all kinds of concepts in our heads, they are imagined abstractions, but they do reflect a reality. Justice, truth, freedom and a million other concepts may be considered more or less abstract and more or less real. Reality is what we might formulate through personal and shared experience as the worldview that we have. Of course, it is hard to have a complete and perfectly coherent view of this world, of which we still know precious little."

"Jane has never showed up outside of my tablet. Is she for real? Is she a simulated reality? And will you show up out of the tablet, so that I can touch you and smell you, and see you directly, without the interference of a device?"

"A device is always somewhere in between you and me, if you are more precisely what the brain in your skull is or does. You see me with your eyes, but they are only the devices that take my image to your brain."

"Jane was on my brain for a long time without me seeing her directly with my eyes. It was like I had a separate pair, the eyes of my mind working there."

"That's how our memories function. Even if we don't know much about that, we do have some hypotheses on what's happening in our minds."

"You mean to say that you installed a chip in my head containing a huge amount of memory without knowing what you are doing? Isn't that a bit awful?

Scandalous? Utterly outrageous? Downright terrible? Bloody preposterous and appalling!"

"As you see, we have done it right. You are a champion, far more powerful than the DEEP BLUE super-computer that beat the world chess champion."

"Big deal, a game of chess! Kasparov was right to ask for a re-match. He beat the machine the first time in 1996, and would have probably beaten it in 1997 too, if the IBM people didn't intervene between matches with who knows what."

"The fact that you know and can communicate with us about it shows that the memory implanted works wonderfully. Aren't you great?"

"What greatness are you talking about? Of my plastic memory?"

"It's a step in the right direction. We'd like to be able to increase the neuronal or brain memory by biological means, but we are not there yet. So, since we understand better how the chip memory works, for the time being we combine the bio with the plio... That is, the plastic chip that's in the bio, the plio."

"Couldn't you have left me with my own memory too? I lost my previous personality in order to gather the new one that I have now, but I really have no idea of how I was before, so I cannot compare myself of before with myself of now."

"You are smart enough to understand how experiments work. The simpler the experiment, the easier is to interpret it. Adding the new memory and letting it interfere with your old one would have created a lot of confusion in our interpretation about your outcome. The effect of you acting with the old memory and your new one might have been even disastrous both for you and for our research."

"You are always thinking about your experiment and not much about me. I understand that such experiments on apes, on Hominids, are banned. They are illegal."

"What is illegal in some cases could be made legal in other cases. For the advancement of science and the betterment of humans, that is, of Hominids, some experiments are necessary and acceptable. After all, look at what a splendid specimen you have become."

"Wasn't this also the excuse of the many criminal acts made by the Nazi doctors on the pretence of creating a superior race?"

"That was a different matter altogether. A superior race was intended for the subjugation of the other races, for their exploitation and even annihilation. In our case, we want to liberate all mankind of the drudgery that comes from not knowing what there is to know."

"But that would make all of you gorgeous humans lazy! Isn't memory supposed to be developed gradually, through beneficial and even not so beneficial experience?"

"We are trying to find a better way for our minds to become more efficient in this accelerated epoch in which information is so pervasive. We just don't have enough time to go by the old methods of learning."

"You are always in a hurry, eh? Repugnant!"

"Why do you see it as repugnant?"

"Well, I noticed the visitors at this zoo. They pass by my cage almost totally immersed in the reading of their hand-held devices, with barely a glimpse to us, the residents and the supposed attractions that they have come to visit. Even when they take pictures of us, it's more to have us in their virtual reality than to admire us as we really are. Indubitably, it's repugnant!"

"So, what are you saying, Onkey, these previously considered by you utterly gorgeous humans have become repugnant for you because they don't give you enough attention?"

"That's the nature of the beast, Janice, and as much as I try now not to be, that's what I still am."

"Can you explain that a bit better?"

"Oh, Janice, what's the use of all those doctorate degrees you have if you don't understand my case?"

"So what's your point? I may interpret things differently from you; that's why we do have this conversation."

"The point is that I'm lost. I'm lost! I'm lost in an ocean of plastic, I'm lost in an ocean of neglect, in an ocean of unreal reality, without a hug from a female companion, be her with or without a beard. You dig into my brain, trying to see what are my deepest thoughts, mostly trying this way to understand yourself. You and your similar simians. Trying maybe to see what are the actual needs of my species, and what might be those of your species. Well, I'll give it to you the short way. I don't need the luxuries of your species. Maybe even you don't need them. Maybe even you need just what I need:

companionship, a forest in which to breathe, drink and eat my bananas, and the freedom to roam. Free. From tree to tree. Be it the tree of knowledge."

"I get it. You are frustrated."

"You got it. Damn' right I am! There is rage in this cage! Actually, there is rage in any cage!"

## CHAPTER 4

You won't believe what happened next, because you are one of those utterly gorgeous humans and I am just a monkey. How can a monkey, even if he is a chimpanzee, closed in a cage at the zoo, find out so many details about what I am going to describe here? Well, it's actually quite simple, considering how clumsy some gorgeous humans can be sometimes. You know by now that my first communication with them after the implant of the XMON in my brain was with Jane, who left me a tablet and helped me master its keyboard. However, it was Janice, her niece, who took over after Jane decided to retire or maybe retreat due to my infatuation with her. What can I say, monkey see, monkey do, which might otherwise need an explanation, but I guess that you get the gist of it. Janice, who is full of doctorates and knows a lot of things about artificial intelligence, is not less clumsy than an absent-minded professor, if it comes for me to reveal this streak of hers. And through a circumstance that you may call coincidence, both Jane and Janice did the same clumsy thing in the same time, for my and ultimately your revelation of what happened between them. Now you may say that there are no coincidences in life, that what happens must happen, that there is some

Lost Among ...

kind of fate in the world or even pre-determination, but I
don't accept all this mambo-jumbo simply because I am
too smart and I know better. After all, nobody is smarter
than me, according to both Jane and Janice, but not
really because I am who I am, it's because I am with
XMON and nobody else is. What's so special about this
XMON? If you cared to read the previous chapters of this
story of mine, you'd understand, but maybe you forgot
already. We, simians, are forgetful. So I am bound to tell
you again. It's a chip full of memory, so full that even I
have sometimes difficulty to go through its content, which
is nothing less than the whole knowledge of mankind in
digital form. This is why I can have the privilege to call
these utterly gorgeous humans clumsy, even if the term
privilege gives me the goose bumps. Why is that, you
may ask, and I am here to oblige: although I am an earlier
descendent from the evolution tree than the humans are,
which makes me a more ... primitive primate, and
although there is a certain hierarchy both in my species
and in your species, I abhor the fact that some members
of these species take such advantage from the others on
the basis of their privileges, as to build with it a pyramid of
injustice and despair.
Here is where the goose bumps come in; only in this case
they stand as a metaphor for fury. I told Janice previously
that I am furious when she noticed that I am frustrated,
and why shouldn't I be? If you can equate privilege with
advantage, and I certainly have the advantage of being
the smartest via the XMON, then why the heck am I held
in a cage like the lowest of the criminals? Of course, if

you are also clumsy and didn't get it yet, (everybody may be clumsy from time to time, even I, so don't feel offended) I'll tell you that it is a matter of security: the utterly gorgeous that you are can do nothing in front of me, when it's bare knuckles against bare knuckles. Well, your ilk does have a certain advantage over me, and, lo and behold, it's not coming directly from the brain, it's coming from the neck, your larynx, the glottis, or your voice box.

Although I have now in my brain all the words that your species have mustered to create, the devilish thing is that I can't pronounce them. The only way to communicate with your brethren, which so far has been just a sisterhood of two, is to type the words and phrases on the keyboard of the tablet. Heck, if I had a voice box... Anyway, I do have my good ears, and it's not true that we monkeys are deaf (I guess that you know the image with the three monkeys: no see, no hear, no talk). So I hear and understand everything from you guys. And here the clumsiness comes in handy. My dear co-communicators, Jane and Janice, were able to leave open both the audio and video channels of their tablets. On top of that, as if it was an arrangement, they placed the tablets in such positions that I was capable of seeing and hearing everything that was going on in the labs where they started to quarrel. And now you know what can a certain amount of clumsiness bring you: revelation! Oh, yes! What follows is what I heard and saw with my own eyes and ears. I'll see later if I can give you the right spin to all of this. Jane started by asking:

Lost Among ...

"How did it go with our chimp?"

"Why do you ask, you must have followed the entire conversation?"

"Well, of course I did, but I'm asking as to see how did you perceive it."

"He's a smart ass of an ape. I can't be sure... maybe beyond our expectations."

"Why beyond? Wasn't this what you expected when setting up the chip for him?" Janice said,

"Percy, the guy I was doing all the work with, thought that he expected some bumps on the road, especially because we still know little about how to connect the chip to the networks of neurons."

"So, aren't you happy of how well things went so far? It's an astonishing success!"

"Astonishing might be the right word, but the fact is troublesome."

"Troublesome, why? You just got exactly what you wanted to get," said Jane.

"That's the troublesome part. We shouldn't have had to."

"Are you kidding me? What's wrong with you, Janice? I'm so proud of you and of what you have accomplished. Just think what a huge field of possibilities you and Percy opened up with this success. We can bring the chimps closer to us behaviourally and convince the world that it is imperative to take care of them."

"You are always thinking at your main heritage on this planet. But I started to be somehow doubtful."

"Doubtful of what ? You are one of a kind, Janice,

54

Laurian Taler

and don't you forget that. You are my niece, after all, and let me be proud of this."

"I'm also proud of you, Jane, and maybe I wouldn't have become what I am without your tenacious, visionary and persistent intervention. But I have my doubts…"

"Is it about how to combine our work? Is that what you are thinking? Enlighten me."

"No, no, the doubts are from too much perfection."

"How do you mean that?"

"Well, Jane, don't you think that such a complex surgery, without us even knowing what we attached where and how, as if by magic, becomes so perfect? It is, to say the least, wrong!"

"Now you really confuse me, Janice, how can such a perfect operation be wrong in the same time?"

"That's just it. It wasn't supposed to come out so well, so I have my suspicions."

"Suspicions? Suspicions of what? Can you be more specific?"

"Well, it's like… How should I put it? If Onkey were to have a working voice box, it seems that he would speak in the style of the people from the Lincoln Park neighbourhood."

"What are you implying by that?"

"It's as if Onkey learned to express himself in writing not like an average English-speaking citizen, but specifically like one who lives near our zoo."

"How did you discover that?"

"It's not a discovery; it's more like a feeling… I can't even be sure of what I'm saying. This is why it's just a suspicion."

"And what else would go with this suspicion?"

"It may sound like paranoia, but that might mean... it might mean that we are actually not communicating with Onkey."

"How can you say that? Don't we see him typing all the time when we discuss with him?"

"So, what does this mean? It's just that he looks busy with the keys, as he has seen you do when you trained him... Monkey see, monkey do... "

"Are you saying that somebody interferes as an in-between, cancelling what Onkey does with the keys, and inputting his or her answers? Are we having an intruder in all our work, like a hacker who is sabotaging everything we did so far?"

"And humiliating us in the same time with all kinds of erotic and sexual advances which, making us believe that are coming from an intelligent ape, might provoke in us a defensive reaction that allows somebody to laugh their heads off."

"Now, now, don't be so dramatic about that. Let's see whether this process of interference can be true or is just a figment of your paranoia. If it were true, it would mean that most, if not all our work with the XMON implant has no value at all. Are you prepared to see that?"

"That's what I'm afraid about. This is where I say that our experiment seems too good to be true. Nothing works so perfectly without a hitch from the first try," said Janice.

"Well, you can't say that. There are some examples

in the history of technology where whatever has been conceived worked flawlessly from the beginning."

"You might give me some examples of that, because I fail to remind myself of such cases."

"I don't have a full list, but of course Tesla with his many inventions and designs, all imagined in his head and excellently conceived, then the first British digital computer, created by a guy named Flower even before the American Eniac, not to say anything about a myriad of other inventions, all built on the shoulders of predecessor creators."

"Anyhow, if my suspicions are supported by evidence, what are we to make of our work with poor Onkey?"

"Janice dear, we need to establish if Onkey is truly the one that communicates with us, and although that might not be quite so simple, it's not rocket science either."

"And how do you think we might do that?"

"Well, it's you who has all these computing qualifications, not me."

"Hmm… There could be a number of schemes that we might employ. The first that comes to mind is to switch tablets; maybe the one he uses has been hacked. If we give him another one, a virgin one, we might avoid any interference."

"You make me laugh," said Jane.

"Why, what's wrong? Is my solution not a good one?"

"Oh, no, it's the fact that Onkey might need a virgin,

albeit one that is only a tablet."

"Why is that funny?"

"Janice, what's wrong with you? I'm amazed how sometimes even the most obvious aspect of humour escapes you."

"Sorry, aunt Jane, what humour are you talking about? I'm screwed up by this interference possibility and you want me to taste some monkey humour?"

"Don't you see, it's the fact that Onkey had a crush on poor old me, and now we conclude that he might need a virgin? As far as you being screwed up, I have no actual knowledge at all. Did you bunga the lab chief?"

"Jane, I can't stand this kind of verbiage; you know that I'm on perfect terms with Professor Panzon. And being screwed up can mean a lot of other things."

"OK, no Panzon for you, it seems, which reminds me, isn't he a Scot?"

"So?"

"Well dear, he doesn't need the pants on, he might wear a kilt! And don't we all know, there is no need of anything else under the kilt!"

"Actually, I've never seen him wear a kilt, although he likes shirts with tartan..."

"See, he's making you an invitation with his tartan shirts, and you don't get it."

"What invitation? Are you serious, aunt Jane?"

"Deadly serious! At my age, if I cannot have a laugh on account of my scientist niece, I should be ready to die. Silly Janice, there is tar in tartan, also tart, there is art, and almost Tarzan!"

"So? Do you want him to be my Tarzan?"

"It's not what I want, poor old me, it's what you want and what he wants!"

"What I want now is to make things clear about our work with Onkey. It's like a bulldozer sitting on my mind."

"That's why you can't connect the dots any more... Relax! Well, maybe you can think about who could want to sabotage your and Percy's work, in case there is any sabotage."

"Why, you think it's all imagined?"

"But you just said before that you have no hard evidence, that it's only a supposition. Don't wreck yourself just yet! You might be a Tesla, after all!"

"Oh, yes... Another thing we should do, maybe in conjunction with the virgin tablet, is to put Onkey in a room that is totally wi-fi insulated, so no outside communication would be possible for hacking his new tablet."

"Then how would you communicate with him?"

"Direct cable between our tablets."

"That means you'd have to be in the same room with him. Unless you use a longer cable. It's a no-no."

"Oh, yes, we could have a lattice of bars or a glass wall separating us."

"Would this be enough?"

"I think we'd also need some well-positioned video cameras to follow all the typing movements that Onkey would make. This way there would be no possibility of having someone refuting our entire process."

"That's my girl! Now I feel that your bulldozer has

been smashed to pieces!"

At that moment the door of the lab opened and a short man, not quite as utterly gorgeous as the women, came in, saying:
"Aha, my best two Jays holding a conference here! What are you twitting to one another?"
"Percy, Percy, please have mercy, we are not just two birdies, are we?" asked Jane with a tone in her voice as if to emphasize she prayed for some higher level.
It took me a moment to adjust when the camera focused on the image of the newcomer and I was able to ascertain those other peculiar and rather shocking attributes of the man. He wasn't only short; he had a wild look on his face, a huge mandible and an almost flat nose; his shirt, opened at two buttons, allowed for a strangely large amount of hair protruding out from his chest. I couldn't believe my eyes: he almost looked like me! Now I might be exaggerating a bit, but if I were shaved and combed neatly and dressed like him, I could pass for his less grown up twin! At least that's how he appeared to me in the first moments after his entrance.
I immediately felt an utter envy. Not only was he taller, but also unlike me, he had a voice! And I immediately perceived that both ladies appeared smitten by him! This brought to my mind a lot of doubtful sentiments about myself. Maybe that's why I had such limited success with Jane, and couldn't even start thinking about any dalliances with Janice. It was this Percy, this doppelganger, this alter ego of mine who was the barrier

to my happiness. I didn't need much for happiness, as I had already explained to Janice, but I didn't need barriers like Percy either. And now, on top of all this, they wanted to test me. They had doubts about my capabilities. Well, they actually had doubts about their own experiment with me, and in all this there was a strange misunderstanding in my mind about how and why Percy and I seemed to have something in common. Actually, it was a bit of a mystery. Maybe there was something more than a coincidence in the way we both looked. What if... Heck! What if... No, that shouldn't go through my head. I wanted to weigh with more care the chances of that. But I couldn't think further about it, because I had to follow the conversation of the trio.

"But of course you are two birdies, just two birds of paradise," said Percy.

"Either you are making us too exotic or you consider the lab to be a paradise, and you are wrong in both these cases," said Janice matter-of-factly.

"We are a bit confused by our analysis of the XMON experiment," said Jane. "It seems that Janice has some doubts of its veracity because, get this, it seems to be too successful."

"What, Janice, are you doubtful of both your and my genius?" asked Percy with an air of acted self-confidence.

"It has nothing to do with genius; it is all related to how the XMON interacted with Onkey's neural tissue. It is as if his brain or the chip, or both knew exactly how to integrate one another for a perfect fit, and that bothers me a lot."

Lost Among ...

"You know something," said Percy, "it also kind of bothered me so much in the last weeks that I couldn't have a proper vacation in the Canadian Rockies. I kept looking at all those wonderful lakes and mountain crests, and what I was seeing was Onkey's brain in which we were inserting the chip."

"Yeah, you were adventurous enough to leave everything in our care after the operation. We emailed you a lot of info on how Onkey reacted after his recovery. You know that he fell in love with Jane, and that he might have certain plans regarding me too?"

"How many kiddies?"

"Stop it just now, you roughneck!"

Jane felt the need to intervene. She said, with her smooth, velvety voice that had impressed many people when she held her conferences all over the world:

" You have serious matters to discuss, not to make fun of each other. Onkey is on both your minds, probably for different reasons. How about finding a common ground?"

"Look, Percy, our level of confidentiality regarding the entire project may be in jeopardy. Call me full of paranoia, call me whatever, but I feel there is something wrong with our perfect results."

Percy coughed a short grunt as if to make sure his voice was not too rough, then answered:

"You have always had some distrust in the importance of memory in the brain. My hypothesis seems to be the correct one. As soon as the brain has enough well sorted and stocked information, it uses all that for

higher level processing in the complexity of its networks."
Jane tried to help Janice, who appeared to follow Percy's
talk with her mouth open:
"The difficulty is to understand how can an ape brain
integrate so fast and so easily processes like reasoning,
language and decision making. To this effect, I want to
remind you that although size matters for the capacity of
brains to have high functionality, there have been enough
cases where high functioning people had a smallish one.
The most cited case is that of Anatole France, the
renowned French writer, whose brain mass was found to
be around 1000 grams, which is low, as average human
brains measure around 1400 grams. Then, it's the recent
discovery of Homo floresiensis, a smallish human that
lived about 13000 years ago on the Flores island of
Indonesia. He had the brain size comparable to that of a
chimpanzee and it is believed, on the basis of the tools
found where he lived, that it was functioning at some high
level of intelligence. On the other hand, parrots have
brains three times larger than chicken, and we know how
smart parrots are. Still, it's totally silly of me lecturing you
on this, as if you were some grade three or four kids
greedy to know all about brains."

Janice wanted to intervene, but was following with
avidity Percy's right hand that kept on pulling tufts of hair
from his shirt opening in a repeated effort to smooth and
straighten them. It was Percy who took over the chat:
" The plasticity of the neural networks and their
capacity to adapt at new situations is well-known.
A chimp's brain is sufficiently rich in neurons to allow it to

Lost Among ...

gobble high densities of data and perform high level tasks with it. That should be especially easy when that data is so highly organized on the chip. The mystery remains in how did the neural networks suck out the data from the chip."

Janice intervened with a level of vehemence that even Jane did not expect.

"That's exactly why I am so suspicious! We don't have fluids to suck up here; we have electric activity at the level of the neurons, and that activity is quite different quantitatively from what happens on a silicon chip. We don't have octopus - like arms scouring through the jars for food, we have dendrites of neurons surrounding a chip that protrudes a few hundred endings into neuronal mass."

Percy interrupted, saying with conviction:

"That's right, there aren't fluids to suck up, but there are micro-fluids happening at neural level. Remember, the current at neural level is just a process of polarization - depolarization based on the flow of ions through ion channels or pores in the neuronal membranes. A flow means there are fluid processes happening, only they are micro and nano processes. They convey a voltage gradient across membrane, which we call electric current. It is a matter of adjustment between the voltage gradients of the silicon chip and the voltage gradients of the neurons, for which the immense plasticity of neurons is called in to work. That's why Onkey had to maintain his comatose period for a while. It was to allow the neurons to act like the octopus arms in jars, connect actively with the environment of the chip." Janice retorted:

"I knew that, thanks for making Jane think that I was out to lunch about chip - neuron interfaces. What I still object is that everything seems to function perfectly without the existence of an evolutionary process of adaptation in neurons to silicon. That's why I feel that we need to take precautions in testing Onkey's capacity to communicate with us. It is bewildering to see it all so perfect!"

Percy started to laugh loudly. Jane and Janice exchanged critical and surprised looks. What could be so funny? Janice even asked this question after a pause:

"What the heck do you find so funny in my paranoia? Do you think I'm mad? A mad scientist, that's what you have in front of you. Hello, hello, am I mad?"

Percy's answer came with a chuckle:

"Of course you are mad, you are madly intelligent and wise and ... and gullible, that's what you are! I think that somebody has put into your perfectly balanced wisdom the not so wrong idea of perfecting through smooth evolutionary process; because of that, now it's impossible for you to see jumps in this process, especially when intelligent creatures like us intervene."

"Percy dear," said Jane this time, "you need to consider Janice's point from another angle. We do have transcriptions of all the written communications between Onkey and us, but they are not irrefutable proof of his language prowess, as hacking into his tablet is still a possibility. We need to think on one hand, who could have interfered, if that's the case, and on the other hand, we need to prepare that irrefutable kind of proof through testing that will make sure nobody could deny our valuable experiment."

"So, you seem to embrace Janice's fears," said Percy to Jane.

"Since she brought this thing up, it occurred to me to wonder how come, XMON being essentially a memory chip, Onkey has jumped to such a high level of functioning. It's like he just needs a fully - equipped lab and he will start showing us what he can do creatively, surpassing maybe all that has been created so far in the most advanced labs. And this just on the basis of extended memory? I do have a problem with that," said Jane, with more than a shadow of preoccupation in her voice.

"Then, what are we waiting? Let's put Onkey through the wringer and see how clean and clear comes out on the other end," said Percy with an air of irony in his voice.

I knew what a wringer was, so it occurred to me in the first instance that I wouldn't feel that great passing through one. This Percy wanted to flatten me, extract all the juices out of me, and make me like a sheet of paper or a tablecloth? No wonder I hated his guts all of a sudden, although something unclear, an unexplainable warm and fuzzy feeling seemed to burn a hole in that hate of mine. My hate level danced up and down for a while in me like a sinusoidal representation of an acoustic wave. Notwithstanding the speed of my reactions, it took

Laurian Taler

a while for something in my brain to click: Percy's wringer was just a metaphor, what he said only meant that he accepted the idea of having me tested thoroughly. I took a gulp of air in my lungs. Percy didn't seem to be the devil incarnate. He actually believed in my capabilities, more precisely in my brain's capacity to adapt to his or their chip. Actually, now it was my chip. Unfortunately, the work on it was so much of the last moment, that there was nothing in my memory about its architecture. I assume that if I knew this architecture, I could maybe become consciously more capable of enhancing its properties, that is, make it even more effective. Not that I had to complain about its qualities. Well, of course, as I mentioned before, there was one thing that the chip didn't or wasn't capable of doing: direct speech. I'm not thinking at the robotic voices that could be found in so many computerized devices. I 'm thinking of my own tenor or baritone voice, with which I feel I could express so much of what had been accumulated in my ancestral heritage.
I wish I could talk, sing, shout to the world what the world needed to know, but didn't: I am just accidentally a beast. Maybe reading this will make you laugh. Well, laugh as much as you can, but if you think more deeply at what I wanted to say by that, you would realize that this is no laughing matter. After all, at this point I am, in a way, less beastly than anybody on this planet. All the intricacies of your human relations, as have happened over eons in your history, are encrusted in my head. As such, I may be considered more human than any of your confreres. Of course, a large portion of my personality depends on my

genetics, which have evolved in the complex relations driven by the changing forest conditions over many millions of years. Beast as I must be, I do have my own sense of who I am, and with that comes a profound feeling that I could have been quite easily as gorgeous as you are, reader, if not for the above mentioned accident of history. I could have been a contender to the title of gorgeous myself, if the jungle disappeared at one moment in time and gave me the chance to walk the walk and liberate my arms from the hustle and bustle of grabbing tree branches all the time, to build what you have built with so much success, the tools that improved your life and mind; if I encountered fire in the savannah and used it to cook my food, if my vision became more adept to see far in the distance and allow me to anticipate and prefigure out what's coming in the distance of space and time. My horde and I would have become for sure more like you, with a skull well - balanced on a neck less weighted down by huge muscles and more prone to develop the fine organ that I miss so much, with its wonderful voice. If I had a voice I certainly could have made myself more explicit in my good intentions and that's how I would have displaced, little by little, my beastly features. So, do you agree now that I am an accidental beast? What I still do not understand, even with my vast repository of your knowledge, is how come you were not able to displace your beastly features along your complex history? It is as if you learned and forgot, again learned and forgot, as if your own experience was valuable less for you and more to our close brethren, the bonobos. At least for them, it's only 'make love, not war', while for you is make arms, more destructive, more obliterate-able of everything that's life and reason on this piece of blue earth.

The lack of this singular quality, the missing of the voice, seemed to me of such paramount importance that it overshadowed whatever huge capabilities I had through the memory chip implant. What was the use of such glorious intelligence if I couldn't connect directly with the world and express it in all its varied forms? I thought that the expression of my singular voice was important for demonstrating all that has been encrusted in my species history over the million years of viewing and probing and living a bestial life, surrounded by the shadows of the jungle and limited by the capricious accidents of our evolution. In this sense, I was now doubly lost among the utterly gorgeous humans. Away from my jungle, away from my societies of chimps, but still essentially away from these humans that want me to help them enhance themselves beyond what they are now, and of course, beyond what I became through the use of their memory, I felt that there was so little a place for me in this world. It occurred to me, by coming to this word, world, that all of a sudden, I was thrown in a larger, vaster, limitless space with billions of solar systems, billions of planets, billions of jungles and maybe billions of creatures like me, who were all asking themselves where they were in this world. As for me, I was in a Chicago zoo cage. I was beyond lost.

Lost Among ...

## CHAPTER 5

Here I am now, waiting for my co-creators to approach me in their tricky, spy-like ways to test my communication capabilities. I say co-creators on one hand because I know now that there are at least two who went so far as to surgically implant the chip in my head; on the other hand, with my previous memory erased, I hardly can figure out who my mother was. Of course, I shouldn't pretend to know who my father might be, as chimps are not very attached to the concept of monogamous matrimony. Not that knowing my parents might help in any way, since I am actually completely isolated from other chimps, except for Oldey. Well, Oldey could be a father-like figure for me, not so much as a bloodline connection, as for the fact that he has taught me the value of being altruistic. Simply put, I didn't expect something like this from him, especially since, with my newest acquisition in my head, I kind of felt so much more superior. At least up to the moment he has shown his superior physicality to me with the nonchalance of a champion. If you missed anything up to now, or if you also have memory problems like many who are endowed not only with it, but also with many years of passing through the gates of forgetfulness, I will make it short and

Lost Among ...

easy for you:

I am an involuntary chimpanzee resident of the Chicago zoo, and I was involuntarily operated on my head to install the most advanced memory chip in the world, the XMON, which contains most if not all the mankind's information on it, for the initial benefit of making me the smartest everything ever. Of course, I am playing the role of a guinea-pig, in that I have to demonstrate the possibility of implanting the same kind of chip in humans in order to make them vastly smarter than they are now and presumably smarter than I am. I can communicate with Jane and Janice, two of the utterly gorgeous humans that started to keep me company through a tablet on which I can type with rather high speed whatever I want, when in contact with these ladies. Jane and Janice are aunt and niece, respectively, the first one an icon of research in Primates, the second one a doctor in almost everything and a brain surgeon, who did what I just said to my brain, together with a guy called Percy, with whom I did not have direct contact yet, but it looks like I will, because this triumvirate will put me through some tests, to be sure they can claim that I have become who I have become. They call me Onkey, and since I am the first chimp with typing manners, they gave me the first name of Adam. Did I miss something? Sure, the chip keeps recording any new data into my head, so you can understand how easy it was for me to write all this. At least, I hope you won't be too shocked to see that a chimp is a writer, daring to even put his name under the title of a book. Unless, of course, you have that elitist smug attitude so typical of the utterly gorgeous with regard to all the modest, hard-working animals under your control, the so called domestic ones. It is rather well known that when confronted with the ones that are not your 'domestics', the ones less distracted from their nature, the wild ones, the utterly gorgeous humans become utterly diminished unless or even when they have a drastic weapon in their hands. I give it to them, they are mirific when it comes to weapons and tools. After all, the tablet, as a tool, not only gave me the opportunity to establish a high level of conversation between our species, it also allowed me to see and hear, from a distance, as shown in the previous story, what you are plotting to make me: an indefatigable witness of your prowess in the usefulness of the chip. Well, nothing of this kind would have been necessary if you could have provided me with the great tool that all of you have since birth, a functional, truly natural voice machine. But no, you either couldn't do it, or you were thinking that for you humans it was of no need, since you already have it. So, you might have thought, to hell with the poor chimp, he shouldn't be raised to your level of communication, perchance he'd make you uncomfortable with his intellectual attributes. After all is said and done, you must accept that at least physically you are so much under the weather in comparison with us, the chimps.

Now that I've seen Percy talking to my friends Jane and Janice on my progress and on their possible suspicions, I am more and more preoccupied by his appearance: he is looking too much like me, or, if you prefer, I look too much like him! Not that there aren't enough differences, especially in his height and shortness of his arms, in his better balance on the ground and mine definitely in the trees. So I am rightfully suspicious too with regard to this resemblance. Am I one way or another more related with him than with the other humans? Is it just a coincidence that we are as we are? How come it is particularly he who arrived, albeit together with Janice, to the point of experimenting with my brain? Some people see in coincidence the hand of God, while others might wonder why that name has the same letters, at least in English, as those for dog. If I am permitted a view on that, it is what it is: incidence, happening somehow repeatedly. People may give it significance from 0 to 1. With an established pattern, it becomes significant indeed. So, I muster to say that highly evolved minds are looking for significance where it may be and may not be. But I am still allowed to ask, how come? Actually, if I put myself in Percy's shoes, and Percy in mine (not that I wear any, so far), I wonder if he is not asking himself the same questions I do.

Since I am respectful toward you, reader, I cannot let you completely in the lurch about this. I am sure that you already have made a few suppositions with regard to the resemblance that I have described: I may be simply the son of Percy, who might have had a moment of amorous encounter with my mother; or he might be just my uncle, the brother of my mother, who might have blossomed with me from who knows what kind of impregnation; or Percy might be one of the living Neanderthals that happened to slip through thousands of generations and eons of so - called higher civilization; or he could be a blessed with high intelligence mutant expressing genetic characteristics that in the utterly gorgeous humans had receded in time. There might be, of course, other possibilities, but I do not intend to write a full novel on that basis alone. It just irks me that my life, already full of mysteries connected to my lack of previous personal memories, gets even more complicated now at the encounter with one of my makers. Well, I don't want to appear as a know-it-all, but somehow I can claim the fact that in my case there is more than one maker, or even better, in a view that goes beyond the biological, more than two makers. Bluntly put, I am a bio - technological marvel. Only now I must be tested to prove it to the entire world.

My neighbour Oldey has been observing me from a respectful distance with increased curiosity for a while, seeing that I was so entrenched with my fingers and eyes on the tablet, sometimes sitting comfortably on the branches of my tree, sometimes just on the ground of the cage that we shared. With my focus to the tablet's keyboard, I couldn't notice that actually Oldey was finding his way to my back and was trying to understand what I was doing with that strange device in my hands. When I realized that he was spying on me, I pushed the tablet in front of him and took his right hand to lead it toward the tablet. He was tense initially, but I was resolute to show him some of the devices' capabilities. I got hold of his index and made him touch the icon for the images. The screen opened up with views of the jungle. Oldey smiled appreciatively. He liked what he saw. I made him change the images one by one. We both looked happily at other inhabitants of the forest, some like us, some different. It took very little time to see that Oldey was flipping alone through the images, presumably with the same wonderment that I had experienced at the beginning of my trials with the tablet. I made a few pictures of Oldey and of myself and made him look at them. He grinned knowingly. Obviously, he was a clever individual. The apes are known to be capable of recognizing themselves in the mirror, but the tablet wasn't a mirror, at least it didn't give, through the images, that immediacy that a mirror would return to someone. However, the apex of the ape was reached when I got him on a video image. After looking at the video intently, Oldey insisted that I take other sequences with him moving agitated in the tree, dancing frenetically or swinging from one branch to another, turning into a truly stuntman, that is, a stunt-ape full of willingness to act. It was as if he discovered his true calling a little too late in life and tried hard now to compensate. It's impossible to give you a full list of his approving grunts, even an audio book wouldn't be able to present them with complete truthfulness. I definitely made him come out of his depression; I know that because since his encounter with the tablet, Oldey was using his colourful shirt in a much different way than before. Instead of rubbing his head and chest with it, Oldey would throw his shirt in the air between branches, swing rapidly to another branch and return in time to catch his testamentary toy with gusto.

I was amazed at this change of mood. I wondered to what extent could I teach him how to use the tablet. One impediment, that actually came from my extensive human memory, was the idea that it's hard to teach an old chap new tricks. Oldey was much older than I was, but you wouldn't give him too many years if you were taking into account his pirouettes in the tree, his fast swinging and his excitement of acting for a video. I was ready to prepare him for some learning sessions with the keyboard and showing him a video for its usage, thinking that maybe his brain plasticity, combined with me, one of his own, as tutor, might allow him to overcome both the limits of an aged individual and especially the ones related to his, that is my, species. As it happens many times with good intentions, they remain just that, because our little paradise living in a cage was interrupted by Percy's and Janice's arrival. It was shocking for me, because it was for the first time that I was seeing both in un-mediated appearance, in their own flesh, so to speak. Of course, I immediately guessed correctly why did they come: to escort me into one of those rooms they set up for my comprehensive tests. As if Oldey too understood the importance for me of the moment, he froze exactly like me at their arrival. Janice looked intently through her large glasses at our frozen tableau for a longish moment, then broke the silence:

"Hello, Onkey, good to see you again. This is my associate, Percy, who will be doing with me some testing

at another location. Show him with a wave of your hand that you are friendly!"
As if in a puppet show, Percy, Oldey and I waved our right hand in  about the same time. Janice, realizing the ridiculousness of the situation, burst into a loud laugh. We all grinned at the same time. If a neutral observer had noticed the scene, it certainly would have appeared as if we all understood each other perfectly. Percy pulled out a banana from his large lab coat pocket and threw it to Oldey, who caught it without problem. I looked a bit strangely at Percy. He said:
"Onkey, my friend, your banana will be served at a table. By the way, be so good to go through that opening door. You will see on the floor a yellow line. Follow it to your banana. Did you understand me? Please confirm with a yes like I do now."
With this, Percy started to slowly shake his head up and down a few times, then he looked intently at me.
"Wait, wait!" intervened Janice, "please take your tablet with you!"
I stretched my left arm to the closest branch, where the tablet was resting by its hook. I took it, pressed the video icon and made a dancing movement with my behind. Oldey understood and started to dance. I directed the tablet to take him in. After a while, I turned the camera toward the gorgeous. Janice grinned again, but Percy was pulling his tufts of hair out of his shirt opening, as I saw him doing through the video channel when he was talking about me with Jane and Janice. I stopped the camera, turned to Oldey and made him a sign with the

right thumb toward the left. I repeated the sign, this time moving my whole body through a turn in the same direction as I was showing with the thumb. Oldey stretched his fingers toward the tablet, and with a careful movement, touched the rewind button for the video. This time I looked intently to the newcomers, who were, and I am not making this up, standing beyond the bars of the cage with their mouth open, utterly surprised. Turned again toward Oldey, I made a small grunt, shaking my left shoulder to the front. Oldey pressed the start button of the video. He grinned, as he was seeing himself dancing, then grabbed the tablet and brought it toward the gorgeous two, showing them his and their act. It was clear to everybody that Oldey was one ape of a kind. Obviously, he became such because of me. Well, I know that in the older human parlance, pride is one of the major sins. But as proud as I was, I wanted to show even more to the gorgeous that were observing us. So I embraced Oldey, who was as happy as a champion on the highest pedestal; he used his large, clever grin, only this time in a frolicsome manner. I wish I knew what he was thinking at that moment, but I must recognize that I don't have any mind-reading attributes. However, I knew that the utterly gorgeous could become impatient; I took the tablet from Oldey, gave him a short farewell grunt and exited the cage through the door that had opened in the wall behind the trees. The long yellow line was there on the ground of the hall, indicating me where to go. It took me just a few seconds to reach the place where it bent toward a room with a small table and a chair for my tushie. As promised, a banana was expecting me on the corner of the table. I installed myself on the chair, put the tablet on the table and grabbed the banana. While I was peeling it off, a very intense feeling that I was observed overtook me. But by now I knew much more than at my first sittings with the tablet. I knew that I was in this room for the specific purpose of being spied, tested, wrung through a battery of trials and interviews and recordings to prove that indeed I am who I am, the chimp with the mind bigger than a blimp. What I had just demonstrated with the video recording of Oldey and my knowledge transfer to him was neither sufficient, nor proof that I could communicate with the speaking species. They needed hard evidence that was indubitable, certain, unassailable and true. As true as the banana gobbled in my mouth. I relaxed. What else could I do? Soon, my co-makers will come and will put me through the rolls.

The room was separated in two by a glass wall with several small round holes in the middle of it, presumably to allow the sound to pass from one side to the other. Beyond it another, larger table with some devices on it was visible; among them I recognized, according to my grand memory, nothing fancier than some ordinary laptops. On the walls, however, as obtrusive as possible, two video cameras were facing me from different angles. I looked around to the walls of my room. Geez, there were three of the cameras, again at different angles. The ceiling had two other similar devices. Since I was curious, I looked at the floor too. There I saw a cable that protruded from the room in front of me through a small cut in the glass separator above the level of the floor. The cable reached my table, where it was tied to a leg of it with plastic connectors. I realized what its attributes must be, remembering the discussion between Jane and Janice that I had followed previously. They wanted a direct connection between my tablet and their laptops. Eliminating the wireless, they hoped to combat the possible contention that somebody might interfere between our computer devices wirelessly. That could allow somebody to pretend to be me. In other words, a hacker could steal my identity and fudge all the answers, putting in his/her answers instead of mine. Of course, that would be horrible! Humans claim that we chimps steal food from time to time from each other. It may be true, I cannot contest that because my personal memory of before the implant is gone, but what horror stories did I find in the chip about what humans do to one another! It validates the fact that gorgeousness has nothing to do with morality. Identity theft has reached humongous proportions since the advent of the Internet. And with that comes the instant disappearance of values of all kind, from money in accounts and property titles in real estate, from copyrights infringements of artists' rights and pay, to plagiarism in the media and who knows what else. This part of human memory that I have in my brain does not put a nice nuance on the collective or individual behaviour of the gorgeous. On the contrary. So, it is clear for me that the elimination of the wireless communication between my tablet and my counterparts' devices is a necessity, in line with what my co-makers want to pursue: the truth and the proof of it. I can say that I am ready for it. Just for the moment I have a hard time finding where exactly should I push in the cable's connector. My hands might be nimble, but not quite for everything. I know, from others' experience, how easily it is to bend and break these connectors. Should I better wait, otherwise who knows what might happen with my request for another banana? Eh, let me try again.

I must have lost my sharpness while eating the banana and inspecting the rooms, because I should have noticed the number of chairs behind the table with the laptops: there were four of them. It meant that I would probably have a cohort of four utterly gorgeous to test me. Who might be the other one or two, as I didn't see Jane coming to show her amiable presence? Well, I didn't have to wait for too long, as the door behind the table and the chairs opened and in came my co-makers, together with an unknown person of male semblance. He sat at one of the chairs in the middle and without waiting to be introduced, which I felt was more than a level of rudeness from his part, asked me with a voice that felt like the epitome of arrogance:

"Do you know who I am?"

I lowered my eyes to the tablet in front o me, ready to start typing, but something deep inside made me stop.

I raised my eyes toward him and inspected him more thoroughly. He seemed more aged than Percy and Janice, but not as aged as Jane. He was wearing a tartan shirt under his lab coat. With his piercing blue eyes of a pale nuance, he was looking straight at me in a most unpleasant way, as if trying to work his way beyond my eyes, through my optic nerves directly into the different compartments of my brain. It wasn't just an analytical look; it was one from a severe master toward his slave, with an air of dominance and disdain. It didn't make me feel good at all, but the level of unpleasantness appeared to transform itself in me in a large smile, uncovering the unmistakable, powerful set of teeth that I decided to shine at my interlocutor, after which I concentrated to write on my tablet's keyboard, with capital letters:

"R. U. D. CHEF PANZON, OR COOK SCREW-THEM SIR HERE?" - after which I left my chair, jumped on the table beside my tablet and with a sudden move, pushed my head as close as I could to the separating glass wall, trying to make my eyes look as penetrable as possible. The newcomer reacted violently at my move, pushing himself away from the table and knocking himself down from the chair. His demeanour changed abruptly from that of a domineering one to that of a clumsy person caught in the middle of a stupid act, which was not entirely far from the truth. I felt a degree of satisfaction that I didn't know was available for me, almost something orgasmic, if I were to cite from the vast library in my head. Janice and Percy, who didn't even have time to sit on their chairs, were also astonished, each one in a different way: Janice had put her right hand over her mouth, and bent backwards from her waist up; Percy got a panic attack in which he started to turn on his heels, a few times clockwise, a few times the other way around. That was quite enough for me. I descended from the table onto my chair again and grabbed my tablet. With a controlled fury that I didn't know I could muster so well, I started typing my new message to the utterly gorgeous and astonished:

"Should you wring me or should I wring you in the wringer now?"

CHAPTER 6

My taste for being tested wasn't too high at that moment. I was sure that I had already astonished my testers with my previous behaviour. More than that, I practically scared them off, both when I jumped onto the table and when I asked them if they wanted to be put in a wringing machine. I guess that being very smart, Janice and Percy might have figured out what did I mean with that proposal, something that might have come back to them since they themselves have used and heard that notion when discussing about my testing. As for Panzon, their chief, he might have needed an explanation, which I wasn't prepared to give yet. And since I decided to avoid a cumbersome set of questions and instructions from them, my smallish brain was working feverishly at finding an alternative. I was keeping an eye on the three utterly splendid ones in front of me, of which Percy was somehow less close to perfection since he looked a bit too much like me, and another eye on the tablet's icons.
I had experimented before with the one with an artist's palette on it and I thought that it held a lot of promise. Clumsy as I appeared initially at handling its different tools, when I realized that the saying 'a picture is worth a thousand words' was so true, I was hooked. On top of

that, I was sure that adding a few words to a picture could be the excellent proof of what my testers would have wanted me to demonstrate. But first I had to convince my co-creators that I had the wherewithal to be provided with what I needed for my future demonstrations. So I didn't want to mince on words and phrases, I wanted to go for the jugular, so to speak. I held up my right palm as a signal that they interpreted correctly as 'wait', because they interrupted their chat after their last astonishment and followed me with interest. With my left hand I showed them the tablet, after which I pressed the icon for painting. The screen became white. Almost without looking, I chose a hefty brush, and still keeping the screen visible for my audience, I drew with a few simple brush strokes a pipe. Under it, with the same brush, I wrote in not too calligraphic manner, with capitals, 'THIS IS A PIPE', after which I uncovered with total satisfaction my teeth using my largest possible grin. Percy was first to react, turning to Janice, hugging her and laughing, then starting to jump together with her, while she was still having her jaw fallen down. Panzon pushed himself again away from the table, this time managing to remain on the chair, his eyes ready to exit their sockets. I was certainly amused of the reactions I elicited from my spectators. I liked it even more when Janice, then Percy, started to applaud. Obviously, it was a triumph for them, as it was for me too. I didn't know what to make of Panzon's way of showing his amazement. It was still early in the game for me to understand him, although the first impression wasn't too positive. I raised my right palm again, asking them to wait, after which I found enough white space under my first caption and added 'image', this time in small letters. I was sure the video cameras were recording everything, so I felt a pride I didn't know I could have. After all, it seemed to me that I was not only drawing and writing, I was clarifying the deeper concept of truth and its symbolic representation.

I wasn't interested in creating a paradox like Magritte did when he wrote under his pipe drawing, "Ceci n'est pas une pipe".

I was even less interested in starting a longish explanation of what did Magritte achieve with that legendary legend under the drawing, as Foucault did in his intention to philosophize on the 'strangeness' felt by the seer who is confronted by something that is and isn't in the same time. My intention was clear: my reality was what I wanted to impress with, and for that I needed to exit the realm of cages in zoos and electronic recording and tablets. Once being able to show that I can put meanings to images in the form of words or legends, I could become legendary myself. But I needed to do it in front of a vaster audience than that of the splendid trio that I have already astounded. So I erased my imperfect pipe and wrote with the same brush on the screen:

"Real demo - need brushes, canvas, paint, easel."

Panzon was the first to bring himself back to conversation, asking:

"Why not continue with the tablet?" to which I responded, using the keys this time:

"It's not direct enough. May be construed as tricky.

Lost Among ...

Paint, brushes, canvas are all palpable and completely un-mediated. I paint, I write, I demonstrate my might ... of the mind." Percy intervened:
"Will you do this in front of a crowd?"
"And reporters, television, whatever," I replied.
"What if they will think of you being just a dwarf dressed in an ape's costume? People can be inordinately incredulous," added Janice.
"Let them be, I'll show them what no dwarf can do up in a tree," said I with complete assurance.
"People can be annoying, throwing with things at you through the bars of the cage. How will you react?" asked the lab chief, afraid of any mischief I might provoke or the crowd might create. I was slightly amused by his question, to which I answered with a grin and the following:
"What are the chances for me to misbehave, now that you know a little more about me?"
"Didn't you jump on the table rather aggressively at the beginning? You made me fall off my chair!"
"Your falling was not of my making. You just forgot about the glass wall separating us."
"You sure are smart, but there is much more separating us than a glass wall, rest assured of that!" retorted Panzon with the characteristic hubris that I couldn't stand.
"And you are not the hub of the Universe either. Just an accident waiting to happen."
He rushed to ask further:
"What exactly do you mean by that?"

"You better learn how to sit on a chair, mister chairman. I myself can sit on a branch in a tree and not fall off like you. Anyway, for a lab chief in a zoo you certainly exceed the average level of high horse haughtiness acceptability. Are you too much of a bourbon drinker, or you think of yourself related with the Bourbons?

Janice and Percy exchanged looks signifying something I didn't catch, after which Percy dressed up his voice to say:

"One in favour of the ape, chief. To tell you the truth, I always wondered if you had blue blood in your veins. You see, it kind of sounds bluish when you think of it: Panzon, blazon, Bourbon..."

"Look at me and at my belly and tell me if life isn't doing it wrong to me: Panzon in Spanish means large-bellied person, somebody paunchy. On top of that, you make me aristocratic too. What did I do to deserve all this?"

"You were well born and noble, at least that's what your parents thought when they named you Eugene, forgetting to add 'ius' at the end," said Janice with a faint trace of sarcasm in her voice.

I felt the need to intervene, not so much to save Panzon from the barbs of his subalterns, as to speed up the process that depended, probably, on certain expenses to be approved by him as the chief of the laboratory:

"You cut a fine figure, sir, but speaking of that, would it be hard for you to spend some money on paint and brushes, or you could just borrow the stuff from the maintenance team? You do have a maintenance team here I think, don't you?"

"When did you learn to be so diplomatic, Onkey? It looks like you show these two smart-alecs who attack me how to handle a hot potato. I have to apologize, I was having doubts about your intelligence. I still have doubts about your capacity to handle yourself pacifically in front of a larger audience. What guaranties do we have that you will refrain yourself from any acts of violence?"

"It is in the nature of the beast to be violent. It comes with the desperate need that it must catch something, that it must conquer to survive. As you see, I am only desperate to express myself, artistically this time. Is there a better guaranty than this?"

"How did you come to the conclusion that you must express yourself artistically?" asked Percy, and continued: "It must have been some moment of inspiration, maybe a form of feelings sublimation that we don't understand where could be coming from. Can you explain?"

"Do you want me to start an analysis of the origins of my aesthetics or to dwell in the neural processes that brought this tendency?" I asked, giving him two wide topics to choose from.

"My interest is in the neural processes, but if you could touch on both topics, maybe we would understand everything better," said Percy, as if waiting for clarifications from a guru.

"I think we could approach the matter after I show you what I have on my mind, artistically speaking, through a few sessions of drawing and painting with an audience. At least this way we would both have material to refer to, something you might call hard evidence. So, better prepare in a hurry some canvases or at least enough paper. Don't forget plenty of fruits. Until that happens, I suspend my writing on the tablet."

And to make it clear, I left the chair and found a corner in the well - appointed room with video cameras where I sat on the ground, giving no more attention to the trio of questioners. I knew that it appeared rather rude to leave them like that, but my intention was to convince them of my power of decision. I hoped to have inspired in them a sense of my strong personality. If they knew that I was decided, what else could they do?

It looks like somebody always works during the night in this zoo: apart from finding my tablet always recharged, an important matter to which I did not give any attention up to now, the next day when I woke up there was an easel holding a large horizontal cylinder of paper at its top, a portion of paper already pulled down from the roll, as if inviting me to draw. Several large coloured chalks were resting on the lower part of the easel. It seems that the previous day trio had decided that paint could be too much of a hassle if some open cans were to be toppled by who knows what kind of accident. A still life was already waiting for me in the form of a small table loaded with fruits. Oldey had been up before me, but smart as he was, knew to keep a safe distance from all the new objects in our cage. Although he certainly had the upper hand in brute force, he appeared to show a very polite behaviour toward me, maybe recognizing my advantage in certain things, especially since our using of the tablet gave him so much pleasure. I guess that he was diplomatic enough to abstain from ravaging the attractive display with fruits, as if knowing that it would make for some strained relations between the two of us. I didn't want to keep him on the edge for too long, so I chose one of the mangoes displayed and threw it to him when he was looking toward me. He must have had his own sense of aesthetics because the mango looked too good for him together with the other two on the table. He moved shyly around the display, back to his tree and again to the display, where he dropped the mango among the others and chose a banal banana in exchange. It made me wonder, was he also one of the many neglected prodigies of the ape world, or was this just an expression of modesty from his part; did he simply prefer bananas to mangoes or did he sense a difference in ripeness of the two fruits? Hard to say, but what impressed me still was the fact that Oldey appeared to reconstruct the harmony of the still life by replacing the mango among the other fruits. I really appreciated that, and to show him that his choice was right, I too chose a banana for my breakfast. With it in my mouth already, I tore a large piece of paper from the roll and dropped it near his tree, after which I took a few coloured chalks and put them beside the paper. With one chalk in my hand and another given to Oldey, I started to apply colour onto the paper, by holding the chalk horizontally, to cover a larger area. I changed chalks a few times, trying to blend several colours into one another, then started drawing the yellow mangoes on a layer of green leaves in the middle of the paper. I made a pause to see his reaction. He looked up to the table with fruits, on which, apart from the mangoes, were a few bananas, two avocados, some grapes, but no green leaves. He seemed confused. After a number of movements with his hand over the chin that appeared as if he was scratching not only his face, but his brain too, Oldey decided to complete the scene on the paper with the fruits from the table. He first drew a line over the bunch of the green leaves with his chalk, as if trying to get rid of them. Then, dropping his chalk, he carefully carried the bananas and the avocados, placed them more or less around the mangoes on the paper, and then finished with the grapes in such a way that they almost hid the layer of leaves drawn by me. When he finished, he looked at me, waiting for my reaction. I didn't know what to believe: was he trying to equate the mangoes still on the table with my mangoes, the ones drawn by me? Was he validating this way my own reproduction in the drawing of those fruits? Or he was just more adept at seeing all those fruits closer to his little reign, near the tree that he inhabited? Fact is that seen from a proper distance, the ensemble that he had built was not bad at all. It had mainly the same positioning of the fruits as they had been on the table, which at least was showing that Oldey had a good memory for places and for colour. This was practically a perfect test of his capacity to mimic, but what if there was more than that in his exhibition? I would have wanted to reflect further on this matter, but it was time for the zoo to receive its visitors. The large hall in front of our cage had been partially reserved for the press and television, so I realized that we were not too far from having a show soon.

Whatever might be your experience with shows, you probably realize that both the audience and the performers are getting through a more or less feverish period before it. It must come from the level of unexpectedness that is typical with most shows, with their unpredictability. I don't know what kind of announcement the trio made in a hurry to the media about what was going to be shown here, but it became obvious that the media was hungrier for circus than for bread. The spaces for the public had been accessed by the paparazzi with sophisticated cameras of all sizes, sign that imagery was the order of the day, and I was supposed to fulfil their expectations. Probably something must have transpired from my gorgeous interviewers. When they appeared, I knew that we were on with the start of the performance. What was it going to be, their or my performance? Well, they were indeed my co-creators, but still, they were nothing at this point without me! But I wasn't in any way interested to sabotage their high hopes, so I knew that I was going to go along with all those expectations. After all, it was my desire to show to the world that I was an important part of it. Think of it whatever you want, reader, but don't we all feel this necessity to get out of this deadly anonymity, at least from time to time? What I didn't understand well enough was this rush toward idolatry, inscribed in my memory from the innumerable rock concerts and other shows with stars of all kind, not so much from the part of performers, as from the public at large. It conveyed to me a sense of loss of balance, a kind of madness for which the only explanation I could find in my head was a mass wave of hormonal surge that completely overwhelmed with exaltation some members of the audience. It was a form of rapture, maybe less its artistic equivalent, as its mob one. Well, I wasn't prepared to raise any utmost exultation from my audience, especially from those with their hands and eyes busy on the cameras, people who probably have seen almost everything that could be seen and as such, must have been blasé beyond belief.

It was Panzon who started the proceedings, as if he were my show promoter and I was under contract with him to perform. Without saying anything about my chip implant, he just explained to all present that after I will show a number of my artistic creations, there is going to be a question and answer period for the further elucidation of my prowess. When he turned to me and gave me a head inclination, I understood that I was supposed to start being the artist. It occurred to me that the previous day trio was so convinced of my talents that, apart from the drawing of the pipe, they didn't ask for any more proof of what I could do or show. Besides, they had understood rather fast that I wasn't inclined to show them anything else. So, was I going to be able to further impress them, not to say anything about the larger audience? Now that I had carte blanche, I thought to do just that. A streak of showmanship was rising steadily somewhere in my body. It felt, strangely, more in the guts than in the brain. I went with my left hand over my face a few times as if to straighten some hairs. I turned to the easel and pulled the hanging paper up and down to show that there was emptiness on both sides of it. I turned to Oldey and pointed to the fruits on the ground, then made him a sign that he understood perfectly, as he rushed to replace all the fruits back to the table. Wow, he became a willing assistant. Smart ape you are, Oldey! I went to him and gave him a hug, then another banana. Most of the audience was taking pictures, but some applauded, and all had a variety of exclamations. They liked what they saw. It seems that the most powerful way to convey and provoke feelings in an audience is to show them such feelings. Nothing beats that. So I was on a good start. Oldey ate his banana full of tact. I took the piece of paper with the mangoes drawn on it and gave it to Oldey to hold, not far from the easel. Seeing two chimps on their two feet was already spectacle enough; the group in front of us had been already well warmed up. I took two pieces of chalk and created a blended background similar to the one on the paper held by Oldey. With a speed that even I didn't know I could act, I re-created the aspect of the fruits that lay on the table. I turned to show them the result. There was a collective AWE coming from the audience, apart from the innumerable clicks of the cameras. It was time to give them the coup de grace.

Turned again to the easel, I found enough space to write with capitals, one at a time, and turning to the spectators after each letter, the legend: STILL (EDIBLE) LIFE.

It took a few seconds for all the clicks to die out, after which the entire audience looked stoned. Perplexed. Wounded. The complexity of what they just witnessed was blocking their capacity to fathom the unimaginable. Where was the trick? What if there was no trick? How can it be? Is this really a monkey? Can't be! Can't be! No, it can't be! Perfect training? What perfect training? Never in a million years! Never? Mutant? Man-ape? Hybrid! Manzee? Humanzee? Who the hell...? In Chicago? Can't be, can't be, can't be! But it's here! What is? What? What? I didn't bother to rip off the drawn paper, I just pulled further down, under the horizontal bar of the easel. With a brown chalk I started to draw Oldey holding the paper with the mangoes. It was just a sketch, under which I wrote

OLDEY IS SMARTER THAN YOU
          THINK!

Was I deliberately mischievous this time, by putting the last word on another line? Well, isn't art supposed to create controversy? Yeah, OK, but from an ape?

I turned to the perplexed and made a rotating sign around the right temple with one of my fingers. Somebody from the group, a woman, fainted. A deep preoccupation was showing on the faces of most present, which gave me instantly the feeling that Jane, good darling Jane Doogirl was both right and wrong. She was right to try to save us from the dangers of extinction. She was wrong to think that humans were ready for accepting us. Certainly, not as equals. Maybe as freak - show entertainers? I turned again to the easel and pulled down another amount of empty paper. Oldey noticed his image go down and decided to go down with it. He set on the floor with the back to the spectators, reaching about the same level as his drawing hanging from the easel. Although just a sketch, he seemed to recognize himself in it. I started to draw, this time with short looks at the people behind me. The camera clicking started to sound again. In no time at all, what was behind appeared to be also in the front of me, on paper. What was I going to add under this sketch to further astonish them? I decided for

CHICAGO CROWD CACKLES CHIMP.

The result was that two other people, this time two men, fainted and were pulled out for fresh air. I wasn't at all embarrassed, but Janice was, because she came in front of the group and started to explain:

"Our main protagonist is in good form today. We will continue without delay, but we need to be sure first that everybody is alright and not prone to passing out." Since nobody moved, Janice continued:

"There is no trick in what you just witnessed. There is only science... and a good dose of luck, I believe. We are lucky to see that a specimen of Pan troglodytes, the scientific name for a chimpanzee, can express himself not only artistically, but in writing too, and show a humongous amount of humour, if you want, well, even sarcasm... This is not a mutant, it is not a hybrid, it is not a trained monkey see, monkey do."

Someone in the audience interrupted her bluntly:
"You just told us what he is not, can you tell us what the heck he is? Is he a well-disguised dwarf? Heck, three people fainted here!"
Janice was unperturbed. She continued with her equal voice:
"We are very sorry for the strong reaction, such things, even if they could be anticipated, cannot be easily prevented. We assure you that there is no disguise of any kind involved. Our highly functional chimp has received through implant a new, revolutionary memory chip developed by our labs in collaboration with the University of Chicago and certain Silicon Valley enterprises. Due to the excellent way in which the chip was accepted and enmeshed in the neural network of the brain, Onkey, because this is the name of our star, has a prodigious memory and an IQ that we did not measure, but assume to be, how should I put it, astronomical."
"You mean to say that he is smarter than us?" jumped a thick voice from behind a tv camera.
"When I said astronomical I meant huge, huge, huge... No idea how much, but we assume that he knows almost everything there is to know."
Another voice, this time extremely irritated, tried to speak for everybody when asked:
"What do you mean everything? Does he know my name?"
"I have no idea, maybe if you give him a hint," said Janice.
"What hint? Hey, 22 Hobbie Avenue, near Seward

Lost Among ...

Park. Pay me a visit!"
I turned to the easel, pulled down a swath of paper and
wrote in capitals,
WHEN, MR. DRUMMOND? SEYMOUR DRUMMOND?
"That's not me, that's my brother! I am Daniel. He
doesn't know everything! See? Huh!"
"Just a moment, on whose name is the house at that
address registered?" asked Janice.
" It's my brother's home. I moved there from Frisco two
months ago."
I turned to the paper again and wrote
773.494.3322 and 415.649.8585

"Darn, the first is my brother's cell number, the
second is mine. What's the trick? Unbelievable!"
"It must be a trick! They are having an arrangement!
It's impossible!" started to say a man in the group, and
several others were approving tacitly.
"Ask him something fresh. What are the news of
today?" intervened a press genius.
"Sorry, gentlemen, his memory doesn't contain
today's news or news from a while before the implant,"
was Janice able to say in the uproar.
I went behind the easel and picked up the tablet from a
branch of my tree. I touched the icon for the web, entered
N Y TIMES and watched what came upon the screen.
I went then to the paper and made a drawing of a
zeppelin, under which I wrote,
USED FOR CARGO.
Indeed, there was a story in the Times saying that large

blimps, for long desired to be used for heavy transport, were now in use. I inflated my cheeks, then released a good laugh.

"Amazing, he used the Internet! Can he fly too?" asked a voice sarcastically.

"He is an ape, not an aeroplane. And yes, we know that he can use a tablet in a variety of ways," said Janice again.

I noticed the guy who made the last remark. Did he want sarcastic? Let's give it to him! He was a youngish type, the only one in the entire group who was wearing a simulation of a goatee, something that seemed more like a hairy crescent moon on the thin brim of his chin. I made an easy sketch of him floating in the air, knees up his chest, back slightly slanted backward and arms stretched. Under his sketch, I drew myself with a leg up in the air, as if kicking him in the bum and making him fly. Everybody started to laugh. I was pleased enough that I decided to show them a bit of flying too. I jumped up to my tree and started a few rapid stretches and hangings from several branches, and then ended my acrobatic work by descending with a vault right back near the easel. Oldey emitted some grunts and threw a chalk at me, which I caught with dexterity.

"He is bloody creative, but is he a Rembrandt?" asked another voice.

I didn't have time for a detailed painting, although I kind of liked the easy handling of the chalks and the acceptable blending of their pigments. I decided to be literal, so I pulled down more paper from the roll and wrote

Lost Among ...

## REM NO, I AM A BLOODY CREATIVE CHIMP BRAND, REM GOT IT?

I wasn't sure the message would be sufficiently understood. There were several possible interpretations for rem, but in this case one at least was obvious for those who did some computer programming. Rem there stands for remark at the beginning of a line that is just that, a remark. In my case, switching the first three letters in Rembrandt's name to a remark followed by a remark, I thought I was creating something clever, not to say that this way I also emphasized that I was my own brand. And "got it?" stood for " Are you clever enough to figure this out?" which wasn't a small feat either. I was again pleased with myself at that moment.

A young woman put her hand up, waiting patiently until Janice signalled for her to start talking. She said:
"I am really confused. You said that this chimp got a memory chip implanted in his brain. What does this have to do with his obvious high intelligence? We were pushed in school for ages to avoid memorizing facts. Now what? An ape gets smarter than us just with some extra memory? Where is that chip, I want it too!"
Janice smiled imperceptibly and made a gesture toward Percy, who up to that moment was modesty itself. He made a few steps to occupy the centre of the hall. He brought up both his arms with his indexes stretched towards the group, then pointed them at Janice, saying:

"If you want an implant, look for Dr. Janice D. She is the surgeon with the nano-touch and the nano-glue. If you want the chip, c'est moi who you want... and a good number of other contributors. Now let's see if we can make some clarity in some brains here first, before any implants go there. Madam, Miss or Lady, we are all delicate vegetables without our memory, as you must know by now. Your brain is a water mill that cannot mill anything without the water and the grains. It is computer hardware without software and without the data to be processed. If you want to be smarter, then move more data through your brain highways and centres. To do that, you need more to carry, proper data, properly organized and properly rendered available for operating with and operating on. There is a quantum of brain size, capacity, volume, sophistication, at which all this data could be well, highly processed. It appears that our smart ape has that quantum and it needed just the data to be what you see he has become. A smart ass of an ape, at this point practically smarter than we are."

"Sorry to interrupt, Mr... you didn't say your name."

"I am Percy. Percy Letabou, computer scientist." The guy who interrupted took over again:

"Is that your real name, Percy? Letabou? Are you restricted or interdicted or something like that? Tell us the truth: did you hump the chimp's mama? Where is she? What do you hide from us, eh?"

Some rumours started in the group; at this moment everybody seemed ready to embrace any version except the official one. A more enterprising type in the group

made an effort to quiet down the hubbub and asked: "Sir, do you have a price for that chip? Can it be readily available, and when? If not implanted, how else could be used? For when do you plan other implants? Can you give us some dates?"
Percy brought up his arms to make the group listen, but to no avail. He started to rub his forehead with both hands, waiting for a proper moment to answer. I got the feeling we all needed a lighter atmosphere.
I took the tablet again, put it in Oldey' s hands and pointed to the group. He grinned, but waited for more from me. I had to point to the picture - taking icon. He grinned again, jumped on his feet and started to run from a side of the cage to the other, taking pictures of the group beyond the cage bars. The utterly splendid realized that they were this time the objects of an unusual photographer. In a way, for the moment, the roles had been reversed. Oldey' s act gave pause to the visitors, as if a whiff of 'Planet of the Apes' was floating over their heads, if not in their heads. Still, it was we, not them, behind the bars of the cage. My ears were repeatedly ringing with the sound of the phrase uttered by Percy, 'practically smarter than we are'. How much practicality was there in me being smarter, when I was acting like a clever clown for an audience that wasn't inclined to accept knowledge as intelligence, and who mistrusted a scientific breakthrough? So I was drawing and writing, big deal! In a world filled with an opulence of images on the Internet, what kind of value could be given to the authentic artistic creations of an artist like me, when the

art market, like any so called free market, was actually manipulated for at least five centuries? It occurred to me that with this session, albeit short and not very productive, I could become really famous as a being, as an artist, as an artistic somebody. Shouldn't I turn this incipient notoriety into something practical? If the market was what it was, shouldn't I exploit it like the lowest or the highest of the speculators? I scratched my head with preoccupation. To what scope should I do that? Only to express myself? Did I have an itch that did not give me peace without doodling whatever came to my mind, a mind that wasn't even my own any more since the chip implant? Was I so full of vanity before or just after the implant, or only after I heard my co-creators recognizing me as being smart beyond the pale? To what purpose should I direct my notoriety? Where is Jane to help me with her vision of a world with love for chimps like me? Maybe that's what I should try to do! Be like Jane, a defender of my own in a world in which there is so much arrogance from the part of legions of unrestrained affluent that even the more normal splendid ones became accustomed to believe in the normalcy of an unbalanced, unfair society. Why would they accept the status-quo? Because of being scared of change? Was the fear to lose what they have stronger than the sense of correcting a plethora of inequities? Or these elites of the splendids were incapable of change because the real splendid were the few who measured and cut, controlled what was to be controlled, that is, of all the others.

The splendid democracy is in fact the plutocracy of a few

very rich splendid ones.

And I, what balance should I try to achieve? Maybe if I continue with all this questions, I will lose the opportunity to be pragmatic. For the time being I should focus to join forces with Jane or at least with her vision and use the language that the utterly splendid understand the best: the language of money. I turned to the easel and pulled down a fresh length of empty paper, on which I wrote, this time with a red chalk in a large format:

> ART AUCTION FOR
> JANE DOOGIRL FOUNDATION
> TIME AND LOCATION SOON IN MEDIA

The cameras started to click again. I waited beside the easel for my announcement to be registered, recorded, and almost as sure as death, I figured, soon to be printed and exposed everywhere. I decided to pull down the curtains on the circus myself, so to speak. The easiest way was for me to turn the easel around, after which I called Oldey to sit down with me near the table. We had a little feast to finish.

## CHAPTER 7

It went like this: the hall got emptied of visitors after Oldey and I started to usurp the edible still life, and other visitors to the zoo were channelled to different sections, away from ours. Janice remained to find an auspicious moment in order to enquire about my plans for the auction. She wanted to know whether I intended to prepare a number of pieces way before the event. I had to pick up the tablet again and explain in writing:

"What value do you think will have a ready made object presented as mine, when you saw how much confidence the crowd has in my talent?"

"But what will you be able to do within the limited time frame set aside for an auction?" asked Janice with the usual preoccupied tone in her voice.

"My intention is to act like a chess grand master playing simultaneously with a number of opponents; only my opponents will be the twelve canvases on which I will paint in front of the intended buyers. This way there will be no possibility of pretending that the results are not my art. As for the value of it, we'll see if the prices will go to the roof or not..."

Janice seemed to have a problem with my approach, because she insisted:

Lost Among ...

"I see at least three negatives in all this, but maybe you can enlighten me: first, the works might come out rather uniform in this way; second, you might not be able to put enough detail and skill in the works in order to satisfy the possible buyers; third, you might have a hard time impressing them enough with the coloured chalks to make them pay for your effort."

"Don't worry about uniformity. As for detail, it will come out as much as I will find out to be possible within the time frame available. However, instead of chalk, get me paint and brushes, please. Not in tubes, in pails or cans. I'll manage with five pails."

"What five pails? What colours in them?"

"Did I say five? Get me the rainbow, white and black; that makes for nine pails. Also three kinds of brushes, maybe ten of each size, with a standing holder for all."

"Anything else, Master Picasso? An assistant or two, more edible still life, maybe some nude models?" went on Janice ironically, a bit overwhelmed by my requests.

"Don't forget an overall tailored for my size; I don't want to get paint on my fur. Even some gloves wouldn't be a bad idea, what do you say?"

"At your disposition, Master. I'll get you a painter's beret too. For when the next event?"

"Two days or three days from now will be enough, if you can get an appointment with a reputable auctioneer. We want the frenzy that the media will create to be hot. And since this is hopefully just the first of the auctions, we'll have more time to prepare for the others."

108

The media didn't waste any time. Although it was going through a process of deep modification of its output due to the increased use of the online editions and the advertising money that was migrating back and forth between the paper and the online formats, several newspapers took out evening editions, an unheard and unseen event for years, only for the purpose of scaring off the public with another invasion, this time from super intelligent apes. Percy came a few hours later to bring me several of these newspapers, where my drawings and many other images with Oldey and me were printed with bombastic so called explanations of what had been witnessed in the morning. I examined the output with care. The journalists were trying to beat each other with effusive combinations of epithets.

PRIME PRIMATE PAINTER

declared one art critic in a newspaper, other was asking

DO YOU BUY JUNGLE ART?

The one that seemed the best advertiser for our future event was occupying almost an entire page in large format printed over a picture of mine. It said

ACE APE ART AUCTION

which I thought wasn't too bad, since I was convincingly grinning in the picture. Actually, even more than the grinning, what I liked was how well the picture captured the deep expression of my eyes. It made me remember of Jane again, as I thought her eyes might have had from time to time the same expression. I became slightly agitated, I felt that my eyes were turning watery and I had again the impression that there was a huge emptiness somewhere in my guts. In spite of the fact that this day I had become a celebrity, there was a lot that was kept away from me, there was a lot that I was missing, and the terrible thing was that I couldn't put a finger on it. Well, you shouldn't take that too literally, reader, although I needed both the mental clarification of what I was missing and the actual contact, as touch or hug or who knows what else. I went to the bars of my cage and stretched my right arm between them toward Percy. He looked bewildered of my gesture. I realized that my open hand was too much of an invitation to a dangerous move from my part, so I closed it into a fist. He approached me cautiously with his closed fist and we touched. He said, with a strangled whisper:

"Oh boy, you are something else!" and pushed again his fist into mine.

I ran to my tablet to scribble, BRING JANE HERE. He looked long at me, and then uttered,

"She is sick, didn't you know, Onkey?"

How could I know? Nobody told me anything. Since her last appearance, we were busy enough to not give attention to other things. I had spent a good amount of time exploring the wonders of the tablet, trying to practise a variety of skills that the tablet's apps were requiring from me, and finding out on the Internet about things that my memory seemed to be without. I didn't want to give up easily, so I enquired:

"How bad is she?" not waiting for an actual medical report, but for an encouragement from Percy for her recovery. He mumbled, without much hope in his voice, "I've no idea, I should ask Janice."

With this he departed, taking out a cell phone from his lab coat and pressing a few buttons. Rats, why didn't they give me a tablet with phoning capabilities? I should have been able to use the Skype' s lines, but for some unknown reasons, my tablet did not allow downloading of software, so there was no access to Skype for me.

I thought of looking at the news, or finding some snippet of information about Jane' s health somewhere on the web, but there was nothing. With "ape painter" in search engines there was plenty of data. I actually noticed the huge number of websites that were holding something with such content. Most of them were about me. That could mean possibly a high interest in the art auction.

I just had to do more there than what an ordinary, regular ape could do. I had to do more than Congo, or Betsy, or Sophie, the apes that were mentioned on the web as the ones that created furors in the world of art long before my time. In a comparison with the cave paintings of the humans' ancestors, their art received, at least by one anthropologist and animal behaviourist, the highest consideration as the real expression of the nascent concept of art. Of course, they had been regular apes, while I had such a strong memory in my head that each detail of a painting or of a design was embedded on my chip as a photographic memory. I could reproduce anything, given the right amount of skill for blending colours and depositing the proper shades wherever they were necessary. Still, I wanted to stay away from the effortless aspect of art production. I imagined it was the kind that provoked many modern art museum visitors of saying repeatedly in their heads:

"I could do that too in no time at all!"

This is why, even in spite of the fact that some of this stuff had been valued at staggering levels, I wanted to plan my output, by choosing just three or four typically successful styles that were amenable to show not only some skill, but also some depth of meaning. That kind of planning was actually more difficult than I thought initially, because heck! My memory kept on slipping from time to time, maybe just because there was really too much to gobble with the impressive array of images that were flickering through my mind. Twelve seemed to me a good number to create a high intensity bidding for my output at the auction, but with four styles it meant just three products per style. The question was, should I go on painting three canvasses in one style and pass then to another, or should I try to paint three or four completely different paintings, one of each style, then repeat the process? And should I wait after a series of three or four paintings, to see how are they valued and how would the bidding go before starting another series? There was madness in the method, but madness needed to be achieved for getting the highest level of exaltation from the part of the buyers. Certainly, I didn't have any direct experience in auctions, but I had some information from what some articles in older newspapers were mentioning. I particularly didn't like the tricks arranged by some auction houses for trying to raise higher and higher the bidding by planting fake bidders among the buyers. But who was I to analyze and criticize the strangeness of the art market, where a stretch of canvas painted in one, two, or three mostly uniform colours could fetch tens of millions of dollars, as if those millions couldn't receive a better, more practical use? Of course, for those buyers it was practical enough, as the mere holding onto such an item for the right period of time could increase its selling value by an incredible amount. As in many other endeavours, timing was of the essence here too. For the auction houses it was also utterly practical, what with their fat commissions on such increasingly ballooning purses. It was the artists who were faring less, especially since their recognition and valuation would come mostly after their demise. 'You have to be dead to be good', was a tacit saying in this market. As for me, I wasn't in that category. At least not yet. I was a celebrity by other considerations, which were more related to the rarity of the phenomenon, the almost impossibility of acceptance from the part of the gorgeous of such skills as coming from an inferior species and the mass hysteria that a mob insanity would feed during a well manipulated auction. Still, the fact that I was ready to accept the game didn't make my ape conscience less heavy with guilt. I felt not only the pressure of the huge spectacle on which I was about to embark. There was the added feeling that with my future performances I was actually going to take away a certain thick portion of the pie from the embattled artists who were trudging without recognition and sometimes without any pay. Try to find fairness in that! I didn't want to feel blasé about it. Of course I knew that I couldn't easily change the world. I just thought of enrolling myself in the good work that Jane and her followers were doing for the survival of my tribe. Wasn't that something meritorious enough to bring me peace and balance for the event that I was preparing with the help from Janice and the others? As far as money is concerned, it looks like there is always a flow of it from one side to another, a process simple enough and still, sophisticated enough that very few people are able to understand and control. Since I never handled money, it seemed ridiculous to me that so many books have been written about this subject. My only understanding about this was that you certainly could buy a lot of bananas with money, even plantations full of banana trees, and in some instances, even a few banana republics. Actually, the republics went easier with the appearance around their coasts of a few warships. However, it also appeared strange that while most governments were making money by printing more and more of them, people were using some plastic cards instead of money for their payments. This I understood: for a certain degree of convenience, which was showing how limited was sometimes their reasoning, people preferred paying more through a process that was chaining them to the mercy of the real owners of those plastic cards, the initiators of credit. So, why should I be surprised that rationality didn't seem to be the strongest characteristic of the behaviour of many participants in auctions? And since there were such large numbers of utterly gorgeous buyers with huge amounts of money to waste, why not let them do it for my own useful

purpose? It wasn't a bad purpose, after all, it was for saving the ones in danger of extinction, the ones that happened to look less gorgeous and be less vocal and think less of how to enslave and exploit others.
I smelled a certain odour of monkey business in these auctions, so I thought that I have arrived at the right place. Let them have it!

Janice had an impeccable taste for my wardrobe. I couldn't have done it better myself, not that I intended to pretend now that I was an expert in the art of fashion, which in my modest opinion, was another kind of monkey business. Happily enough, my repository of images about the fashion industry was totally static, otherwise what kind of reactions could I have exhibited at the visual promenade of almost naked models dressed with transparent frou-frous that were neither here nor there at covering their impossibly skinny bodies. So, it was clear, I was no fashion guru, but I embraced my cream and tan coloured overall as the best custom made item for an ape. Although it was an obvious contrast between my blackish fur and the creamy, tanned nuance of the textile, I thought that it was lively, light, and rather close to the expensively looked-after tans of the exquisitely gorgeous that were practically covering the upper decks of so many yachts. I chose a yellow beret from the several Janice brought me. It went well with the pair of thin, creamy gloves to cover my hands while painting.
The only unpleasant thing I had to accept was a long chain, covered in rubber, attached to one of my ankles,

which Janice convinced me was absolutely necessary to obtain approval for my action at the auction. The other end of the chain was firmly connected to a large plate of iron, which had been screwed in eight places on the pedestal from where I was about to paint, in front of the select audience with high interest in monkey art. The white canvasses on the three easels were ready to be painted, the nine cans of paint, four between the middle and the left easel, five on the other side, were open and waiting. A state of the art palette stand with a large number of brushes was handily accessible near the middle of the stage, without covering too much of the action. A few meters behind the easels, a table and a chair were visible. On the table there was a good stack of canvases. My tablet was also there, handy for whatever dire necessity. Separated from my raised platform, the auctioneer's desk occupied a corner area of the large room filled with impatient cognoscenti of the art market, ready to make a fast killing. The attraction has been extremely high because the auction had been announced as a unique event in which the art would be produced in front of them. So, it wasn't only an auction for ape art, it was also a spectacle, which combined with the brouhaha created already at the zoo by me, appeared to be clearly eclipsing even the most ardent political events in the city. The previous evening newspapers had brought out a number of commentaries pro and contra this event, some animal lovers criticizing the preparations for chaining me to an iron plate, while others finding the whole auction an exploitative measure toward animals in general and apes in particular. The union of plastic artists expressed their interest of being present at the auction in order to protest what they called the neglect of government and art market establishment toward the precarious situation of the artists in the city and everywhere. A public protector of the journalistic kind was asking if enough measures had been put in place to keep the audience safeguarded from my cannibalistic tendencies, suggesting that at least a few lion tamers with nets and sharpshooters with the most proper guns be at the ready in case of danger. That's why I was still pleasantly surprised seeing the capacity of the auction house fully exhausted. I was even more surprised when Janice appeared dressed with a similarly-coloured overall as mine and with a red beret to complete the arsenal. I was eager to start, determined to alter my plans according to how I will feel the reaction of the crowd.

The auction director whipped up the show with a few grandiose words about love for the closest relatives of the animal world and about the extraordinary value that art can do to facilitate the understanding of the deepest chinks in the soul. Janice took over to emphasize that most proceeds went for the Jane Doogirl Foundation for the saving of species in danger of extinction and the fact that the auction house decided to reduce their succulent commission from 15 to 7 per cent for the same purpose. She also said that it was my decision, at reading some comments in the newspapers, to allocate ten per cent of the proceeds to the union of local plastic artists, which provoked a real storm of applause in the auction house. When I appeared from behind an easel I heard some chuckles, then a complete silence. I chose a brush from the standing palette, raised my hand with it, and then bent over as I saw on the web with the help of my tablet, how a conductor was doing at the beginning of a show. I wanted to convey from the start that I was polite. I also wanted to give everybody a hint of when I was going to begin and end an act. I stretched my left hand to get a second and a third brush. With my swinging gait I turned to the paint cans and dipped in paint all three brushes, each in another can. I attacked the central canvass with sure movements. It took only a few seconds for the crowd to recognize at what was I working, even if I hadn't had time to change the brushes yet. The trick however was to make them realize that I was not copying any of the master's paintings, just his style. I added several brush strokes to bring the piece to completion, and then I wrote at the bottom of the canvass in black: MIRA MIRO. The first moment of stupor was replaced by an out-roar of approval. It was an invitation to appreciate a style that I did in front of them. If I had chosen to write Juan instead of Mira, it would have been a pastiche, and they recognized that I cleverly avoided that. A murmur going on between the cognoscenti was an obvious sign that they wanted to share with others their high understanding of my cleverness. I proceeded to make another inclination in front of the audience, to which they cleared immediately the air of any noise. I approached the left canvass after changing the brushes and dipping them again, this time in other colours. I created a deep blue background on which I sketched a woman's figure. I dressed her with a white blouse on which I added some folksy motifs in red. At the bottom I added: MY TISSE U? Was this too far fetched? I heard several laughs coming not as disapproval, on the contrary. Again, I did not pretend to have made a pastiche of a Matisse. I just gave them the style, saying that it was my way of creating both a Matisse - like painting and a tissue with a misplaced U that was also standing for 'what about you?' At my third inclination everybody applauded merrily, firmly convinced that I was totally repressing my potentially aggressive tendencies while exhibiting a double flair, the one for invoking masters and the one for calembour. For the third canvass I went again to create a light background with several strokes from a large brush and then multiple strokes with a middle brush. On this creamy-reddish background I sketched an oval face with rose cheeks supported by a longish neck coming out from a more robust body. I added the darker colours of the dress and of the coiffure, the deep, sad eyes of the model or of the imaginary nostalgic sufferer, with the inscription at the bottom: MOODY LIONESS. After my last curtsy I made a sign to the auctioneer and retreated to the chair behind the canvasses. It was time to hear the canons.

The offensive couldn't start too low because there were percentages involved that needed to clear a more robust amount. It couldn't start too high either, as it was still a monkey product that was auctioned. The sniffer of

Lost Among ...

the proper amount was an old auctioneer whose age implied, with his aura and prestige, certain recognition of the importance of the event. He started with the last painting offered for $ 3000. In a matter of minutes it went up to $ 85,000. A real Modigliani had gone in the past for over 30 million, but my simulacra was not supposed to be in the same league, it was still just an ape who painted it. The young dealer who got it seemed to have rather strange thoughts about what it wanted to do with it, because after it all ended, he was asking another auctioneer if it was OK for the ape to erase MOODY LIONESS from it. I don't know where this came to me, but when I heard about it and he was waiting for my answer, I could only show him my left fist, arm bent, with the right arm resting over the left elbow.

The second painting, the "Matisse", started directly at $80,000. Certain decorum for the value had been created by the first sale. My preference would have been actually for this one to start the auction, but obviously I wasn't in charge here. I want to say that my Modigliani, in my humble opinion, was a more valuable piece. However, the "Matisse" went stratospheric and ended at $ 650,000, taken by a French advertising company. Good luck to them, I had no idea that it could make them money by using it in their ads. What else would they do with it? Well, theirs was also some kind of monkey business, so it fit. The easiest piece of the first three, the "Miro", on which I didn't put much hope, started at $ 200,000. People got crazy here. Maybe it was the purity of the three colours in their so tight combination, with the blobs of paint overwhelming in their vivid explosion on the canvass; maybe it was the heavy bidding for the second painting, or the crafty pressure created by the auctioneer, I don't know. Maybe the audience was inclined to pay more for the abstract than for the figurative. It ended at 1,35 million. And that was just the beginning of the craze that followed. I went immediately to add more abstract pieces to my output, staying still with recognizable styles. The next six pieces went for between 1,6 and 2,4 million. Janice started to massage her face, as it almost remained in a rictus from too much silent laughing. The frenzy was showing itself in the speed with which hands went up and in the speed with which the auctioneer was pushing up again and again the price of my two minutes of canvass smudging. Maybe these utterly rich and truly spoiled guys by the randomness of life had each a money - printing machine in their basements, maybe their sense of value was perfectly altered by the company they kept, or maybe they were seeing an investment in what others were seeing as just an irony of sorts. Well, apart from the chain at my ankle and certainly all kinds of other chains, visible or not, at other people's ankles, it is a free country, free for craziness, free for wheeling and dealing, free for excesses and limitless 'limited' limits. The obvious fact that nobody was robbing anybody in this sanctuary of art display and evaluation made the whole process appear as a perfect form for merchandizing in the art market. The highest irony came from the fact that the participants were, without exception, totally versed in the complexities of the procedure and were happy to be acting in view of what everybody, sooner or later, would gain from it. Still, somebody must gain little or nothing, or worse, lose a lot because of it. But not the ones present here at the meticulous practice of creating a new niche in the ape art market.

My scant knowledge about high prices in this brush and paint business stopped at the dizziness - provoking 142 million for a triptych of large proportions. The three remaining canvases that I had were of small dimensions but could make for a triptych, just that my vision for such something stretching from one canvas to another tended to avoid the subjects that invited such use. It would have been preposterous for me to start painting some saintly, sacrosanct figures having anything to do with the trinity. That trinity was a concept that not only sat badly with my present view about the world, derived from the so many advances in science and philosophy that occupied a good part of my memory, but it was harshly contested as clear absurdity even in some circles of theology. Being an ape, I wasn't supposed to have religion, and of course, even if I had it, it certainly wouldn't have been recognized as such by the gorgeous. It would have introduced again the questions of whether I had a soul and whether such an ape soul, in case I had it, could be saved. Not being religious, could I dare to paint a religious subject? How would it be looked upon, coming from an ape? Maybe as monkey business? As an affront to the religious? So, what the heck did I have to do on a triptych if not a religious subject? But of course, the three ages of man! Even better, the three ages of mankind! Or both! But how? Childhood, maturity, senescence, these could be done easily. What were really the three ages of mankind? Maybe manual stupidity, industrial stupidity, informational stupidity? Hardly something to delve into in front of the local Maecenas, especially coming from an ape. Don't get me wrong, I do not take the view of the arrogant that all these ages were dominated by stupidity. It was the dominators who dominated and imposed a grand level of stupidity in the masses. In spite of that, it was the masses that generated, through arduous work and experience, the progress of mankind from one age to another. Maybe a different way to look at the three ages could be before - history, history, and after it, or beyond history, if we can define it somehow. Yesterday's mankind, the one of today and tomorrow's mankind. Will there be a tomorrow? The vision of trans-humanism paints a future in which humans will go beyond what they are nowadays, through technology, through genetic modification, through education. What is the essence of today's humans, and what is that of tomorrow? Will they actually be able to transcend their irrationality, their greed, their fear for pain, for adversity, for death? Take irrationality, for example. Humans are error-prone, avoid reason in favour of emotions, in that they prefer to do as they like, not as they think. Even when logic tells them not to venture into certain risky business, they do it without consideration for probable outcome, which is failure. They prefer to win and hate to lose, so they choose with preponderance situations that only might become favourable, in spite of the facts inclining to be adverse. Humans are stupid several times a day, although their brain wiring is the most complex thing in the world. And believing just that makes them even more stupid, because they throw themselves in complexities that their wiring cannot handle, thinking that they can do everything. Look at their environment, at their inability to handle the economy, at their dismal results in holding on to peace among themselves. But then look at how they handle themselves at this auction, bidding like there is no tomorrow for a piece of varnished cloth, having in mind just the fact that they actually hope to resell that cloth in the near future at even higher prices. A triptych do they need? Let's give it to them! On the left canvas I painted a pig roast on a stake on top of a roaring fire. On the middle canvass I made a huge can, not much different from Warhol 's soup can. On its label I wrote 'Frantic BACON with NUTS'. On the third canvass I went for a square array filled with multicoloured zeros and ones, the main food of the future. It was simplistic, but effective. One way or another, the triptych was food for thought.

Practically everybody in the auction room realized that I wasn't just an ape, I wasn't even just a painting ape. With a strange mix of awe and money, they have put me in a new category: the ape philosopher of art. The triptych alone went for 4.9 million. The old gentleman who had conducted the auction decided to dismiss all precautions by leaving his platform, stepping up on mine and giving me a hug. After that, visibly distressed by emotion, he turned to climb down the four stairs of my platform, tripped and fell. I couldn't help him because of the shortness of my chain, but the audience noticed my intention and applauded. Four helpers came to remove him from the floor. Janice also took her life in her hands by running up to the platform to hug me and say into my ear:

"Onkey dear, we'll fly to New York first class!" I took off my beret and exchanged it with hers, and then I put mine gingerly on her head. She looked at me quizzically, trying to understand my gesture. I slowly closed my eyes, spread my arms, and then gave her back the embrace. Only my hands, due to my short stature, rested pleasantly on her bum.

Lost Among ...

## CHAPTER 8

Percy missed the whole hullabaloo from the auction house. When Janice called him on the cellular to give him a short review of how things went and how much they accumulated, I heard everything because I was still holding her tight in my embrace. She might have liked my grabbing of her bum because she made no effort to remove my hands from there. Instead, with a vivacity that I didn't know she possessed, she got her cellular from the chest pocket of the overall she was wearing in my honour and made her call.

"Percy, Percy, hear me out. We 're rich! Can you believe it? Onkey has gone super, hyper, extra-tops with his paintings. I think we might clear about 16 million bucks when all is summed up. Onkey was fan-tas-tic! He is still holding me in his embrace, and I tell you, Percy, he deserves it. Oh, you should have seen him acting like the gentleman he is: polite, smart, genial. Even the old man who conducted the proceedings was so impressed that couldn't help without coming to embrace him first. ... What security? Yeah, yeah, just like that. And the poor man was so moved, I can understand him, you know, he has seen enough in his life, but such talent from an ape? And such exquisite behaviour from an animal? ... Yeah,

yeah, I know, we are animals too, just a bit different. How about conveying your congratulations directly to him? Wait a moment..."
With this, Janice lowered her head toward me, who was still holding her soft parts.

"Onkey dear, do you want to hear Percy telling you a few words? Just listen and when he's finished, look at me and close your eyes to signal he stopped."
She put her cellular to my right ear. Although my right hand was in a very good position, holding a cellular by myself was a novelty, so I had to let go of such pleasant flesh. I started my first telephone conversation with my hand over Janice's hand and delivering some HO!HO! HO! grunts to Percy. He must have learned to be patient when on a call with Janice, especially because the lady had such a torrent of crystalline phrases flowing out of her mouth. When he heard that I stopped my grunts, he spoke with his initial cough to clear his throat:

"Adam Onkey, you son of a gun, you are a formidable dude! I hear that you mesmerized the whole audience! I can't wait to be with you and Janice at the New-York performance. I'm working on getting a charter plane for our trip there. Congratulations! Will you please pass me Janice now? Thanks, mate!"
I had to reward my left ear with at least a moment of using the cellular, so I switched it from the right hand to the left one, but that meant that I had to get rid of holding you know what, which is a shame, because I immediately regretted that. Janice found the move liberating, as she was able to go down the steps from my platform. She

made a curtsy in front of a smaller number of people who have not cleared the room yet. One of them, a tall, handsome guy in a very well-cut outfit, holly grip! of the same colour as both mine and Janice's overalls, came to shake hands with her and to tell her that he would be so pleased to be of some help. I immediately smelled a competitor, because this guy just looked like one. After a short conversation with him, Janice took him by the elbow to direct him toward me. She said:

"Please let me make the introductions. Onkey, this gentleman is Armin Offer. He is an art dealer in Paris and Berlin. He says that you would be very welcome there in case you desired to perform in Europe. He also says that your amazing skills at painting are surpassed only by the immensity of your wit and capacity to make the right point. Mister Offer, I present to you Adam Onkey, our art and everything genius, who happens to be also my very lovable friend."

Armin Offer must have had guts of steel, because he also decided to step up the platform in order to shake hands with me. I didn't want to be impolite, although his courage could have been taken either as foolishness or as haughtiness. With his size he was towering over me. He stretched his hand toward me, but I first preferred the fist touch while looking intensely into his eyes. Seeing my fist, he accommodated me by closing his own hand. Once we touched, I wanted to feel his grip, so I opened up the fist. He grabbed my hand and started shaking it effusively, saying:

Lost Among ...

"I think I can speak for most of the art dealers of Europe when saying that they would be as welcoming to you as I am, since we do have an old tradition of supporting painters from different backgrounds and origins. Please be assured that I, personally, would like to extend my very deep appreciation and support to you and to your team. If it is not much trouble, I would like to offer my private aeroplane for both the trip to New-York and the one to Paris, if you decided to do so."
As circumspect as I was, I couldn't find any fault: the guy's hand shake was firm and totally lacking of tentativeness, his eyes were having an expression of self-assurance blended with respect, and his voice had the tones that my mind was, alas, dreaming of having for my own so silent speech machine. He was a really complete package, hard to take any other way than positively. Well, I wanted to give him a sign of my own capacity to be myself, so I slightly increased the grip of my handshake while watching his reaction. He became quite aware immediately of the pressure and responded in kind. Certainly, he wasn't a wimp. My experience with human handshaking was equal to one as far as numbers went, but relying on my memory, it was very clear that such an experience gave one, if not both hand shakers, a sense of theatrical loyalty. It occurred to me that this was a man of great action, immediately confirmed when I heard the conversation that followed:
"You guys shake hands as if you are at the signing of a pact or something. How many places in your aeroplane, Mr. Offer?"

"Just four, excluding the two for the pilots. Do you fly planes, Miss Doogirl?"

"As in piloting them? No, never, but I bet that Onkey knows something about that too. I mean, theoretically."

"That is no... mmon...major business, if you have the practice. Theory is never enough when you are, so to say, in the air..."

"But flying over the ocean, isn't that too much of a challenge for you, Mister Offer? You at least need an extra pilot, if you also pilot yourself, don't you?"

"I do have a reliable one, always available, almost perfect in most conditions. It is an automated pilot, and it comes embedded in the controls. This way, if I want, I can have five seats for passengers."

"We haven't organized anything for New-York, let alone for Paris, so I cannot see holding yourself available for dates that are not even considered yet."

"My business will take me to L.A. and Seattle for the next five days. I'll give you my business card having the contacts with which you may want to keep me up-to date. As for Paris, I assure you that with one call by me to my associates, it will be smooth sailing for your team, at any time. Just let me know when do you want to go."

"Please excuse me if I am coming a bit too frontal to you on this, but how can you explain this sudden and super-generous offer to haul us from a place to another, from a continent to another, from an auction house to another? You must have some well-hidden interest in doing that, just so, out of the blue. What's in it for you, Mister Offer?"

Lost Among ...

The man grinned with a strong set of white, perfectly aligned teeth.

"Apart of glory, nothing. I am well-known in the art community on both shores of the Atlantic, even on the shores of the Pacific. But nobody else knows me as a celebrity would be known. By taking you and Onkey over the ocean, I would enter into the history of aviation for the first small plane flight with an Anthropoid on board, which is also a model of super-intelligence. There is no money that could buy such advertising as the one preceding and following our flight. On top of that, my direct connection with you and Onkey would augment my position as an exclusive art dealer among my clientele. Isn't that motive enough?"

"You certainly are a shrewd businessman, Mister Offer."

"Please call me Armin. May I call you Janice, Miss Doogirl?"

"I don't see why not, after all it looks like we are going to share a small cabin for a while, and I'll be completely at the mercy of your piloting abilities. My colleague and collaborator on this project is Mr. Percy Letabou, who is just now looking to find some airline to accept Onkey and us on regular flights in the cabin, with not much success."

"Then we are set. Count on me, Janice. You already made history, and this way I'll be part of it, too."

With this, the art dealer turned impresario-cum-long-range pilot slipped his business card in Janice's hand, squeezed her hand and mine good-bye and left. Janice turned to me to see how impressed was I. Shaking my head to show approval, I made an expressive face and I also chuckled. It was my way of saying that he seemed genuine. He couldn't be otherwise, having a sophisticated aeroplane to take him everywhere without an extra pilot. It meant that he knew what he could do. Indeed, flying solo over the Atlantic Ocean was not for the faint of heart. He must have some explorer blood in his veins for this kind of venturesome exploits. Still, we needed to be circumspect, so I took the tablet from the table and wrote on it:

"Great job, Janice, but we must check on this guy by all means available, and not just from the internet. See if you have connections with the police, art dealers, and in the piloting communities to find out if he is the real McCoy. New York suits me a week from now, and I always wanted to climb the Eiffel Tower."

It took Janice two full days to find out that our new acquaintance was totally reliable and possessed a palmares of achievements in both art dealing and avionics. She was also capable of setting up at short notice an auction with the reputable Gander auction house in New York. The super-major houses didn't want to have anything to do with us, as they were damn speciesists, but mostly for being fearful of being tainted with the extra-label of monkey business operators. Maybe you aren't aware of what a speciesist might mean. One like this is really mean in meaning. Well, if you guessed that it sounds close to racist, you are right, only it applies as supremacist, that is, discriminatory, to other species. When Percy came with the lists of restrictions and conditions for transporting non-human Primates by commercial airlines, both Janice and I realized what a wonderful offer was available for us from Mister Offer's part. Sure, with more digging one way or another, Percy probably could have arranged for any transportation, now that we also had the dizzying amount of cash from the first auction and hopes for increased quantities of the easily printed green bills. But why splurge when it was enough to exchange favours in the right place in order to obtain free and optimum service with the person who could be our Virgil in Europe, not that I expect this part of the world to be hellish in any way. It's true, Europeans, like all humans, from time to time kill each other with great aplomb and with no better reason than an extra square meter of land, silk or pizza, but look how well one of them has described the others in the many circles and trenches where they belong.

When Armin Offer came back to Chicago, we were ready for him and for the rest of the world. He had the idea of giving us a short, accommodating flight over Chicago, with which occasion I had a good view of the city that was my birthplace. Not that I had a nostalgic attack, but that reminded me of the fact that I was an orphan who had no knowledge of who my parents were. Armin, who was trying to be jocular with me, seated me beside him and let me have the controls of the jet. He then took a few pictures of me with his smart phone and asked Percy, who was seated behind him, to do the same with his own smart phone. Janice was having a blast behind me, as she felt obliged to take over the colourful interpreting of the flight with explanations for the different skyscrapers that we were encountering. At one silent moment Armin asked her to let him explain something to me. He told me to pay attention and pushed a button that engaged the gps screen. He asked me then to show him where on the world map could I find St. John's, Newfoundland. That was easy, I touched the East extremity of the so-called Rock and a map of the island appeared. I touched again on its right side and the city's map, together with its airport, appeared in full splendour. He then showed me the three main buttons that I needed to engage in order to take off, fly and land there. He told me that the buttons are self-monitoring their status, so if I still push the take off and fly ones while I am already in flight, they assess the situation and stay inoperative. After that, he asked me to assume that I am already there and that I need to fly over the Ocean to Iceland. But first he turned off the gps, so I had to start from the beginning. Guess what? With one flick of a button, I turned on the gps screen, I went for the global map and I found Iceland on it. After I touched the point for Reykjavik. I also engaged the three buttons that he showed me previously. The jet took a gradual turn, trying to direct itself toward the target. I looked at the guy. He was smiling at me. He then found the Chicago on the map and asked me to return. Again, at the touch of the map and the re-engaging of the three buttons, the aeroplane took a gradual turn and approached the city. Armin gave me a slap on the shoulder, saying:

"See, the aeroplane knows what to do if you give it the right instructions. A few more lessons and I can go to sleep."

We were ready to leave for New York the next day.

Although I didn't need a passport, as in the eyes of the gorgeous I was still not quite a person, a good number of health certificates with fancy stamps and even fancier signatures from the right veterinary authorities had been prepared just in case. After all, I had to go over borders, which was not so much of a problem, except that those borders were manned by border officials, who are quite a separate species, all by themselves. You see, border and customs officials are the guardians with unlimited powers of interpretation. They claim that they have extra sensory perception powers. They claim that they can read minds, and they can define all the shades of green as being red. So, if they want to stop you, they stop you and there is no way they can be mollified by verbal arguments. Ah, the pleasure of applying power in a simple and mostly straightforward manner! Barring somebody from entering a country is among the most refined pleasures of this species within a species. And I, being a non-human Primate, could be easily taken as a persona non grata, which on one hand would consider me a person, but on the other hand would bar me from entering a country. The utterly gorgeous had a point with the health certificates, as certain spreading of terrible viruses had roots in populations of African monkeys. However, humans were transporting agents as well. Do they carry lots of health certificates when going over borders, as I am required to do? Find any consistency in that logic. So guess what happened when we landed at New York's La Guardia airport? As soon as we stepped in through a private gate from the tarmac, most of the people who saw us in the lounge started to run away, including airline, border and customs officials. Such a blow for my celebrity status! Mister Offer was able to show his athleticism by running after an official to ask him why is everybody running away. The official stopped, pulled out a napkin to cover his nose and mouth, and asked through gestures that his interlocutor do the same. Only when both were 'covered', the official told him that two days ago an African delegation landed and after passing through the customs, somebody from the delegation asked for a doctor. That was enough to trigger a panic. And now, my furry aspect had created, by analogy with Africa, a similar panic. It was good that Armin had a great relationship with one of the customs managers, as he passed often through their offices with lots of paintings. Still, the powers to be wanted to have a blast with me, especially after one of the officers remembered the fuss created around me in the Chicago newspapers and not only there. So, claiming that they had to check thoroughly onto the many health certificates that Percy was showing them, they used the time to pester me with questions about my immunization shots, about where and when did I had taken them, and if I became agitated when pricked. With my tablet hanging by a long belt from my neck, I was able to write some responses, to which they were grinning much more idiotically than I thought possible. One of them decided to even say:

"You are a smart ass of an ape, but not as good as a customs officer." To which I couldn't stop without writing:

"I agree, you are a better smart ass." At this, the guy became violet in the face and slapped my papers on the counter, but the other officers laughed loudly, hit him friendly over the head and pulled him away from there. We were finally free to go, but not without having to pass through a small barrage of photo-reporters who were at the ready for whatever occasion. That wasn't too bad, as the hullabaloo in the media was immediately added to the advertising set up by the auction house that was our host. A limo took us to Manhattan, where we had reservations on a hotel on the 26th Street. It was at walking distance to the Gander auction house. The only stipulation their management had in the contract with our team was for me to paint at least twenty paintings at the auction, no matter how long it would take. They figured that if with twelve paintings in Chicago we were able to gather about sixteen million bucks, with twenty works in New York there was a chance that the total would amount to thirty or forty million. Their purse, at fifteen percent, could reach six million. They'd laugh all the way to the bank, not without making a big press conference about it in order to salt over the fresh wounds of the bigger and haughtier auctioneers.

What can I say? It was a blood bath. Armin used a projector at the beginning of the presentations to show the pictures that both he and Percy had taken with me at the controls of his jet. I decided to start by doing the same, that is, to paint myself in the cabin, with the varied flying devices neatly visible on the canvas. Encouraged that the painting was immediately sold at 3.6 million, I went on making two similar ones, but in completely other nuances. They both went for almost 5 million. From there it was smooth sailing. Nothing under five, nothing over six. I peppered them with De Kooning, Mondrian, Rothko, de Vlaminck, Richter, Lichtenstein, Burri, Gorky, Pollock, and a few other modernists.

It looks like I found my price range for the time being. On the other hand, nobody, but nobody in the world of art has amassed over 105 million from one single artist producing work in one session in front of the potential buyers. I was truly a champion, at only my second auction. More than that, I was a unique piece of puzzle, because out of nowhere I elicited from all these maniacs of financial wizardry a recognition of my power to compete with them in the art of the occult domain of supply and demand. Only my scope was definitely more moral than theirs.

Armin, Percy and Janice were ecstatic. I wanted to show my affection to them, so after the auction closed, still in the presence of the management of the house, I made three small paintings in red, green and blue, each with all three of them smiling on the canvas. I wrote on the tablet: "My friends, this is my way to show you that we are a team. From now on, each of you own an authentic, genuine Onkey."

Money is always a problem to handle properly. Janice's three doctorates were not so helpful when she came in front of 120 million bucks. The amount was supposed to enter automatically into her Aunt's fund for safeguarding and preservation of wildlife in danger of extinction, except for a 10% pledged for poor artists organizations. All this big amount needed manual handling by Janice, who asked Percy and her chief, Eugene Panzon, for their input. However, in this matter they were as helpless as she was. The chief financial officer of the zoo refused to get involved, claiming that his hands were tied by the insurmountable intricacies of the huge changes through which the zoo was passing at that period, both structurally and financially. It was tantamount for him to recognize that he couldn't handle anything over his burden. Well, he couldn't be blamed too much about it. In a surprising move that nobody saw coming, Panzon told Janice on the phone that since my memory capacities were as large as demonstrated already, a few extra bookkeeping favours could be asked of me. And didn't I have enough knowledge in my head about the best investment wizards of the planet, the hedge funds that turn one slender billion into three with their léger-de-main skills? What other alternatives were available for the rising of the dough? Should the trio of Panzon, Janice and Percy hire an expert in investments or hire a group specialized for that? Obviously to me, getting one person to work exclusively for us would have some advantages, but the risks were too high. On the other hand, the hedge fund way was too costly and the risks were not missing from there either. I suggested to the three of them by way of my tablet and email a three way compromise: one third invested in major exchange trading funds following the big stock indexes, one third spread to three different hedge funds with various management rates, and the last third divided between a few solid banks, precious metals producers and realty management companies. Simple, right? Let's say, five plus three plus three plus three plus three, that is only seventeen names to follow and adjust. So, now I became also a capitalist, with my suggestion of investments supporting those same financial institutions that are regularly and perfidiously screwing the majority of the population out of their money.

There is a limit to what anybody's mind can handle, and most of it comes from the way in which we use our vast capacities for moving in and out what we call information. Bluntly put, it's a matter of memory. That's why I grin with a full set of teeth when I think about the limitations of the gorgeous. To put it another way, I don't have memory problems like they have. For them, getting into the fads of dismissing memorization in favour of creativity was and still is a deadly kiss for the development of a good, highly functional memory, without which creativity has very little chance of having what to handle. Not that all schools took this approach, which might have been suggested by the think tanks that were apprehensive at the real possibility of getting too many paupers at the helm of the society, this way usurping the hegemony of the old elites with who knows what radical consequences. That's how, drumming up to vast swats of public education the easy and fake creativity pie in the sky that has little to do with the heavy machinery of societal control, the education manipulators could maintain the hold onto the grip of power to the moneyed layers of society, schooled with more conservative learning. After all is said and done, memory is a concept hugely related to conserving. Conserving the how and the how much and for whom. Do you get it now?

Of course, now that I entered the rarefied zones of making money hand over fist due to the nebulous and mysterious covetousness of the art trade, I may be considered one of the nimble capitalists; only I do have no rapacity in my genes. I found the proper scope for this mound of gold.

Armin Offer must be a serious risk taker. After unloading a number of art works ordered personally by his well-to-do American customers and after receiving my two minutes toil which made him an even richer art possessor and trader than before, he thought of going over the vast Atlantic Ocean with his totally new load as something rather ordinary. True, his jet was state of the art, but it was still a small plane. What was a major risk for others appeared to be an opportunity for him, because he spent a number of hours before the departure with journalists, where he emphasized the fact that he had a very special passenger for the risky journey. That was I, the simian painter and super smart individual, who has taken with him flight lessons and, according to Armin, will be at the controls of the jet for part of the travel. The guy was a shameless self-promoter, because, although he was talking about me, it was he who was benefiting from the entire advertising of the event. His stature among the European art traders must have increased by a factor of ten. I wasn't envious at all, I just wondered if there might be any diminution of the potential revenue that we started already to envision from the European tour of auction houses. But a real risk was that before our take off, some pilot licensing board might invalidate his licence and block the entire voyage. So we were soon satisfied to fly away from New York unhindered and, after two refuelling stops, make it safely to Paris, where a crowd of photo-reporters spent almost two days waiting for our unscheduled, not at all secret arrival. By this time both my and Armin's artistic reputation exceeded whatever the American newspapers were able to concoct about us. Even Percy and Janice were described, in truth very meritoriously, with highest accolades, as parents of the procedure that made me who I became. The scandal tabloids and not only them were full of our pictures with positive blurbs about our auction victories in Chicago and New York. It seemed that the extraordinary press set out in Paris tried to reverse the lost position that the city had long ceded in favour of the huge American market for art. And that with the help of an ape?

Armin's confidante and secretary, Carlo Trulli, was

waiting for us at the Orly airport and tried hard to extract us from the vortex of reporters. Of equal height with Armin, with a decided but elegant manner in all his movements, dark and handsome and blue eyed, Carlo inspired a reserved and forceful presence. You couldn't think of him as a body guard because he looked more like a star actor than anything else. He took the two larger suitcases that belonged to Janice and Percy and placed them in the trunk of the Jaguar, while Armin handled the smaller one that had been devoted to my belongings that, I must confess, were very few. Carlo asked Armin if he wanted to drive, to which he responded that he preferred to seat behind, having Janice in the middle between him and Percy. That made me the happy occupant of the front seat beside the driver, obviously a premium position for absorbing a good part of the landscape of Paris parading in front of my eyes. It was early in the morning, the traffic already heavy, but the incomparable show of the large boulevards densely built, with shops and people seen everywhere, with building of importance that were not imposing by size, gave our entrance into the middle of France's capital a luminosity and a grandeur that was still easy to accept. It gave the impression of a world with a measure stick that was not overwhelming, not much beyond natural. It was maybe the density of the trees parked on both sides of the streets, the large windows of the shops at the first floor, together with the limited height of most buildings that gave the seer and the walker and the rider a sense of comfort, in spite of the multitude of cars and bikes everywhere.

"We are located quite in the middle of the city, not too far from the Luxembourg Gardens," said Carlo after a while to break the silence which established enchanted smiles on the three visitors' lips. After passing through a number of large boulevards, the car took to a smaller street and entered through a forged gate into a small park with a mansion surrounded by tall trees.

Armin tried to explain:

"There was no way to install you anywhere else but in this place of mine. Hotels over here are anything but comfortable, some too cozy, some too noisy, and some too public, if you know what I mean. This will be the right thing for all of us."

Janice appeared to be impressed by the size of the place, even if she understood the high life that her host must have carried in order to entertain the spoiled and picky crowd of business types and arts visionaries to make a living in this branch of economic endeavour. She tried but still couldn't stop a surprised comment coming out of her mouth:

"What, all this for just the five of us? I'm lost already!"

"Don't worry, you won't get lost. And actually, there is more than us around, as you'll see soon," said Armin.

To this, Carlo completed:

"Armin needs an army around him to function at full speed, and I guess you noted that he likes speed."

Percy retorted:

"Do you call that speed? He didn't move at all his hand from Janice's knee!"

Lost Among ...

Armin laughed loudly and explained:
"Paris creates a commotion in the first time visitors. I had to reassure our new friend that she is in good hands." A young man opened the door at the car's arrival in front of the house. He carried the luggage into a large hall that could accommodate a cohort of guests. Once in, Armin made the presentations:
"Janice, Onkey, Percy, this is Vania, our house administrator and down-to-earth holder of many things, among which it is an acute sense of good taste for art. I rely on him for his intuition on what new trends in art may become valuable. Please let him take you to your rooms. I will be busy for an hour to oversee with Carlo the plans for the next week. See you at brunch."
After this, Armin and Carlo entered through a door that opened just opposite to the large hall. Vania directed us newcomers to a staircase that went to the second floor, where three rooms were ready for us. Janice took me by hand to enter the room in the corner, near the one that she chose and the one that Percy was occupying. She told me:
"You'll show everybody what a civilized being you are. Be gentle and use the bathroom as trained. You are now an ambassador of the future realm of smart apes. Do you like your room?"
Instead of answering, I grabbed whichever of Janice's legs was closer and pushed my face into her bosom.
I would have preferred to share a room with her. She was my mother by operation only, but I was at the age when a female was something extraordinary for me too,

146

something to cherish and unite with. I felt that my sudden freedom, coupled with the possession of an entire room for myself, opened up untold but certainly much wished fantasies. The struggle between the rules of decent conduct taken from the utterly gorgeous as expressed in the chip's memory and my own species desires and reproductive calls needed an outburst, a resolution. Was this outburst supposed to be just expressed through art? What about my rooting for something more real, more down to earth, more carnal? Should I rebel because of the lack of this output, should I become angry and savage because of this repression? An angry chimp can be a terrible thing, especially for these feeble gorgeous who seem to have muscles made of dough. Now that I was much more than just a chimp by virtue of so much accumulation of history and knowledge and skills and human behaviour as encapsulated in my chip, could I betray my newly made relations in this astonishing world of art, artificiality and artifacts, granted, kind of decadent to some extent, but still astonishing? Was a carnal call more powerful than all what humanity has learned from its history, the need for self–control and rational contemplation before proper decision for action is taken? Or was I endowed with true wisdom by this chip of mine, countering my youth calls of the flesh, or it was just a natural tendency of mine to be both shy and full of temerity in front of the major decisions of life?

I could have stayed longer in the partial embrace. It was partial because Janice was still holding my hand while I was holding whatever I could grab of her leg, and my heightened sense of touch realized that it was the better part of it, that is, the buttock. She must have felt desired, a sentiment that many people can hardly resist when coming from the right counterpart. Now that I was not only super–smart, super–artsy, but also super–productive in one of the most lucrative niches of the transfer of riches, maybe she considered me a partner-able partner, not only in her and Percy's process of improvement of species, but in that of high–breeding? Who knows what and how much goodie may come out from such a cross–breeding? Alas, my dreamy period came to an end when Janice pulled me closer for a moment, and then gingerly separated herself from me with a delicate movement that I was unable to counter, as I was probably expecting the feel of a new embrace coming from her.

"Now be a good boy and make yourself completely comfortable in your room; I'll do the same in my room and see you in a while. Make sure not to wet your tablet if you intend to take a shower. Bye, dear." And she kissed me on the forehead and she left me dumbstruck in the middle of the room. As if I wasn't speechless enough!

I really couldn't say right away what Percy was doing at that moment in his room, but I can figure it out now, after so many other things happened and have a quite vastly different view of who was what and who wanted what in the whole scheme of things. You see, Percy was kind of secretive with regard to his work. His brilliance has never been fully recognized in the academic circles or in the corporations that he worked for from time to time. Apart from creating the chip that I was wearing and setting it up with the right amount of memory through an incredibly sophisticated software, his two other achievements about that chip, which he did not divulge to anybody yet, were in the capacity of that chip to re-energize biologically, that is, without needing any outer electrical input, and its capacity to act as a blue-tooth device. That allowed my brain to read or receive any information that was also available on the internet through a modem-router device. Practically, I could use anybody's near smart phone to attach myself to the web. Conversely, Percy's smart phone, which was paired with my chip, could extract and read from me whatever readable data to him. It made for a powerful information weapon with complex implications. Percy had this way a certain capacity to control me, or at least to give me instructions that I could follow or not. But it wasn't only him who could communicate with me, I could also choose to see what was going on in his smart phone, if he left the device open to my spying. This is how I soon discovered that he was interested of finding out what kind of communications were going on in the mansion in which we were guests. So, while Janice was taking a shower and I was lounged on my humongous bed, I saw and heard through his smart phone that Carlo was contacting a hospital equipment company in Paris, Vania was dealing with the auction house that was preparing our show both in Paris and in Berlin, and Armin was promising somebody an important amount of money. In short, inadvertently, I was spying on the spy who was

spying on the house. If Percy was doing it on purpose or not I couldn't realize at the moment, but it seems now that in time it served us well. You see, I was curious enough to wonder who was the person to whom Armin promised such an important amount of money. With his cell number in my head and a bit of browsing, I realized that Armin was talking to no other than one of the most prominent neuro–surgeons in the country, Dr. Sebastien Lacan.
I guess that Percy must have become at least as suspicious as I became, putting one and one together, that is, the neuro–surgeon and the hospital equipment. One and one and one, because there was also the amount of money. That should have added to three, only there was an unknown called X, which added to four: why would Armin pay a neuro–surgeon a huge amount of money, and why was Carlo ordering hospital equipment, sounding more like a full operating room? X meant that there was an operation planned, and that had nothing to do with paint and art auction. Operation, what operation would a neuro–surgeon do if not on a brain? As far as I was aware, I was the only one around with a hole in my skull. Was Armin envious of my skills residing in my skull? Was he interested to lift up my chip? To insert it into his own brain? Was all his excellent service available only to approach us for getting close enough to my chip? He had practically all that humans needed and much more: health, youth, handsomeness, riches, strength, contacts on all continents. What was I missing about what he was missing? Who the hell needed an extra hole in his brain? And not just the hole, but also a strange foreign object

that nobody knows for sure what it could do to their brain. And what about me? If they stole my chip out of my brain, what would happen to me? I already lost my own ape-ish personal memory from before surgery and implantation. Without the chip, I would become a vegetable. Unless my own brain cells retrieved at least some part of the memory out of the chip. How that situation could play out nobody would know before the chip extraction. Well, well. I wasn't ready to accept any of this. After all, now I was somebody. And not alone. There were Janice and Percy with me, they could shield me from all this. Unless... Unless they would play Armin's game. He could afford it, he was very rich, he could get even richer after the auctions in Paris and Berlin, and who knows how gullible or corruptible all these people are? I was stretched on a pleasant bed in a great bedroom in one of the most beautiful places on Earth, with all kinds of superlatives in my head and in my deeds, and I was having a morning nightmare. Again, I seemed to be lost.

Lost Among ...

CHAPTER 9

Armin's mansion had the form of an inverted T. Our rooms were located on the left side of the T bar, and the dining room was under us, on the first floor. Vania came to invite us for brunch, and with this occasion gave us also a short visit through some parts of the house. The central piece of the house was continued in the leg of the T with two floors, both which contained private art galleries and a warehouse, which also served as a carpentry workshop, mostly for the intricate frames of the paintings. We weren't shown the right hand of the T bar, but were told that it was used as offices downstairs and other bedrooms upstairs. The galleries were not for public visiting, but we were among the exceptions that Armin would invite for special occasions. He had another gallery, a public one, on a street close to the Opera, curated by two employees. Vania gave us a short presentation of the lower part of the gallery, saying that the upper one will be shown to us by Armin himself. Even with my memory working at full tilt, I couldn't recognize many paintings on the walls, although it was clear that they were quite impressive in the sure manner and forceful expression in which they were painted. Vania explained that they were a collection of Russian paintings from a period that wasn't publicized much and as such, were practically unknown, but they formed with others a trend that became increasingly sought after by some collectors. He said that he had a hand in convincing Armin to collect them, as he was more familiar with that market.

The dining table was large enough for sixteen people, but we were only seven. Armin was standing when we came in and introduced us to Beatriz, a Spanish woman in her mid forties with a very pleasant demeanour.

"She is my main angel for the entire operation," said Armin. Carlo found necessary to complete the picture, by saying:

"Beatriz knows everything about all the collection, and everything about all our clientele. She already knows who has each of your paintings, Onkey, and for how much."

Armin, at the top of the table, invited Janice to sit on his right side and Beatriz on his left. I was seated beside Janice, facing Carlo, and with Percy beside me, in front of Vania, the arrangement seemed appropriate, except for the fact that all the four members in Armin's household appeared to have exactly the same height. Janice was making a nice figure, but Percy and I seemed much shorter because of the comparison with the ones on the other side of the table. As for me, I was hardly reaching the table. Armin excused himself for a moment and left the room. We didn't know what to do. Nobody was saying anything. It was embarrassing, as I thought these people must have had some conversation training. I jumped on the chair, sat on my knees to better reach the level of the table and pushed the plates towards the middle to make space for my tablet. I typed on it for some moments, then showed the results to Janice. She started laughing, then told the others, with interrupted laughs almost after every word:

"Our boy says that he is going to eat one of you if you don't give him something to eat right away. He also says that he might start with Vania, as his flesh might be more tender, and leave Beatriz for dessert."
Seeing their contorted faces at what they just heard, I started to clap my hands with glee. They realized that I was just joking and that I was actually enjoying myself of the macabre threat. Janice's relaxed mood at what she had read off my tablet was supposed to give them at least enough assurance that the threat wasn't at all serious, but a potentiality must have remained somewhere in the back of their minds. My species had given them reason enough to be terrified at what a small ball of fur and limbs can do. However, I was something else. I had a strong sense of humour, black or of any other shade. And I had a set of rules. Was I capable of savagery in spite of these rules? Of course I was, but I needed to reassure my table companions. I wrote on my tablet and then pushed the tablet in front of the stunned ones facing me. Beatriz read aloud:

"Rest assured, I am more human than you three are. I am the voiceless voice of reason. You are safe with me. Am I safe with you?"
I watched attentively their demeanour at her reading of

my words. Neither of them seemed to be shocked in any way of how my reassurance sounded. I assumed that Beatriz and Vania might not have any actual complicity in preparing me for surgery. Carlos, the one ordering the surgery room from a hospital equipment manufacturer, might have had an inkling on what that room was needed for, but surely didn't show it. Maybe he had a poker player's face, maybe I couldn't read much on it, maybe his order had nothing to do with me. For the moment, I couldn't dig deeper. Armin returned with a children 's high chair and asked me if I wanted to change my seat.

I nodded approvingly and jumped on it with joy. Finally, I was reaching the table's surface with ease. I suddenly felt I was taller.

"I don't know about your diets," started Armin, showing the table empty of any food, "but for a while I tried only fruits on an empty stomach, and guess what, I am much more energetic now. Granted, I won't force you to such a diet, I only wanted to make it known to you before anything else is put on the table."

With this, as if by magic, a portion in the middle of the table opened up to allow for a large porcelain plate filled with a huge variety of exotic fruits to be raised from nowhere. Percy was so enchanted that he started clapping. It must have been for the surprise apparition of the plate, or maybe for the really fabulous composition of the different colours, nuances and textures of the fruits on the plate. Janice stretched her right arm behind my back and gave Percy a small hit on his shoulder, saying:

"Come on, man, behave yourself! These people

here would think that you've never seen fancy fruits in your North American cave."

"But I can't eat them! Don't you see, they are a splendid work of art!"

Saying this, Percy grabbed a spoon and filled his plate rapidly with blueberries, dragon fruits, and cherries, obviously ravaging the whole arrangement. He also used his spoon to help me, by letting me approve the tentative selection that Percy was trying to make for me, by pointing with the spoon to one or another of the fruits on the plate and waiting for my head's bending approval. Janice was next, also supplementing my plate with a few fruits, knowing quite well my appetite and predilections. Armin followed, and then the other three table companions took their servings, as if a clockwork established the clockwise order of filling their plates.

"Leave some room for the sea fruits, unless you are afraid of your cholesterol levels going up," said Armin, and as he finished saying that, the fruit plate lowered itself in the hole at the middle of the table and another plate appeared from there, carrying this time king crab legs, large shrimps and oysters. This plate had in the middle of it a raised, smaller, empty plate, with a function that became obvious a bit later.

"May I suggest that you take the oysters first, they are hot from the oven," said Beatriz, and showed everybody that she was very familiar with how to engorge herself with one of them.

Janice turned to me with a worrisome face and asked me,

Lost Among ...

"What do you think, do you want to try them?"
I raised up my shoulders and pushed my lower lip more
prominently, as if trying to say, "Why not?" and grabbed
an oyster with dexterity, brought it up over my head, and
with the mouth open upwards, let the mollusc slid off its
valve in my entrails.

"Hey, Onkey, you are a natural!" exclaimed Vania,
and followed my example with an exaggerated gulp. After
that, laughing and making small noises, everybody went
for the same sumptuous movement. Carlos took two crab
legs and started drumming in the plate's rim, after which
he started to suck profusely from one end of a leg. More
tactical, Armin proceeded to cut with a pair of scissors the
crust along the axis of a crab leg in order to get to the soft
flesh from the inside. The method appeared more
effective to all, so everyone started using the scissors
that they only now recognized as part of their own table
set. It was quite obvious that while Beatriz and Armin
were familiar with the procedure, the others were having
a blast at trying, gayly and vociferously, of being more
and more successful in getting to the delicate meat.
When the lower plate got exhausted and the upper plate
filled with the hard parts of the sea fruit, the mechanism
of the clever table engorged them and made space for
what, another plate, this time with drinks: coffee, tea,
juices. and toast.

"I was about to fall asleep without my portion of kick
in the butt," said Carlo and threw himself onto a good
amount of espresso. "Mannaggia," he added for himself
in his nonna 's language, "mi servirebbe un serbatoio

intero per svegliarmi!"
Beatriz offered immediately to clarify the atmosphere by translating for the others:

"Don't mind him, it's an accepted vulgarity to say 'Dammit' in Italian. He claims that he needs a full tank to wake up. A full tank of espresso, that is."

"Carlo, as a doctor I need to tell you that, although coffee may be good for your heart, espresso in too large quantities is a killer," intervened Janice with a frowning look.

"How large, dear Doc, 'cause I'm ready to beat the World record for espresso drinking, with you as a referee." After a small pause, he added with a smirk,

"With five oysters and five espressos, I can become a locomotive, and I invite you to try to stop me if you can!"

"As if I didn't know, these Italians are like my Spaniards, so full of macho that they leave a wet track of it behind, wherever they go!"

"What about you, Vania? Are you Russians also macho?" asked Janice to involve him in the chit chat.

"We are the strong, silent types," declared Vania with a smile, then added:

"And although, according to Cehov, we are sinners, as everybody else in this world, we purify ourselves and get rid of our sins. How else can we be, but pure? After all, we constantly purify ourselves with vodka, the little water with huge fire in it. But since I said that we are the silent types, I must shut up!"

Janice turned to Armin with an air of devilish humour to ask:

Lost Among ...

"Where do you stand in these matters, Armin, I mean, what's your, dammit, dynamite drink?"

"Oh, you want to go for an under the belly hit, won't you? Try to find my weak spot, eh? Well, as my name implies, I have an arm in good cognac, but that is only occasionally, and as my other name implies, only when I can offer it too, or share it with the right person."

My tablet was open, so I wrote as fast as I could, and then directed Janice to the screen. She read:

"Tête á tête, va en quelle bête?"

Janice blushed all of a sudden, and then turned to me, saying:

"You have to curb your extravagant humour, we are guests here and everybody expects us to be well behaved and with the proper use of our tongue, tongues, language, oh, well, whatever!"

After which she blushed again, this time to the top of her forehead. Beatriz tried to move onto another page with the topic, announcing:

"Carol the twelfth of Sweden was much more frugal with his meals than we are, but then, we are not the belligerent types. Our schedule for today is to visit the Louvre first and La Défense after, to roam around the city a bit and take in the atmosphere of the main boulevards. Armin, Carlo and Vania will join us in the evening for a light dinner in Montmartre, say at six at 'Les Enfants Perdus'. We have tickets for a ballet at the Opera at 8 o'clock. I hope you'll soldier with me. I guaranty you'll be in bed and sleeping at 11 sharp."

"Sleeping or dead?" asked Percy.

160

I moved higher my ears. Was Percy joking now? Was he trying to be defensive? Did he know or had he some dark intuition of what might come, what with all that hospital room and neuro-surgeon that I had heard about earlier? As nobody reacted with any hint of acknowledgement into his remark, I tried to assure myself that I was not actually paranoid, and that for the time being I needed to dig more deeply to find out what was concocted in that surgery preparation and for whom.

"What about tomorrow," asked Janice, "will we be soldiering again or get to practice for the Paris Marathon?"

"My dear Janice, you'll be so happy you did this marathon with me, you'll ask for an encore. With this tour we'll find out more about what and who ourselves are. This is an exceptional occasion that Paris gives every visitor. I was one such visitor at some time and I must say that more than I learned about Paris, I did really learn about myself."

"Oh, Beatriz, I'm sure that you are going to be the best guide for our stay here. I just wonder if I could, from time to time, pull up my soul with me."

"That's a strange way to speak for a neuro- surgeon and scientist like you," said Carlo, then decided to continue, "What do you actually mean by the soul, and how could you pull it with you, as you just said?"

"You are asking big questions, Carlo, don't you? Without getting into a dissertation about the subject, I must say that the way I see and understand the concept of the soul is strictly materialistic, that is, as deriving from the complex workings of our brains, but with some influences from the rest of our bodies, and even more powerfully, from the web of relations that we establish all along our lives with the world around us."

"So, according to you, there is no mutability of the soul outside of the body? No immortality of it?
No transcendence?"

Percy decided to enter the fray with his own views:

"Dear Carlo, you live in a house that is full of immortality, at least a relative immortality. I refer to the art products, which in my view, confer to their creators a kind of immortality. It is a form of memory, if you want to see it this way, of what came out of their activity. Just imagine yourself as a being without memory and you'll understand that there is no way of talking about the essence of yourself, expressed in the soul. Now, if it comes to mutability of memory from a mind to another, there is no better example than what you have right in front of you, our extraordinary phenomenon which is Onkey. Only his memory is much more different than what we, as poor individuals, develop over a life time. His is a collective, assembled, artificial, systemically created, effectively nano - molecular memory of our civilization, implanted in his brain. Ask Onkey if he has a soul."

"Hey, Onkey, what do you think, do you have a soul?" went Carlo inquisitively, looking directly into my expressive eyes.

Everybody was focusing now on me. I was about to crack a joke in order to put myself in the right light, but would it have the same effect if only written instead of expressed with the proper voice intonation, one thing that I certainly couldn't do? I went for the written variant anyway. First I shook my right index finger at Carlo as if he was a child that needed scolding, and then I put up my arms to signal a kind of hooray coming out of my chest. I typed, with capitals in my tablet,

"APE -SOUL-UTELY!!!" and under it, with a thick underline, the words:

"I have the soul of humanity in me. With an appetite for an ape soul too, but that's ancient history."

"Well, then both of you seem to be correct," tried to conclude Vania. "The soul is of material provenance, is a memory of self, and being a memory, can be transported somehow."

"Vania, don't confuse a memory of a person, such one that gets evolved in a process of maturation and existing intrinsically within the neural network of the brain, whether in the proteins of the neurons or in the practising habits of the synapses between them, with a dry amount of data spread like butter on a piece of bread."

With this, Janice stood up and made everybody understand that she ate enough and also had enough of the previous discussion.

Armin helped her by pulling back the chair on which she had set. He proceeded to get me a hand to jump off my high chair, as if I actually needed one. He addressed me:

"Dear Onkey, please allow me to ask forgiveness for a number of things that you may be exposed to, due to our limitations as stupid humans. Not everybody in Paris knows of your presence here, and even those who do, are ignorant to the fact that you are a perfect gentleman. Some authorities may allow you in certain places only if you wear some proper attire and a leash. Beatriz took care of a number of these things and together with Janice and Percy I hope that you will enjoy your before–auction days with us. See you at 6 for dinner."

With this, Armin pushed his right fist to meet with mine, bumped me again twice, turned and left. Vania inclined himself ceremoniously in front of Janice, then Beatriz, then me. Carlo put one hand to his back, another to the scruff of his neck, after which he made a few tarantella steps in front of the ladies, did a side jump in front of me, and then performed the very distinguished old salutation as if taking off his hat and offering it with two waving movements from his right arm to the present audience. Janice took me by hand and we followed Beatriz into her chambers to make me a more acceptable Parisian. As for Percy, he announced that he will wait for us at the entrance.

Well, Beatriz must have had a sailor lover on her mind, because she pampered me with a blue sailor costume and a white beret with an anchor insignia in front. I also got a less obvious belt around my left wrist to function as a leash. My tablet was on my chest, hanging as usual from my neck. A conspicuous white napkin was settled in my left front pocket, just in case. We were ready. The ladies got themselves sunglasses and large hats to provide them with some shade. It would have taken less than three minutes, but Beatriz wanted to let

Janice try a few of her jewelry. That got me making a few grunts, so the ladies finally gave up and left the room. We took a less pretentious, convertible Renault from the herd of cars in the subterranean garage. I was seated, of course, in front, near Beatriz, who cut a nice figure in her peachy, vaporous dress. Percy was behind, and Janice, I assume that only to see better through the space between my seat and the one in which was seated Beatriz, appeared dangerously close to Percy. When I say 'dangerously' I only mean it so that you may understand that I had a faint nuance of jealousy, even if I wouldn't have minded putting my left paw over Beatriz's right thigh. What can I say, the air in Paris seems to have a lot of hormones floating around freely. No wonder they call it the love capital of the world. Whether that's love or something else, I 'll let you decide.

It's not my intention to make a description of the Louvre, because the museum has a lot of everything, from ancient antiques to modern sculptures, from clay tablets to diamonds and crowns, from papyrus to paintings and oh, well, the newest of the newest, the so called installations. Actually, you cannot even enter the Louvre without going through the biggest of them all, which is the glass pyramid. I have to confess that it really got me, although I knew about it in some detail. A pyramid gives you a sense of stability, of accumulation, of conservation, of focus. For me, somehow all these qualities get related to the faculty with which I had been extensively endowed, that of memory. What is a museum,

Lost Among ...

if not an exercise in conserving some of the memory of a
civilization? Beatriz was efficient in other places, but the
Louvre was a monster of a museum which gobbled up all
and every visitor in no time. So, what to do in such a
case, with barely two hours to go through the so called
points of highest interest? Victoria of Samothrace, a
Hercules, Mona Lisa, a famous frozen in time disc
thrower would be mostly whatever the regular visitor
could handle, apart from the sense of crowding and
immensity of the place. There was too much to absorb by
the little human heads.
Curiously enough, leaving the Louvre in order to reach La
Défense, a newish business neighbourhood established
at the opposite end of the so called Historical Axis of
Paris, gives you the same feeling of personal smallness
because of the grandeur of everything encountered:
Place de la Concorde with its Egyptian obelisk, the
Champs Elysées, a fabulous boulevard with super
expensive real estate, Place de l'Étoile or, with its newer
name, Place Charles De Gaulle, containing in its middle
the magnificent Arc de Triomphe, where a dozen straight
avenues intersect, forming a radial traffic hub. The
Historical Axis continues from the Arc de Triomphe to
reach a length of 10 kilometres, ending with the incredibly
monumental frame of a building named La Grande Arche.
It is a Gallic enormity at its best, although my data set
says that it has been designed by a Danish architect.
    "Stupendous!" exclaimed Janice several times on
our reaching any of these tumultuous constructions,
created with specific designs to encompass humanity's

smallness and France's capital urban greatness.

Acting both as a chauffeur and as a travel guide was easy for Beatriz, as she must have done this for many other high valued of Armin's guests from other parts of the world. She would say a few words when the car was stopped in the criminally insane traffic, completing with an explanation on whatever she was showing previously to her audience. When approaching an important building or monument, she would just stretch her right or left arm to point at it and say its name. While she was stretching her right arm, I found it pleasant for me to touch her shoulder and follow with my walking fingers the length of her arm, trying in the same time to assess her reaction to my touch. She 'd smile almost imperceptibly, but find the proper moment to caress my left cheek and place my wandering hand closer to my own body. For me it was the most fun part of the whole car travel. I liked the intense darkness of her gaze and the "je ne sais pas quoi" of her attitude toward me. Decidedly, she knew how to temper my small efforts for effusion, without being at all reserved or cold. The pedestrians that we encountered, although in the habit of seeing and being unfazed at the many peculiarities of a metropolis of that size, couldn't refrain gasps of surprise at my view. It was more difficult when strolling through a number of places after parking the car. As soon as we got to a side-walk, the stunned onlookers appeared frozen from the neck down, their heads only turning toward the little sailor monster that pity–patted on their turf. Our group had to learn how to navigate through the maze of human statues blocking our advance.

Lost Among ...

Beatriz showed her athleticism when we started going up the stairs towards the renowned Sacré-Coeur basilica in Montmartre. Happy to escape from the constrains of the car seat, I started to run up those stairs, and Beatriz, holding the leash that was attached to my left wrist, looked like a mountain goat while keeping up with my exuberance. Here we had to slalom upwards amongst the hordes of tourists and local time–wasters that populated the entire grandiose scene.

A good part of Paris was stretching down from the little piazza in front of the basilica. Waiting for the slower Janice and Percy, and taking in the panorama of this marvellously structured yet artistically conceived capital, we kept our calm and proper poise while all the video and photographic equipment on the huge mound that gave the name to the neighbourhood was targeted at us.

I wandered if I could confide in Beatriz with a number of key questions. Seated on one of the top stairs, with Beatriz beside me, I took my tablet that was hanging, as usual, from my neck, and typed for her:

"Can I trust you to be totally discreet and honest with me?"

She made a surprised stricture with her lips, but recovered immediately and asked:

"Why, of course, darling, what's on your mind?"

"What kind of loyalties do you have versus Armin, Carlo and Vania?"

"You little rascal, you want to know everything with just a question? Armin is just my employer, the best I ever had, so you get the picture. Vania is a sweet, totally innocuous man for me. Carlo was my lover for a while, if that's what you want to know, but we are both cool now."

"Fine, it's grand for you to be so open. Now, are they totally inoffensive toward me?"

"How can you ask something like that? Of course they are!"

"Fine again, but what do you know about plans for acquiring a hospital surgery room?"

"You astonish me. What gave you this idea?"

"I heard Carlo negotiating in the morning for it."

"Onkey, don't fib. I was totally honest with you, why are you otherwise with me?"

"My powers of hearing are different than yours. It's the truth. You still didn't answer my question."

"I'm totally in the dark about this, and don't even see the connection with you. Wait, Janice is a neuro–surgeon! And you, you have been operated by her! Maybe it's a present that Armin wants to make to Janice? Believe me, he can afford such gestures, although I don't see the point."

"Well, since I trust your faculties, just think a bit more. Dialectically, if you may. And please, keep me up–to–date."

Huffing and puffing, Janice and Percy got to the top, smiling sheepishly. Turning to take in the vista, Percy spit through the teeth:

"I saw from a distance that you are both in a confession mood. What the heck are you sharing without involving us?"

"Eternally ostracized, poor Percy, isn't this your picture?"

"Yeah, everybody keeps me in the dark about everything, this is why I became a computer hacker in my youth, and believe me, it served me well."

"It's marvellous looking down from here!" exclaimed Janice, although she heard quite well that the topic wasn't the view.

"Percy tries to make you jealous of me, as I became so intimate with Onkey."

"Our hero can be very persuasive; if he enchants you using one method or another, you hardly stand a chance at resisting him."

"He did enchant me all right, and I find both his touch and his gaze very, how should I say, sensual?"

"Then it's not sensual, it's consensual!" exclaimed Percy, and grinned with the maximum amount that his lips allowed. They were all looking at me now to see my reaction. I typed:

"As beastly as I am, you know quite well that my sentiments are positive and totally benign toward all of you. I love you all."

"Proof positive that Paris turns all beasts into lovers," added Percy. "Should we all start making declarations to each other?"

"Oh, Paris, point me toward my true love and let me perish in its whirl," recited Janice emphatically.

"Is that Browning?" asked Percy. As there was no reply, I typed:

"No, it is Rian Tal."

"Rian Tal? Is he the guy who wrote 'The Vile Comedy'?" asked again Percy.

"Nope, he wrote 'The Depth of Azurite' and other stuff," came my response on the tablet.

"Heck, you are not funny anymore! The man cannot say a word without you correcting him. Bookworm!" exclaimed Percy again.

By this time we were already encircled by a good number of onlookers and camera clickers that were obstructing our view and although still respectful, they were putting a bit of stress onto our group. It was time to move on. Beatriz looked at her watch and then said loudly:

"Guess what, if we don't rush, we might be late at the restaurant. The walking, the exiting of the parking and the traffic may delay us a lot."

"Catch me, Percy, if you can!" challenged Janice and pushed him sideways, after which she started to jump down the stairs of the massive staircase. As Percy followed her, Beatriz remained behind with me. I took another jab at my tablet:

"Will you help me with the surgery conundrum?"

"Don't be ridiculous! Oh, in this light, I misread that last word! You are safe with me, Onkey. You are nobody's property."

"That's a Freudian slip, isn't it? Both the word misreading and the 'safe with me' expression makes it a double slip."

"Clever, clever, tease forever. Onkey dear, I 'd do

anything for you. I mean, anything reasonable."
    "That's what I want to hear. Just keep me abreast, at your breast; oh, I'm getting soft already."
We descended slowly the staircase, letting each and everybody around to admire our proud parade.

    The restaurant with the strange name wasn't too far. The guys were already there and had ordered the usual entrées when we came in. We got seated under a fresco with a forest, some shadows on a hill and two angelic girls, a black one and a white one in foreground, suggesting maybe some lost kids. I wondered if Beatriz was making a reference to my tribe in choosing the dinner place with this name. A window was showing a good view to the Villemin Parc nearby.  Armin excused himself and made a clear sign for Percy to follow him.
I saw them outside of the window, Armin offering Percy a short cigarette, puffing together and having a conversation with the torsos bent forward, as if the content of what they were saying needed to stay very close to one another. From the way they were moving their lips, the word "chip" came rather easily to me. So, that was connecting a bit with what I already knew: the neuro–surgery room, the French neuro–surgeon, and now the chip. Obviously, it wasn't French fries or potato chips they were talking about. And since my silicon technology knowledge allowed me to figure out that Percy couldn't have created just one XMON chip for my brain, it must be reasonable to assume that he retained somehow in his wallet a number of these wondrous memory chips,

one of which made me who I was now. Was Armin obsessed with my intelligence? Was he so competitive that he wanted to be at least as encyclopedic as I was? Would he risk losing his own mind, his own interior diary in order to compete with an ape? Would Percy be so attracted by the high stakes that Armin could offer him in order to give in and let him have a chip? What role had the cigarettes in all of this? Too short for being regular. Was Armin using dirty tricks? Everything was possible.

Except for Beatriz, who was seated with us 'Americans' against the wall, the three musketeers were facing us and the wall with the lost kids. Vania showed his purification procedure, emptying two vodka glasses to everybody's health. The room was noisy enough, so the exchanges in conversation got lost in good part, as other tables were at a much higher decibel level than our table. The bruscheta and the caviar disappeared in no time after raising a few glasses. My glass had been pre-ordered with orange juice, as the junior that I was. Junior or not, I understood only with some difficulty the vacuous propensity of humans for strong spirits, and Vania' s purification claim made sense to me only to the extent that he was trying to kill some germs inside his guts. The forty per cent alcohol in all these spirits might have worked as a disinfectant in many cases, but was also a potent drug that was allowing for a trodden path on the street of perdition. What can I say, it was another curious aspect of human rationality or lack of it. Beatriz had pre—ordered something special, because the chef himself, a

Lost Among ...

friend of hers, brought the plate with 'veau de mer en cocotte', one of his specialities. I can only say that it was exceedingly good because of the very unusual dabbing with spices. Carlo said that he ate something similar, but even better in Trastevere, one of Rome's more colourful neighbourhoods. Janice could not stop herself from commenting of the fact that we are robbing the oceans of their riches and leave for the future generations an environment that may be so imbalanced and so poor that it may never recover. Everybody agreed with her, while stuffing themselves with the well–spiced meat.

The Opera was close, but we still needed a bit of driving to find the right parking. The ushers looked suspiciously at me when I presented them with the ticket that Beatriz had provided for all of us, but I blew a kiss to the one that deserved it most and she raised her shoulders, disarmed. The fact that the seats for all of us were in a loggia near the so called Imperial one might have helped the usher refrain from trying to object to my entry. I felt smaller than necessary while climbing the grandiose staircase toward our seats, from where the view of the entire theatre was indeed breathtaking, especially the ceiling with Chagall' s painting. There was an air of opulence wherever I was looking, in the main candelabra with hundreds of lights, in the heavy curtain of the stage, in the gilded walls contrasting with the red upholstery of the seats, so much so that my sailor's costume didn't appear that strange anymore, at least not to me. I felt slightly opulent myself, a feeling that should

174

have bothered me a bit, but at that moment it didn't. I felt as if I was the tamed wild Africa itself, raised to the power of light. The modern dance pieces that were presented on the stage reminded me of the need and efforts of all beings to express themselves one way or another, and of the more or less explicit code that stays at the base of all communication. In this sense, whether the pieces had a stronger or weaker decadent connotation, whether they were having a transferable meaning or were just movement happenings concocted by the choreographers and the dancers, it was for each spectator to decide. All in all, an art experience much like so many others from the pantheon of modernity.

When returned to the mansion, I found a moment after everybody retired to their rooms and knocked at Percy's door. He opened it just a bit, and when he saw me, told me to wait for him in my room for about an hour. It put me on a guessing game of who might he be occupied with for that hour. So I decided to be generous and let him have two hours instead of one. To no avail, as he appeared at my door in 60 minutes sharp, as if an inner clock was in control of him. With my tablet in front of me, I started the nocturnal conversation:

"Armin seems to have a special interest in you. What did he want from you outside of the restaurant?"

"He's a smart guy, I have to give that to him. He realized that I couldn't have produced just one XMON for you. He wants to buy at least two loaded ones from me."

"Did he tell you for what purpose?"

"That's where he tried to remain mysterious."

"I think I might find out what the mystery is. What do you intend to do about his request?"

"Well, as you perfectly know, the chips have value only if implanted. This brings up the question of who can do that, and to whom?"

"It's obvious, for the first question the answer is Janice. She is the only one to have perfected the procedure. The murky part is for whom would the implant go?"

"One way or another, Armin appears to be the perfect manipulator: not only has he access to an exceptional art trade arrangement through you, he has got both Janice and me in the same sweep for whatever he intends to do with the chips. I confess that I agreed to let him have what he wants."

"But he didn't convince Janice yet to offer him her skills, did he?"

"That might be more difficult, considering that it's a six hours micro and macro surgery, and that we have no idea about the target."

"I can tell you that there is a surgery room about to be delivered here in the next hours, and that a famous Parisian surgeon had been co-opted for something related to this."

"How the heck do you know all this?"

"You forget that I'm your creation with vastly exceeding capabilities than what meets the eye."

"So, you know thyself better than I do."

"It's just that you humans have a huge propensity to

176

forget what's good for you."

"Mister Genius, I embarrassingly admit that you have surpassed me in many ways, but as long as you recognize that I am your creator and not the other way around, everything's OK."

"Well, I did wonder at some time whether you have boinked my mommy and as a consequence I became the result of one more natural experiment than what came after, that is, the implant."

"You have a dirty mind, Mister Genius, especially with your capacity for permutations of all kind. I am only your chip creator, and that is all."

"So, will Janice fold in front of Armin's impetus?"

"It depends if she can agree on the basis of ethical acceptability. Otherwise, Armin can convince a stone to share..."

"Sharing stone? Sharon Stone? Are you making a joke or you are into day dreaming?"

"Well, it's late and I'm exhausted. I had my own sharing, you know..."

"Yep, go to bed dear Creator, we'll find out more tomorrow."

Lost Among ...

## CHAPTER 10

I do not pretend to be psychic, but my eyes were seeing that the atmosphere at breakfast this morning was both languorous and filled with a certain delicate aura of satisfaction. The seating arrangement has changed, with Janice at Armin's right, but facing me, so I could see all the almost imperceptible relaxations in her visual muscles, saying what most people couldn't read. Beside me was Beatriz, who was facing Percy. He tried to appear as non-fazed as a Formula 1 pilot, but he was doing it all wrong: his eyes were looking everywhere else than at Beatriz, and his rib cage seemed to have doubled overnight. Vania was at the other side of Beatriz, and Carlo was missing. Armin explained that Carlo had some early business and had asked to be excused. With a voice that seemed more melodious and decidedly louder, Beatriz tried to prepare us for the points of interest that we were supposed to see today, the second in the three as guided visitors before my performance at a well known auction house in Paris. When she got to the part where she had started to extoll the vastness of the Versailles palace and gardens, Armin interrupted her, saying that size and opulence don't always need to be seen as signs of quality. I couldn't refrain myself at that, grabbed my tablet and wrote:

"Beethoven said that he doesn't recognize any other sign of superiority but goodness. On what scale do we measure that?"

"You cannot get too technical in a house of art, Onkey! You do know that there is a certain evanescence of metrics for what and how we make appreciations, that's why quality is not that easy to grab."

"Speaking of evanescence, where did Carlo disappear?" asked Janice, trying to get more than the previous, vague explanation offered by Armin.

"It looks like we need to put all the cards on the table," said Armin, considering that there was no need to keep things mysterious any more. "Carlo is getting a hospital room installed here today. Janice has agreed to operate in it, together with our own specialist, the famous Dr. Sebastian Lacan. Percy put forward two of his XMON chips that will be implanted in my parents, who are both advanced Alzheimer sufferers. I take all the risks for everything, ready to go to jail if it comes to that for these illegal surgeries. If the results are successful, Onkey will have two grateful, not as robust, but somehow similar friends. Onkey will remain the unique specimen that he is, and will enter the annals of science for opening the road of recovery from the dreadful disease."

Hearing all this, it was only Vania who reacted with a heavy dose of doubt in his voice, maybe thinking at the terrible impact that would happen if Armin were to end up in jail.

"I understand, within limits, your suffering and your

parents' suffering, but how do you see things so totally optimistically? What if the implants are not working out as in Onkey 's case?"

"You can't get from A to B without some level of risk. Janice and Percy and Onkey here are testimony that risk is sometimes very fruitful. If they understand the risks and hammer along with me to get rid of the scourge of Alzheimer, how can I not take the path less travelled? My parents are and always will be my personal heroes, and if I can do this for them, it's not only them who will thank me, it will be the entire world. So, it's personal, but not only."

Beatriz entered the fray with an invitation for me:

"What do you think, Onkey? You are after all, the smartest person here! You must have an opinion, and it could be the right one, what do you say?"

I didn't want to throw myself into an answer, especially because I already knew more than they thought I knew, and wanted to keep my secret capabilities secret. I had time to peruse enough info about Dr. Lacan through the web to realize that Armin has chosen the right surgeon to assist Janice. He was not only a superb operator at macro and micro level, but like Janice, he had entered the nano-level of brain surgery. With the proper devices available, he could tie parts of brain tissue like nobody else except, of course, Janice. But the works of the brain, especially related to memory, were still little known. The flow of neural currents in Alzheimer patients is thought to be disrupted by an amyloid–beta protein that acts as an obstacle, specifically in the activity of the sodium channels at membrane levels. An enzyme complex called beta - secretase and gamma - secretase produces such protein, and   if that enzyme complex can be inhibited, there are chances of reducing the effect of the disease. However, there are more aspects unknown in the forming and retrieval of memory in neurons and probably specific memory centres, which maintain a foggy curtain on the understanding of what's going on in the brain. My written response tried to be at least half optimistic:

"Now that I think of it, of my own surgery, I plainly remember that I don't remember anything. I was sound asleep, Janice took care of that. But considering the results, I think it's fair to say that Janice and Percy are my heroes, and they can and deserve to be the heroes of mankind. The big unknown is how are Armin's parents going to react, and what good is an artificial memory that might not travel well enough from the chip to the rest of the brain because of the amyloid plaques and other possible obstacles. My knowledge about this subject is not very specific. However, I wonder, what about trying to put not one, but two chips in strategically different parts of the brain in order to allow for an extra pathway in the travel of the information?"

"That would double the length and the risks of the surgery, but the idea is not as bad as I thought in the first instance," said Janice, and then continued after a pause:

"As astonishing as it may sound, we do not have one brain, we actually could say that we have five. Each hemisphere acts as one, then there are the two smaller hemispheres of the cerebellum, the little brain in charge mostly with movement co-ordination, but also with some aspects of motor learning; finally, more controversial, but still with important functional intervention, is the celiac or solar plexus in the area of the abdomen, behind the stomach. It is vastly connected with the internal organs and it appears to co-ordinate their function."

"It means that when I'm hungry, my solar plexus rings the bell and reminds me to have a snack. They say that even love goes through the stomach. Maybe it goes behind the stomach..." uttered Vania, who must have been the hungriest for love at the table, if I was not counted.

"Fortunately enough, as the XMON chips are very tiny, I've gotten two dozen of them with me, so there is no problem with putting two or three in the brain," added Percy .

Janice sighed, and decided to limit the conversation on the number of chips, by saying;

"With Dr. Lacan 's insight on this matter, there will be a decision to make on the ratio of risks versus advantages in such a complex undertaking. There are quite different sequences in the procedure to be considered when one or two chips are to be implanted. I 'm not able to determine right away the best solution."

"For when the attack?" asked Vania, who seemed to see everything from the point of view of a battle. Old Tolstoy 's big book might have had a strong influence on him. Not that the younger writer by that name was missed in his mind when thinking of modern warfare. After all, the invention of the laser, so much used in brain surgery, had been preceded by young Tolstoy 's conceiving of the hyperboloid, a fantastic device that was presumed to concentrate light into an energetic beam much like that of a laser.

"If Janice and Seby, that is Dr. Lacan, give us the green light, it would be less than a week from now," said Armin with a morose voice.

"Let me know, Armin, how can I help for this process, you know my training," addressed Beatriz forcefully. She was referring to the time when she was functioning as a nurse on a campus fronted by Doctors Without Borders in a forgotten corner of Tanzania. She turned to Janice to explain:

"I had been an emergency surgery nurse for five years before studying Fine Arts. I used to successfully replace a surgeon in more than 50 percent of procedures. Not because I wanted to. It was a necessity."

It was Vania 's moment to jump in, grinning with little daggers in his eyes:

"Now I know why my friends, after a few beers, claim that I 'm a Black Foot Indian!"

"Dirty rascal, I would have sown yours on the forehead, to make you more like a Unicorn. And you would have had to blow it off yourself away from hanging over your eyes," said Beatriz with a big laugh.

"Beatriz, let Vania have his own Indian toy, if he so desires. Your hands are full with our guests and with the strings that you must pull for the success of Onkey 's auction performance. My mind is now all in the surgery for my parents."

From that moment on, the breakfast continued and ended in silence, as if a funeral was imminent.

The second day of visiting started with Versailles. Sure, so impressive, but too monarchic for my taste. As a denatured member of the African wilderness, I am more of a republican, but not in the American party sense. I really preferred La Tour Eiffel, a marvel of construction, included in a grandiose complex that enchanted the eye from above and made me feel as if admiring civilization from the top of a huge tree. We continued with the Dôme des Invalides, which is Napoleon's resting place, and then with the Luxembourg Gardens and the Panthéon, before returning home for Janice's meeting with her counterpart, the famous and affable Doctor Lacan.

"Call me Seby," he told Janice when we all met him, and he gave her a long and plentiful hug, for which I was totally jealous. He turned toward me afterwards and took off his Panama hat with an elegant reverence, but followed that obvious sign of admiration by a friendly, slow knock of my fist with his closed hand. After hugging Beatriz too, he hit Percy on the shoulder as if they had known each other for ages. There was nothing artificial in this man, medium built, medium aged, almost hairless on an elongated head, with a well proportioned measure in all his face's features, except for the eyes, which seemed to be at a larger distance from one another than in other people, the way Captain Nemo 's eyes had been eerily described by his creator. Seeing him grin from one ear to the other, we felt at ease at once with France 's surgical prodigy, a man who had built an aura of famous interventions on comatose, as well as illustrious brains.

"Guess what happened to a friend of mine, also a brain surgeon? He was preparing for a scientific presentation and thought it would be good to start it with a proper joke about brain surgeons. Unfortunately, he didn't know any joke, so he entered 'brain surgeon jokes" into Google. Guess what he got? Twenty thousand pictures and names of dating Chinese girls, all saying, 'I no blain joke!' If you don't believe me, you can try it!"

Janice laughed a bit condescendingly, but didn't want to start a war of words with the man with whom she had to share a double, totally experimental and unique brain surgery on the premise that the great French doctor might be a misogynist and a xenophobe. She scratched her face for a moment because it irked her to come out with something less offensive. She settled for a question:

"Seby, does it mean that both you and your friend are looking to date girls by internet? Is that all you have as social strategy?"

"Oh, Janice, French girls are very sophisticated: once they find out that you are a brain surgeon, they draw the conclusion it is the only organ you are interested in."

"Is there any other organ that counts? "asked Beatriz right away,

"Oh, madam, it's not really the counting that counts," Seby responded with his grin, "it's the cunts!"

"Wow, what a dirty mind you have, Monsieur Professeur!" apostrophized Percy, with a visible pleasure of the way the talk was going.

"Better say good bye to everybody else, Mister Dirty Mind, and let me have you for what you really came here. We have plans to make, haven't we?" said Janice, a bit flustered. Beatriz took them into her office and left them there. So, I figured that the great surgeon was human, after all. I mean, he was not super–human, considering that his frontal attack in the company of two attractive women intended to clarify that he was as hungry for sex as he was medically famous. Well, from this point of view, he was more like me. The problem that I had, quite different from his, consisted in the fact that I had a species barrier following me everywhere. Put it otherwise, I was again lost among the gorgeous humans.

Lost Among ...

## CHAPTER 11

The meeting between the two surgeons took longer than we all expected. That is to say, they did not appear for dinner. On the other hand, around 7 p.m. Carlo brought in six very self-assured nurses, who had been co-opted for the pre-operation training. They all swiftly disappeared in Beatriz 's office, followed by a mobile table with drinks and food, pushed in by Carlo himself. Percy felt redundant in all this time, as Beatriz kept busy with her myriad contacts by phone, email and sms. I knew that I could count on her exquisite skills for doing a good coverage for my next public appearance. Not willing to let everything to improvisation, I thought of questioning Vania about the last trends and fads in the Parisian exotic painting scene in particular, and in the European market in general. While Percy was reading emails on his smart phone, I made a sign to Vania that I'll write something on my tablet. He became more alert, giving me a look that was saying, "Go ahead, I'm all yours!" In short, this was our conversation:

"You must know the pulse of the art market here. What are all the fads of the moment?"

"There are too many to count. It 's really crazy out there, from hyper-abstract to the mono–chromatic and the photographic, from eco–garbage to urban drafting and blurring, from multi–media installations to docu–combis and dial–an–artist."

"What are the last two thingies mentioned?"

"Oh, yes, docu–combis are almost subliminal editing of two, three or more documentaries. You get a fast, dizzying feeling of participation in the several happenings presented. Some people don 't make it to the end, they faint like at a star's performance. As far as dial –an–artist, it's self–explanatory, only this time the artist may perform or produce for you something by the hour, day, month, piece, whatever."

"Well, it seems to be not unlike what I am going to do at the auction, that is, by piece and performance, only it goes to the highest bidder. Still, I wonder what goes better in the eyes of the high bidders, what might they be reluctant to bid for, and vice–versa."

"As far as I know, you bagged a huge performance in New York with exactly the right kind of stuff. I can't tell you what to do, you are the only expert in the world for these things."

"That was because of the initial novelty of the whole business. You, on the other hand, have a feel of the local goings on. Of course, I'll listen to what the others will have to say, but now it's your turn and I'm all ears."

"Then let me show you on your tablet what were the biggest art scandals and sales in Moscow, London, Berlin, and Paris. That will give you a perfect idea, OK?" With a few strokes, Vania brought up on the screen what I was interested of seeing. He emphasized some of the pieces, artists, and prices. I tried to absorb without any critical filter what I was seeing and hearing. It was a good lesson, because although it seemed rather uniform in its diversity, the market had some peculiarities for each metropolis, and it wasn't easy to distinguish what were those. It gave me a base, from where I could further test my understanding of it by making enquiries with Armin and Beatriz. When asked what was Armin doing, Vania told me that he had set aside three times of day, after each meal, when he was visiting his parents in their quarters.

"It is his only aspect of religiosity, if I may say so. When he's not in Paris, or he totally must be somewhere else, both his biological clock and his smart phone remind him to connect with the web cameras installed in their rooms. He is a son for all seasons, isn't he?"

A wave of warmth hit me, and I had to swallow hard two or three times. There was an irony in this. Armin had practically everything, even his parents, only they were hardly available for him, not knowing now who he was, not giving him back any of his sentiments. As far as I was concerned, I had plenty of memory to share, but no parents that I could know and with whom to share whatever I wanted. I could have been named nimrA!

The situation in which I had found myself since I have gotten entrusted with humanity 's remembrance made me have a very peculiar perspective not only about humanity, but about myself. It was a strange, hybrid perspective, because it contained such extreme values and extreme positions too on the tree of human endeavour. An ape at the apex of the tree! An ape in the middle of an elite group of people who respected me for the enhanced brain that I had, and who tried to emulate it at least in the skulls of a lost pair of very rich people, demented by sickness and age. Me, the monkey, up on an inverted evolutionary tree, up on an inverted social tree. I was the one who was supposed to be behind bars, a slave enchained by his wild and aggressive, unpredictable condition. Instead, by this strangeness of repository of such memory, I was the freest, the fastest achiever, the adulated prodigy who could amass fortunes by the minute, the Midas of the art world.

The great experiment at which I was participating meant indeed something revolutionary in the long run, but seen from the point of view of the downtrodden, of the social sole, of the multitude that continued to exist without hope and without horizon, even without access to the roots of a decent living, the availability of an implant that implied treasures was farther then the sky, farther than the stars. How could I, the being from nowhere, the animal without real individual history, without his tribe, without a vocal tongue, mingle and contribute, support and act with a group that rolls in opulence like elephants in the mud? Maybe I better see myself more like Robin Hood returning the riches to the woods. Wasn't his scope in life to take from the exceedingly affluent and return the sweat of labour accumulations to the ones that actually produced them, deserved them and needed them? Such ideas, going through the brain of a monkey might sound terribly pretentious, and they are, because these ideas are not quite mine. They simply roam through my mind because they had been refined by humanity's experience, its social and economic fighting stratification, and its reflexion as memory in the struggle for a better sharing of the world's output. It seems that the progress of technology that allowed for the producing of the XMON memory chip that makes me smart coincides with the more entrenched assertion that humanity cannot continue to function in a world that maintains today's huge disparities between its nations, between its classes, between its consumers of goods, of energy, of education, of knowledge. A lack of rationality in the way the market functions endangers the entire fundament of the world economy, and with it, the survival of the utterly, as well as not so utterly, gorgeous. But in vain I see the faults of a system that tries, like any system, to maintain itself in spite of its crumbling battlements. In vain I fleece the gorgeous by using their own legalized tools for avarice.

I cannot change much this way. As long as my own, my downtrodden, learn not enough to raise their social conscience and learn not how to organize politically against the Everest of financial wisdom and its preposterous accumulations, there is no chance for them. It's the economy that gives the power, but it's the power that safeguards or changes the economy. The inverted pyramid of opulence, in which eighty-five plutocrats amass as much as what half of the planet's people have, can hardly stand without crashing. If or when this might happen, all the world disruptions will reach even the wild forests of Africa, where my tribes of chimps and gorillas have a hard time surviving in better circumstances. Neither Homo sapiens, with its claims of being wise, nor the other Hominids might be able to find refuge in the dog eat dog crumbling of a society based on famine and belligerence. This brings up the necessity of balancing the acts of human endeavour against famine and against belligerence. The term balancing conjures the idea of some forms of moderation, in which extremism of all kind is shunned and controlled. The basic tenets of modern revolutions promoted, among others, the slogan of 'Liberty, Equality, Fraternity'. Seeing that such a slogan has been variously interpreted to fit whatever social or even anti-social movement, maybe the introduction of the term 'moderate' beside each of the slogan's words might give the necessary equilibrium to a better, humanistic development process. Indeed, what kind of liberty may be a limitless one, when practically nothing around us is limitless? How could we accept limitless, or in fact increasing inequality, when this goes so much against the entire balancing act that humanity, unique in its limited wisdom, must realize? As for fraternity, the murderous description in the biblical story of Cain and Abel started the whole concept in a fatal way, on the wrong foot. Could it be that, completely different from all the previous interpretations, the two brothers are not only different in the way of earning a living, but actually in the way their accumulations from that living make them quite differently capable of sacrificial (read bribery) offerings? Abel's richer offerings puts him in a higher class, for which Cain is envious to the point of fatally striking his brother dead. Hence, the birth of antagonistic social classes. It didn't help that the envy in the fratricidal story came from a slanted God's attitude toward the brothers' offerings, positive versus Abel's and negative versus Cain's poor, insignificant one. With such a biased and pretentious God, it's no surprise that fraternity turned murderous. But then, how else could he pretend to be the ultimate, absolute arbiter? Or better still, how else could we claim to understand him if not as an absolute arbiter that protects the kings and the potentates of this world because they need him to maintain their socioeconomic status? Should we amalgamate our class vision to a Max Marx and a Karl Weber to see things in a combined perspective, or should we adhere to the more clear, non-amalgamated approach?

From what you read so far you must have drawn the conclusion that I am a left–leaning, shameless atheist ape with rabid, revolutionary ideas for correcting the world on its way to perdition before it's too late to do so. I am not trying to excuse myself, but you must really understand that it's not my fault, and neither is the fault of my courageous creators. It is what I could gather and synthesize from the amount of information I was endowed with and the statistical analysis of trends in the thinking of modern man. From all this I came to the idea that historically, some people are too fast to dismiss the wavy, contorted progress of social evolution, especially with expressions like 'that's how it always has been and that's how it's gonna always be'. However, they are definitely

Lost Among ...

wrong, and I am one of the best proofs of that.

In the same way in which things precipitate in history through an event that is initially seen as unimportant, but which may reverberate later for a whole epoch, so the quiet evening has been turned into a maddening series of happenings which disturbed the mansion's dwellers and not only them. In order to bring the six nurses to the mansion, driving a large van, Carlo had gone to Dr. Lacan's hospital with a list of names and six contracts. He simply summoned the six nurses to the van on behalf of the doctor, and when all six were there, made them an offer they couldn't refuse: a year's salary for two weeks of nursing under the famous doctor's orders in a private setting. The six women looked at one another with incredulous faces, until Sybil, the one with more seniority among them tore the silence by saying,

"If it involves Dr. Lacan, I have no objection whatsoever!"

"But how do we know that we will be working under Dr. Lacan's orders?" asked Valerie, a petite blonde with very green eyes. Carlo flashed his cell phone in front of them, saying,

"Dr. Lacan will talk to you here and now. He is in a conference waiting for my call to give you all the needed instructions." With this, Carlo placed a quick video call, the doctor appeared smiling and reassured the nurses that they can trust Carlo, who will bring them right away to the meeting. That was the clinch that closed the deal right then and there. However, the women were surprised when Carlo added that Dr. Lacan had already made arrangements for all of them to be temporarily replaced from their work as of that moment, so they would not need to make any calls and would not need to return to their places of work.

"What, do you want to kidnap us?" shouted Valerie, who had a voice that made tremble the van's windows.

"It 's all good planning, that's what it is. Your boss and my boss are very good organizers and they also know how to choose their collaborators."

"Who is your boss?" asked Petra, a well built nurse who exuded confidence through all the pleasant features of her face, of which the regularity of her teeth and the fullness of her lips would have made her a perfect model for advertising tooth paste.

"He is a famous art dealer, young, handsome, rich and unmarried."

"That would make him a perfect boss for us, not for you!" responded Sybil to Carlo's description, to which everybody laughed, removing the initial tense situation in which they had found themselves. Carlo drove off with his precious cargo, only to notice shortly through his back view mirror that Petra had taken out her cellular and was trying to form a number. He braked abruptly, stopped the car and turned to the women. After a short moment of silence, he said, trying to control his nervousness:

"I'm sorry for the surprise brake. Please, everybody wait for the good doctor to give you whatever instructions before starting to contact whomever you wish. He chose you for your professional attitude and for your confidentiality regarding surgery and patients."

"Wow, is this something so secret that we cannot even contact our family?" asked Jeanette, the one sitting right behind the driver, an intense Creole with a complexion to die for.

"You will do whatever you will feel necessary after the good doctor will explain what you need to know. Can we go now, quietly?" asked Carlo, who realized that his role as recruiter of a swarm of women in such conditions was not the easiest thing. He didn't want to impose himself toward them, he was trying to obtain their quiet co–operation. Jeanette, feeling well placed to defend the group in case something went awkward, spoke for everybody:

"You can go, Monsieur, but be aware that I have a canister of pepper spray behind your back!"

"Madame, I'm a normal man in all the ways. I mean no violence from my part and have no eyes at the back of my head!"

"I have no qualms with the right amount of violence from your part, if you do it to me the way I like it! As for your eyes, I saw how you undressed me by looking in the back view mirror! In fact he already undressed us all, one by one!" said Jeanette, ending with a provocative moan in her voice.

"Oh, madame, I'm impatient to get all the proper directions from your part. I'd be happy to be your humble servant."

Sybil intervened with the authority of the most senior among them:

"Go ahead, Monsieur, just don't brake too hard. We are all very fragile, but not at all frigid!" After that, addressing the other women, she said,

"Did you notice his Italian accent? He's a Latin lover! One of the best! Believe me, I know!"

The van took them slowly through the high traffic, while the women changed their mood, each of them evaluating whether it was a „coup de foudre", a thunderbolt that struck all of them with this sudden well paid work opportunity or with the potential occasion of a 'love at first sight' with the handsome man that was driving them into the unknown. Well, partly unknown, because at least the neuro–surgeon was to some extent the known factor. The other unknown was, at least on the basis of the driver's description, the rich and handsome boss of them all, who couldn't have commandeered their not that easy to attain Dr. Lacan without an even more substantial offer than the one they accepted. And then, there was the mystery of what did they need to do, why all this secrecy. At least they were well payed for their nursing. But what if they could also be nurturing the right person? At one moment or another on their way to the mansion, each of these nurses touched her abdomen and brought her hand up over her chest, experiencing non-shareable feelings.

The van slowed down to turn toward the iron gate through which a mansion was visible at the end of an unusually long alley. Paulette, a large-shouldered woman with a strong jaw and a black pony tail, jumped out of her seat, shouting:

"Stop it, I must barf!", after which she rushed to the van's door, opened it and descended. But instead of bending beside the van to release her stomach contents, she started walking along the wall of the mansion, away from the gate. There was a moment of consternation within the ones following her with their eyes. Sybil spoke, somehow expressing everybody's thoughts:

"She must have gotten panic stricken. She has a small kid at home."

"Can you do something?", asked Carlo, visibly shaken by this turn of events. He continued:

"Here, take my phone, call the doctor again and ask him to talk her into coming back. We'll accommodate her any way she wants."

Sybil stretched her hand, grabbed his phone and got off the van, after which she started calling Paulette, while trying to reach her:

"Slow down, you mule! Wait for me, Paulette! Paulette!!!"

Slightly embarrassed, Carlo scratched his scruff of the neck for a short while, after which he turned with a large grin toward the four nurses still in the van:

"It's my fault, I'm not handsome enough!"

"You are OK, don't worry", said Valerie with a smile. "Paulette always needs special assurances. You would need them too, if you were a mother with three kids waiting for you at home. I tell you how you can fix the situation. Give her a solid amount of cash in advance and she would climb Himalaya with you, believe me."

"Shucks, good that you told me. Lacan already did that for all of you. I'll have to run after her and show her the facts." With this, Carlo cut off the engine, pulled the car key out of its lock, set the hand brake and jumped out of the van. He started running after the two women that were already at an appreciable distance. Jeanette pulled out the smart phone from her purse and clicked on it a few times feverishly. Once she saw what she was looking for, she exclaimed:

"Yeap! Yeap, yeap, yeap! It's here! Bingo!" Claire had been the only one who did not say anything yet. However, this time she couldn't stop getting curious of why Jeanette became so excited. She left her place at the back of the van to come closer to Jeanette and asked her:

"Show me, I don't get it, what is all this fuss about?"

"You kidding? Show you my savings? Where is your smart phone?"

"I forgot it in the pocket of my working dress. Do you let me check my account?"

"Sure, be my guest! But first, put a diaper on, you'll need it!" Claire took Jeanette's device and started to thumb in carefully.

A four star general couldn't have been more focused over a battle map than Claire trying to understand what has happened with her account. When she realized that with the last entry she had eliminated her sizable deficit and was well in the black, she put her left hand between her legs and said:

"Geez, you were right, I did wet myself!"

Lost Among ...

Valerie and Petra exchanged conspiratorial looks, as they knew for some time how emotional Claire could be. I found out later that at one particularly difficult surgery, involving a child, when asked to hand over two micro scissors, she clenched her fists for over twenty seconds before she could release the instruments to the surgeon. However, she must have had some other high attributes if the doctor included her in the preferential list of six. In the meantime Carlo caught up with the two women that had distanced themselves from the van. He apologized for forgetting to tell them about the advance and asked Paulette if she had her smart phone on her. He asked her to check her own account and see how fat it became. He also told her that he would personally take care of any and whatever needed babysitting arrangements if she wanted him to do so. But when the woman saw how the numbers looked like in the account, she pulled a hand over her face as if to wipe it off, and then went to hug the man. She even gave him a big kiss over his left ear. Carlo protested:

"One more smack like this and I might become deaf in no time, especially if all the other girls contribute too." He was however thinking already that he wouldn't mind getting more than a smack from the well endowed Petra. They returned to the partially abandoned van, and Carlo formed a code in his phone to open the gates. In the next minute they all paraded through the hall towards the meeting room where the two doctors were conferencing with one another. Passing by me and by Vania, it was only Jeanette who exclaimed with an unexpectedly loud comment:

"Oh, my golly! Isn't this goblin the gorilla that paints like Picasso? Hey, goody, will you make me immortal with a portrait? I'm ready when you are ready!"
I decided to show her all my front teeth with the eyes shining friendly at her. Vania intervened:

"Madame, he is a chimpanzee, and he understood you perfectly. So, from his expression on his face, you may assume that he's ready when you are ready."

"Don't 'madame' me, young man, I'm Jeanette. Ready when also you are ready. What's your name and job here?"

"Oh, excuse me, I am Vania, in charge with the house administration, and this chimp is Onkey."

"Au revoir, Chimpicasso!" said Jeanette with aplomb and then followed the others. Vania turned to me and said:

"See, you already have a model to paint. Would you like her 'desnuda' as painted by Goya or as Venus painted by Velazquez?"
As smart as I had been created, certain things, like finger sex symbols, were introduced in my memory only as an after-thought, with a low level of priority. It was because of that low level that I reacted with some lateness to Vania 's question. I also preferred to be less specific, so I raised both my thumbs, giving him to understand that I would have been happy with both positions.
Not only that, but in that moment I realized that my ardent love preoccupations were actually just a hunger for sex, with me drifting from my longing for Jane to a

Lost Among ...

longing for Janice, to one for Beatriz and now to one for this Jeanette, whose name I had just discovered. It seemed quite natural, except for the fact that this drift could be seen by a more analytical person as what it was indeed, an objectifying of the female. My inculcated superior concepts were coming out from nowhere to shake me up and remind me that in the evolution of the modern thinking there was also a feminist view regarding the relationship between sexes, and as such, I was walking on a very thin wire.

# CHAPTER 12

There is little to do in a mansion where everybody is busy with something else than with you. Left alone after the parade entrance of the six women, I wanted to get a feel on what kind of interaction happened in the office where they were preparing a complex intervention. Sure, I knew on my own skin who was the most experienced of the two surgeons, at least regarding chip implants. Was Janice capable of taking charge of the process of training and organizing the event in a cavalcade of French speaking individuals who at least had enough shoulder rubbing among themselves to know better than listen to a young foreign female who might have been lucky to not kill her patients with her interventions? Or maybe what prevailed was the feminist pride of the seven women, among whom one raised to the top of her career, a career that might have been on the mind of all the other six who at this point, even if successful, were still just helpers for the actual doer, the macho doctor Lacan. It was obvious from the way the six women were recruited that Dr. Lacan had an idol status among them, which meant that it was an almost impossibility for them to refuse his requests, of whatever kind they were. Being curious enough to find out what was going on in the conference room, I used my wireless capabilities to connect with Percy's smart phone, and through it, with Janice's device. With the audio channel open, I could hear Seby, that is Dr. Lacan, trying to explain his staff why there was such a need for all the secrecy in these two interventions. Apart from the fact that the procedures needed an approval from the so called competent authorities that was quite improbable to come, and as such, for the time being, were illegal, there was an undocumented, yet hardly hidden race or competition among the brain surgeons of the world in finding a solution for eradicating the scourge of dementia and Alzheimer disease. The practicality of inserting a memory chip in the brain had been considered, but only Janice had the right chip for it and the right candidate, so far. It was a matter of making medical history by obtaining for the first time a similar result in humans with altered, broken memories. There was no better occasion than the one provided by the exceptional conditions of bringing together all the main factors that might create a success. The nurses were needed not only for the surgeries which would be performed almost in parallel, with a small time lapse between the first and the second intervention, but for nursing in three shifts to cover post-operation care 24/7, hoping that in about a week the situation would become clear regarding the results. As both the patients had been his previously, he had their history and knew that from a physical point of view, they were fit enough to undergo such a complex procedure. At this point, Janice spoke, saying that she has the film of the entire intervention done on Onkey. The team will study the film on the major points in order to get familiar with any unusual, stringent requirements, especially those regarding the positioning of the participants and of the equipment in a double, almost parallel intervention. There was a moment of silence, after which I recognized Jeanette's voice, the one that called me Chimpicasso, asking a perfectly viable question:

"Why do we have to do both these patients in the same time? Wouldn't it be easier to schedule them, say, at a difference of 24 hours to avoid doubling of unknown and undesirable, but possible surprises during the surgeries?"

"Jeanette, you speak like an echo of what has gone through our minds too," said Seby, and then continued: "You see, there are some special factors which have made us go with the parallel procedures. One is the fact that we have two surgeons knowledgeable with the problems involved. Another is the fact that the patients are husband and wife. We count on the doubling of the effect of the eventual reciprocal recognition in case everything goes well. And very importantly, the sponsor and the initiator of the entire plan has convinced us that it is his hope and desire to bring both his parents out of this sickness in the same time, without delay. Finally, if we are successful with both procedures, there will be a total motivation for other surgeons to go ahead in using our intervention as a model for this historical breakthrough." Janice must have seen that somebody wanted to say something, so she addressed her cautiously:

"You are Sybil, right? What did you want to say?"

Lost Among ...

"It seems to me that you don't even consider the possibility of failure," said Sybil, whose experience with many procedures made her a little more circumspect regarding the rate of success in brain surgeries.

"The possibility is there. To put it realistically, the failure is there already. However, it seems that we have here a device which is extremely well accepted by the brain tissues, fuses very easily with the neuronal network and becomes in short time an active memory centre. We will double the chances of the surgery to be effective by implanting two such devices in each brain, at some distance from each other. We hope that through the multitude of contacts that will take place, at least some memory will be re–established."

Seby saw Valerie fidgeting on her chair, so he asked her:

"What's bothering you, Val?"

"Well, doc, we all read the newspapers about this super–monkey who they say it's smarter than a human. They also say that he complains of no memory at all from before his implantation surgery. If that happens with our patients, they will be losing their personality, as I see and understand it. They won't be themselves any more, would they?"

"The difference between them and our Onkey is that they have had a long life, full of collected material mementos, albums of photos and even videos. By exposing them to all these, we hope that some parts of their brains will reconnect to the more profound and maybe unaffected mechanisms of remembrance of their things past, to paraphrase Proust."

"So, do we have to stay here for two weeks?" asked someone preoccupied with isolation.

"Paulette dear, you will be able to go home before and after the surgery, provided that you maintain total confidentiality and that you will be here for sixteen hours every day afterwards for two weeks."

"Now it's clear, doc, I was afraid I couldn't see my three kids all this time. I can be here even twenty, twenty-two hours, if that could do any good."

Janice intervened to mention the next day's schedule:

"Ladies, you will sleep here tonight. Tomorrow you will participate in the refurbishing of a proper space as an operating room, after which we will all practice a number of movements through the room, using the acquired instrumentation necessary for the procedure. Doctor Lacan has trained you already in the use of the high–tech devices that we'll have at our disposition. I think I already mentioned that I have a film, but I also have a so called attack plan, actually a script with each and every moment and movement, every device and every role. We'll work as two teams of four: Jeanette, Paulette and Claire with me, Sybil, Valerie and Petra with Dr. Lacan. This specific arrangement has been decided by your good doctor. The dance will go in parallel as my 1-2-3-4, his 1-2-3-4, but Doctor Lacan will pirouette from his place to my place and back, after which I will do the same. That will be the only time gap, hopefully. I'll work on the lady, he'll work on the gentleman. We'll each assist and control one another. Since my pirouetting is at the beginning and you are all bi-lingual, we'll all work in English. Tonight, only very moderate drinking is suggested, from tomorrow there is no drinking of alcohol of any kind. Food ingestion as per doctor Lacan 's regimen is provided here. If you eat at home, you already know what not to ingest. If you can make arrangements at home to stay here 24/7, all costs will be covered. This way we avoid any incidents, any accidents or who knows what. We are in a war zone against a monster illness and we must be victorious."

"OK ladies, for tonight we have only three bottles of champagne, which will go just right if we invite the creator of the chip to have a glass with us. Until I fight with the corks and Janice calls in the good chip doctor, you may make your contacts with the families. Tell them that you are all together with me in a private hospital and that you'll give them more info tomorrow, when you'll go home for a little while. Give them my cell number too, I'll vouch for you. For special arrangements, baby-sitting, nannies, dames of company, whatever, call Carlo. Here is his number."

I liked what I heard. Lovely Janice, turned Mama Janice, turned Generalissimo Janice, was sounding as if she was actually in charge of the whole process. Seby seemed to me as being her doctor-in-training, although he was a bit older than she was and probably with vaster experience, considering the large number of surgeries that he has conducted. Both were exceedingly optimistic, which was actually normal for brain surgeons, except that now the foe was a Godzilla of an illness. I wondered if their patients would undergo a tabula rasa of precautionary treatment before the implant, the way I had been prepared for it. I also wondered if they had anything else up their medical sleeves that has not come up in discussions yet. Although not as richly provided with research funds as their American counterparts, the French were a formidable bastion of medical research and innovation, and my scrupulous searches through their and other databases discovered lots of new works that referred to the war on Alzheimer. Would my good doctors also use enzymatic infusion, powerful chemical scrapers, vibratory frequencies or who knows what other techniques to dislodge some of the plaques from the neural networks before implanting? I was as hopeful as they were, and kept wondering what kind of relationship I might be able to entertain with the new patients if they could recover their memories and add the one I had already. It would certainly make for rather different entities if their own old memories could be rejuvenated. Wouldn't be a clash of memories within their brains? Wouldn't they become exceedingly arrogant if all were to function perfectly well and they would consider themselves the smartest humans in the whole Universe? Would I be of any value since their cranial capacity, their much larger and more evolved brains, together with their life experiences and probably a high level of intelligence could make for a formidable, unheard of concoction of possibilities, not only in the realm of art, for which they must have had already success during their working periods, but in all other human endeavour? After all, it's not necessarily what you really know, but what you really do with this knowledge that counts. Could the morality accumulated in eons by humanity be superseded by who knows what specific individualistic atavism hidden and casually restored, to bring out who knows what other monstrosities in an unchained memory? As in all the functions available at the discretion of the utterly gorgeous, there is a positive and a negative component, a yin and a yang, a dialectical dichotomy that could be advantageous and perilous in the same time. By virtue of my physical attributes put together with the memory of humanity, I was also a yin and yang of danger and creativity, but for humans, that could go maybe too far. How far is too far? Well, it was too early to tell.

## CHAPTER 13

Everybody might be curious to some extent, but not as much as I am. Three bottles of champagne for nine people seemed to me quite a sufficient amount to unleash tongues and to excite the excitable, and I was anxious to find out who would fall first, so to speak, (although I cannot do that) under the effect of the bubbly. I wasn't looking for a real fall, I was just thinking that, as it always happens with intoxicating ingredients like alcohol, someone in the group would weaken up his or her defence mechanisms, get the inhibitions to the ground and show more than they cared to the rest of them. For finding out what was going on, I had the cell numbers of the three protagonists, Percy's, with which I was always connectable, also that one of Janice in Percy's list, and of course the doctor's number that he gave out to all his nurses while I was quietly listening to their conference. But since Percy was a sui–generis hacker of high calibre, I noticed on his cellular that he discovered the entire video wiring of the mansion and had been able to hook up to it, so I wasn't too surprised to realize that I could navigate through the rooms and see whatever I wanted. Curious monkey business indeed, to wire up your own house! I shrugged. Heck, I didn't do the wiring! Anyway, three bottles had been uncorked and now everybody was sipping from the properly shaped cups. They were already brighter in the eyes, faces smirking and showing how sheepish or otherwise they tended to become when reaching the bottom of the cups. Janice was making conversation with Sybil and Paulette, Percy seemed at ease with Valerie, who appeared quite right for his stature, and Seby, the doctor, was saying something very confidentially, close to Claire's left ear. Petra and Jeanette were forming another group, both very little affected by the drinks and measuring with their eyes what was going on with the others. But when Carlo entered to announce that he will guide everybody to their rooms, it was both Petra and Jeanette who seemed to have the brighter eyes of all. I don't know if some people have a special knack for making the best arrangements, but Carlo didn't receive any opposition from announcing that he was setting up Claire with Valerie in one room, Sybil and Paulette in another one, and the beauties of the group in a third room in the right wing of the mansion.

"Hey, Carlo, are you putting me up with the monkey?" asked Seby, who felt left out. I grinned. He definitely wasn't my type. But Jeanette, hey, what a fairy!

"Don't worry, doc, you are well provided, but I keep your location secret for your own protection."

Percy felt necessary to throw himself in with a line:

"With so many amazons, it's amazing what might happen to you, doc, overnight. More danger than with a well behaved chimp, for sure!"

"You still must give us a map of this place, otherwise

we'll feel like in a labyrinth," said Petra, and Jeanette completed her:

"It's like a castle here, and we have no idea who's the Prince and where we can find him!"

"Oh, there are several here, each one princely in their own way. As far as finding him, first you might have to kiss a toad," replied Carlo with a chuckle.

"I noticed that your eyes are kind of bulging in our direction, is this a sign that you might be a toad?" asked Petra with an interested air.

"Kiss me and you'll see," was Carlo's provocation.

"Will you reappear on a white horse if I kiss you?" Carlos grinned, looking around to see if a horse would fit well enough in the room. Percy proposed:

"We have three empty bottles. Let's use one and find out who is supposed to kiss whom. Otherwise, Petra and Carlos are going to start an orgy here."

"You mean to make a circle and spin the bottle in the middle? Isn't that like for teenagers?" intervened Valerie with an uncommitted voice.

"Oh, Valerie, there is a teenager locked up in my body, I'm sure there is one in all of us," said Seby with certainty.

"What can I say, they never mature, these men, do they?" replied Paulette with a sigh.

"Make a circle!" shouted Percy, then added:

"I'll spin first. Whoever is facing the bottleneck may choose to kiss somebody. The kissed one continues with the spinning, and so forth."

"What if after kissing the three men here we end up

with three white horses in this room?" asked Janice jokingly.

"Or with three toads! Who's going to do the surgery for which we are all here?" added Claire with an unusually courageous intonation for her shy demeanour.

"Bingo! It's me!" shouted Jeanette, then continued:

"Petra, be so good to turn off the lights."

"Are you kidding me? You didn't even choose whom to kiss, and you want the lights off? We want to see some action here, dummy!" That came, surprisingly, from Sybil.

Petra turned and moved toward the door, in order to act upon the switch, when the door opened and Armin stepped in.

"Hey, the real prince of the castle is in!" chanted Janice emphatically, which made everybody freeze for a moment. Petra, almost brushing her boobs to his chest, recovered first, addressing him with her arms stretched laterally, ready for an embrace:

"Prince of the castle, can I kiss you?"

"Enchanté, Madame, just for the moment, may I miss your kiss? There is more pressing matter for us to kiss."

"Is everything all right?" asked Seby, preoccupied.

"Not quite. I've got an alarm on my mobile phone that a security point in the house perimeter had been breached."

"Is the alarm connected with the police?" asked Percy, who seemed to be quite conversant with alarms and their connections.

"Of course it is, but for the moment there are two

problems, one is your security from the possible intruders, and the other is the approach of the police finding all of you here."

"You mean to say we are not secure in both cases?" asked Janice.

"Oh, no, and oh, yes. Both the intruders and the police can be aggressive, albeit in different ways. It is my duty to prevent anything negative happening here."

"So what do you propose, should I hid my team in the back pockets of my jeans?"asked the surgeon.

"I assume somebody wants to get to my art collection. I will see soon on my mobile if that area of the house is breached. So far, the exterior of the house is dark and nobody shows up."

"You mean to say that you can see all the house from your mobile?" asked curiously Valerie. After that, she added admiringly, "That's awesome!"

Armin turned to the door and locked it, then turned to the others, saying:

"The doors are good quality. For the moment we are all safe here. There is nobody else in the building except for my parents and their care-taker, Vania and Onkey. Let's hope the police may come soon enough."

"What if they don't," said Paulette, who was more thinking at her kids left at home than at herself.

At this moment Armin pierced the screen of his mobile with his eyes, trying to see something that wasn't visible enough yet. His mobile rang, so after a short glance, he put it to his ear.

"Yes sir, it's the Offer house, I am Armin Offer, the

owner. We have a breach, and I just saw that someone entered my art gallery with some flashlights. No, I'm not there, I'm in another room, but I have video on my mobile. Yes, OK, we'll stay away from it. Come fast, thank you." He turned to the others to explain.

"It was the police. They asked us not to interfere. Only these guys can be in and out in no time, before the police gets even close." After that, he took another look at the mobile's screen and exclaimed:

"Bastardella! They turned on the lights! What? Four monkeys? Fffrr...rack you!"

I had followed the whole scene on my tablet while Vania near me was busy with some Russian girls on his mobile phone. I won't translate for you what they were saying to him because there were more pressing things to do. When I also saw the four monkeys moving through the art gallery, I realized at once that they were fake. Why they chose not only a monkey mask, but full chimp costumes was beyond me. However, a sense of tribal affiliation and the need to defend it came calling from the deepest of the depths of the remnants of my erased memory. I sprang up, took off my tablet belt from around my neck, left it on the chair, and with a grunt that even the open eyed dreaming Vania was able to ascertain, ran out fast in the direction of the gallery. Vania must have realized that something important had bothered me, because I felt him following me. I reached the entrance hall with two jumps and was able to open the door that was separating it from the gallery. The four monkeys inside were too busy with extracting the canvasses of two paintings from their frames, so they did not notice me in the first instance. With another jump I was close to both pairs. That's when they realized that the count was, literally and quite arithmetically, odd. It made them freeze. They were supposed to be just four. How the heck did they multiply? Was the fifth chimp an uninvited art robber, they might have asked themselves? Only they didn't have time for the answer. Instead, with the speed that no gorgeous can realize before it's too late, I got one of the frames lying on the floor and clobbered all four fakers with it. It was a beautiful frame, a 40 by 60 inches brown with old, antic greenish gold, not exactly my taste for frames, but still a remarkable one. I can't say that I was careful to bash the fakers with the wall side of it, but that's how it happened, so I guess that I didn't even damage the frame. As for the robbers, their attempt to defend themselves was futile. When I dropped the frame over the head of one of them and practically "framed" him with it under the level of his shoulders, I could pull him in a circular movement, that way making him into a human hammer with which I banged the one that was still standing. It only took ten seconds and the robbers were now down. Vania, who had been behind me, jumped onto one who was face down on the floor and started looking for some zipper to undress him of his costume. He must have had some experience with Halloween dressings because he found the zipper and immediately unzipped the guy from his awkward furry coverage and took his head mask off to uncover his face. Vania froze and I was hit with a sense of consternation myself because the guy was actually a really gorgeous young woman with such incredibly fine features that you would be hard pressed to find even among the highest payed fashion models. Somehow the picture didn't fit. Now don't get me wrong. Personally, I have never had the opportunity to meet and admire fashion models, but they were anyhow deeply planted in my memory. I can't say that I am a stickler with style, but even among those fashion models there are so many poor figures. This one however, with her perfectly coiffed gold mane, her high forehead and large green eyes, a determined nose separating healthy cheeks on an oval face that no sculptor could have been able to better find its proportions, exulted a serenity and a harmony of features that made you wonder how come it ended in a monkey costume for the purpose of robbing a private art gallery. Since Vania wasn't moving any more, I directed my eyes toward his face, where I discovered that his expression unmistakably conveyed nothing less than the fact that he knew that woman.

"Katya, ty durak?" That was all he could say when he saw her ironic smile flourishing at the corner of her sensual lips. My Russian translator allowed me to understand that he called her a fool. By her name. So she was from his Russian community. Was he involved with her, were they friends or was it some unforeseen turn of events that life throws at you? He pushed her aside and went to uncover the other three monkey clad robbers who were barely moving, I guess, because they were so much frightened by my presence. Oh, it was a multicultural, multicoloured, multi-ethnic band of robbers. The other three were all young men, a French one, a Japanese, and a Somali guy who seemed to compete in beauty with the Russian girl. There was some incipient exercise of trying to connect some still nebulous thoughts in my mind of how these four ended up, or more precisely, down, on the floor of this art gallery, but I must admit that I had no clues so far. It was too easy to assume a direct tie between the two Russians, Vania as an insider and Katya as the outsider in a plot, especially with the frozen surprise that I read on Vania's face at her unmasking. Of course, a good actor could play if necessary the role of the shocked witness at the discovery of a friend in a robbery, or even better, the role of someone who knows nothing and nobody in such an event. But something was telling me that the whole scheme must be much more sophisticated and that Vania was, at least for now, an unhappy and probably guiltless link in a much longer chain.

We had enough time to immobilize the four culprits with their own costumes by tying the empty sleeves of their costumes from one with the empty sleeves from another until the police arrived at the scene. Alas, the two cops who came first were more curious about me than about the robbery, because they had a hard time focusing at what had happened with the four invaders. The cops kept on looking repeatedly at me, probably thinking on one hand incredulously how come that I had neutralized the robbers by myself, as Vania told them, on the other hand wondering if they themselves were or were not out of danger in my presence. Armin also came into the gallery together with another team of four cops, two of whom started to take a more technical approach to the whole process, maybe realizing that insurance claims of one kind or another must be following soon from such a place. They were clicking right, left and centre around the culprits, at them and at the walls, measuring the empty frames and the paintings, without forgetting to put me in the best light from all the possible angles. Maybe their meagre salaries needed to be augmented through freelance, albeit illegal collaborations with the local tabloids. Since my coming to Paris I had been main fodder for these newspapers. The higher echelons of the police were quite aware of my climbing path in the world of high end arts, so it was with delight that the tech guys had me in their cross-lines now. It has occurred to me for one moment that the whole hullabaloo might not even be a robbery per se, but a perverse arrangement for getting some insurance payments and for putting me again in the attention of the media for the soon to be held auction of my instant, live action painting. It would have meant hitting two birds with one shot. The only thing that didn't quite sit well with the timing of the robbery was the fact that there was a famous national surgeon in the residence, together with a team of nurses and two Americans who had their own particular fame surrounding their names. Was there going to be more enquiries about who else was present here or not? I did not have a clue about Paris police habits around such events, although my head was full of detective literature including investigators like Lecoq, Maigret and Arsene Lupin, more recently the controversial Nestor Burma, not to say anything about the farcical Inspecteur Clouseau of Pink Panther series and the famous Belgian Hercule Poirot, invented by Agatha Christie. With his flair for negotiating and well known position in the world of art trade, Armin could keep the enquiries within the gallery itself, but he couldn't escape a direct question like who else is or was in the building around the time of the intrusion. From what followed I understood that Armin Offer was a subtle and excellent manipulator of the situation, as if he himself had been the writer of the whole detective drama in which I occupied such a central role as the defender of the property. Me, defender of the property? I could not have such claims, nor such biased tendencies. My head was too much inclined to evaluate the last socioeconomic and philosophical trends of the current state of human affairs by conceiving property not exactly as the source of evil for humanity, but dread its coefficient of limitless expansion beyond what the actual Earth sustainability and the proper decency could accept. Of course, all this thinking was coming from my implanted memory, but there was also some primeval ape feeling determined, probably, from my ancestors' equitable sharing of the spoils of the forests where they had to dwell for eons.

"So you are, Sir...?" started the less occupied cop among the four, a medium-built, egg-faced civilian with a strong nose, brown hair and quite shiny hazel eyes under an immense forehead. It must have been the main detective in charge with either the area or with special property intrusions.

"Armin Offer, art trader and gallerist, and the owner of this place. Who are you, by the way?"

"Excuse me for not introducing myself and my team immediately, but you may understand the surprising circumstances. I am detective Daniel Pommier, in charge with criminal and property break-ins enquiries in the 6$^{th}$ Arondissement. My assistant Leon Dumiel and the two techies are Pierre Pantol and Charles Creusot. I will leave with you my card right away in order not to forget. We sometimes have too little time to stay with a situation, so please, do not be alarmed if we have to leave all of a sudden. So, you are the gentleman who brought this... artistic prodigy here from the States, I understand."

"Quite an introduction, Monsieur Pommier, glad to know you personally, albeit I would have preferred other circumstances. And yes, this is the Eminence Grise of the instant art, our good friend and exceptional personality, who saved the gallery from who knows what amount of trouble. I introduce you to Adam Onkey, painteur extraordinaire. Adam, this is Monsieur Daniel Pommier, detective, with his assistant, Monsieur Leon Dumiel."

Assuming that the guys in front of me were not so amiable to a handshake from my part, I took the role of the cabotin by inclining myself in front of them as would do a Medieval knight to his belle, with an elegant reverence and a flailing of my right arm. Of course, coming from an ape was more than a surprise, at which they couldn't resist but to responding in kind. Armin was amused, especially since the whole scene had been

224

caught with clicks and flashes by the techies, all eyes and ears to what was going on around them.

"So, Monsieur Offer, do you have an idea of the size of the damage produced by the perpetrators?"

"No need to worry about that, detective, everything is insured, but as you see, nothing left this room and nothing is really damaged, not even the frames."

"Do you have any knowledge of how come the culprits had been able to break in? We assume that you have all kinds of security measures implemented."

"Oh, you must know much better than I that in this day and age it's all in the speed of action. If Adam wouldn't have intervened, probably the robbers could have disappeared with two or three valuable paintings each. With eight or twelve paintings at maybe half a million Euros, that would have been a hole of four to six million. More or less, but insurance would have covered with no problems."

"Still, it is interesting that these individuals knew enough to get here and not beside your property, where they might not have found such a well concentrated treasure. And what about their costumes, doesn't that seem a bit awkward? A simple mask or a balaclava might have been enough to hide their identities."

"Jeez, it's like they wanted to be caught, and not only caught by the police, but by Adam himself, isn't it?"

"Exactly my feeling, I couldn't have word it better."

"OK, detective, you know what to do, enquire further, write a report and if I could also have a copy, or send it to my lawyer, we'll meet again to see how far our thoughts are the same in this matter. As of the culprits, treat them as you may consider fit, I don't want to bother. They might be young and hungry, or devil knows what actually made them do it so badly. See, I commiserate with them, at one time I was... hm, younger too."

"My compliments for your attitude, but we have a crime here. And even if you do not claim any charges against them, you should be aware that they can turn somehow things around and claim that they were attacked by an animal on your property, with who knows what implications."

"Detective, please let me worry about that. If there is nothing else, my assistant Vania Weinberg will do all the formalities in my place. He is all yours."

With this, Armin took me by the scruff of the neck in a friendly embrace and directed me to go with him.

On our way out of the gallery and away from the police, I gave out a sigh of relief. Who knows how these clumsy cops could interpret my salutary, helpful intervention and take me with them, put me in jail or even put me down for some reason, as they do with rabid dogs or attacking bears. I looked at my host inquiringly. He threw me a wink and said,

"Let's go see the ladies with the not so bashful doctor, he might have operated on some already..." and after a few moments, time that allowed me to retrieve my laptop from where I left it, he continued with a much more serious tone in his voice:

"What do you make of that splendid specimen of a

robber? I had a hard time trying to stop looking at her, and if the cops weren't there, I certainly would have invited her to visit my upper gallery, closer to my bedroom."

It was time for me to decide whether to tell Armin about Vania's reaction at the unmasking of Katya, or to play dumb. Sure, I was intrigued too by the shocking misalignment between her beauty and her participation in a robbery, not because beauty wouldn't go with stupidity, but because you would expect to see such a splendid specimen, as Armin put it, finding a better way in which to exploit her gorgeous features. There must be a simple, reasonable explanation for the fact that she ended up in that gang. But what about her relationship with Vania? Could he be in a perilous position if Armin knew about them? Could he be exculpated? Situations like these are almost impossible to quantify as coincidences, but more like events that somehow, somewhere, are chained together without us seeing what could be fathomable if we had just a few more details. Well, since I did not have those few details, it occurred to me that it was much better for me to let the detectives find out and make light in the respective relationship. Clumsy or not, they would surely investigate further who the four intruders were, what social contacts they have and in what waters were they washing themselves, so to speak. We reached the door where the team had their preparations for the next days, when Armin stopped, put a finger to his lips for a moment, then grabbed his smart phone and sent a short text message with his thumbs running fast over the

Blackberry' s keys. It stirred in me a desire to find out what had he just done, but I wondered if I would be able to decode the powerful encryption of his device. A supposition I did have right away, but I don't want to overbear you with my intuitions. You certainly must have yours, right?

Armin was careful not to upset the group that we were visiting, so he took me in his arms and carried me in as if I were his baby. Although those present had seen me before, the impact of my appearance upon them was much more familiar than even I had expected. A few of the nurses had the courage to wave hands to me, and Claire, who was the timid one but probably very attracted to babies of all kind, came closer to stroke my fur on the back and on the cheeks. I was eyeing Jeanette, the creole with the perfect complexion, thinking that between the splendid Katya and the sculptural Jeanette, I would prefer to throw myself in the latter's lap. She probably was also the least introvert in the group, because she found the right moment to intervene with cheekiness:
"Hey, Chimpicasso, we have an arrangement, don't we? I pose for you and you paint me. From three angles, OK? Each angle, a separate painting, not like Picasso, who used to put them all on top of one another."
"I didn't know that Picasso painted you!" exploded Valerie with a voice that could have cut an ear or two.
"Dummy, I was born right when Picasso died, you hear?"
"What, he also dyed your hair? Awesome!" I would

have liked to say something just then, but instead, a few grunts of untranslatable laughter came out of my so called voice box. I could only close my eyes, bend  my head backwards, release a grin and hit my chest repeatedly with one of my hands. All except Valerie understood. I had fun on behalf of her dumbness. Now guess, who was lost? Among whom?

Lost Among ...

## CHAPTER 14

What do you say if I tell you that I already went over the initial plan of writing only twelve chapters to my story? Bad planning, eh? It's not that. The fact is that I don't really know to what extent should I go describing all those little stories that form the meat of a novel in which I put myself in prime light. Take Vania and Katya, for example. A super-smart Russian guy working for an art trader whose private gallery is robbed by a super-beauty called Katya who is known to Vania. A connection and a mystery. What's behind the connection and how do I clarify the mystery? Wait a minute, why should I? There is a police investigator for that purpose and I already have decided not to interfere. But I guess that I provoked your curiosity now and I must satisfy it somehow. Trouble is that unless Vania or Katya or detective Pommier explain themselves to me about the whole thing, I'd have to become a hacker and hack into the files of the police, and that only in case they do clarify the matter. Well, Vania might tell me something if I press him hard, but I couldn't do that because I like him.

If I had a chance of communicating with Katya, maybe I could have scared her enough to get a so called confession from her, but again, I cannot be but gentle with the most gorgeous sex. Anyhow, she was taken to the police station, so that's off. Better wait for a while to see how are evolving the detective's findings. So, you see, now you have in my novel a detective and mystery component, several beauties that did not decide whom to chose for their, hm, fulfilment, an extraordinary, illegal brain surgery project that you don't know yet how and whether it is going to succeed, an ultimate live art auction in the city of lights and lo and behold, no dead body yet, no car or any mobile device chase or human hunting human event. It's true, there was a fight in the previous chapter, but it was between an ape and four fake apes, so you can see how disproportionate such a fight could be. Had they been not fake, you probably couldn't read now these lines. Well, smart as I am, with expert knowledge in several human martial arts inculcated in my brain, maybe I could have been able to face them and not get torn to pieces. This is why I said "probably" in a previous phrase, but I could have put "possibly" instead.

It was time for all of us to call it a day, but things get darker in the dark of the night, especially with twelve souls full of vitality and overwhelmed by the novelties of the unusual events galloping like racing horses toward them. Three bottle of Champagne might not have been much for the nine people who benefited from their content, but bubbles are known to have quite different effects on the cortical centres of the imbibers. Claire needed no convincing to follow her doctor into his bedroom on the right side of the mansion, adjacent to

Armin's parents room, with the windows opening to the back of the house. So Valerie, who was supposed to be cooped with Claire near Janice's bedroom, found herself alone, just two doors away from Percy's bedroom, which was aligned with Janice's and Valerie 's on the left side of the house. My bedroom was just in front of Percy's, in the corner of the left wing facing the garden between the gate and the entrance to the house. On my side of the hall, two other bedrooms were occupied by Vania and Carlo. Armin's larger en suite was just above the entrance, in the middle of the house and in front of the entrance to his upper, private gallery. Across from Armin's parents bedroom and the one occupied by the surgeon there were three more rooms, one for the permanent caretaker of the elderly couple, and two for the two pairs that Carlo had been so clever to set together, Sybil with Paulette and Jeanette with Petra. When Percy knocked softly to her door, knowing that she was alone, Valerie tried to pretend of being surprised, but after whispering to him, "Are you alone?", she didn't wait for any answer and pulled him in. I was inspecting every movement on my tablet and could give you a succulent description of what happened there, but I was busy observing other doors opening and heads checking the emptiness of the hall. Petra was the first to step into it barefoot and rush past the middle of the house to not even bother with a knock at Carlo's door, as if by some telepathy she knew that she was expected. And she was indeed, as Carlo was holding two glasses of Champagne in his hands already and didn't have to do anything but hand one to her. She took it with her right hand and stepping forward, put her left hand around his neck, readying herself for a kiss.

"Par bleu, Madame, let's drink for a voluptuous night!" said Carlo and clinked the two cups.

"Par bleu, Monsieur, call me Petra or I'm going to bite you!"

"Ah Petra, you are going to bite me anyhow, but let me bite you first," and he inclined himself to reach her fully formed bosom.

If I'd continue here you would miss other possible action somewhere else, but being truthful with myself and with yourself, I don't want you to think that I am transforming this book into some kind of erotic, scandalous, depraved description based solely on the fact that I possess such a wonderful tablet. On top of it, as sexually obsessed as I am, I don't find it my role to enter, so to speak, into the low, dark entrails of the participants' frolicking acts. I just state some facts in order for you to get a fuller picture of the foreground and the background for what follows. In the room beside mine, Vania was calling Jeanette on his smart phone; he had everybody's numbers as a back up in case Carlo was somehow unavailable for dealing with the nurses' contracts.

"This is Vania. You said earlier that you are ready when I'm ready, so that's how I am."

"How are you? Ready? For me? You think that was an invitation to go banging all night?"

"Oh, no, only as much as you'd feel comfortable."

"You are full of it, aren't you? Are you coming?"

"Not right now, only after I reach you. Bang-bang!"

That of course was followed by Vania leaving his room and tip-toeing to the extreme right of the mansion, where Jeanette kept the door open for him. I wondered if Armin was as curious as I was and followed the entire set of manoeuvres on his smart device. Strangely enough, he had his own room on video surveillance, which might not have made much sense, except for the situations where he might let somebody else occupy his en-suite or to check whether his service people were too curious with whatever he had there. I saw him pacing from one side to the other of the large place, looking thoughtfully to the carpet and rubbing the scruff of his neck with one hand, while holding his forehead with the other. Was he busy concocting something? Was he trying to decide something and kept on measuring the pros and cons of the act, or he simply tried to figure out if he is going to see alive and communicate again with his parents after the planned surgeries? He grabbed his phone and pressed a code. In her room, Janice responded promptly.

"If it's not too late for you, I wanted to invite you to visit my very private art collection that is just two doors away from yours."

"And so conveniently placed right in front of your room, right? I see an architect 's mind in the design of the entire mansion, and I presume that the architect took your suggestions as an order."

"I didn't have to order him, I had to order to myself. I might have forgotten to tell you that, yes, I have a degree in architecture too, so it wasn't such a big problem. But to tell you the truth, my private collection is fit to be visited in the evening, privately, and hosted by myself, as it has a more specific theme that I was able to gather with a certain curatorial... intention."

"That makes me think only at the probable intimate nature of what you want to show me. Did you actually curate only, or you even posed for the art?"

" I sense that I was able to make you curious. I am at your disposition."

I saw Janice making a pirouette in her room while dropping her cellular on the bed. Oh, how easy it is to open up the the gates of the illusory promises for an emotional uplifting experience with an evening invitation to an art collection that is located just three steps from a well – appointed bedroom owned by a well – appointed prince charming! If I were a woman, I certainly wouldn't have the strength to refuse. But not only I wasn't a woman, there was nobody to invite me. Armin opened his door and stretched his hand toward the door of the art collection gallery. Using his smart phone as a remote controller, he opened the handle-less door just as Janice appeared in the door frame of her room. He went to her, offered his hand with a simple but gracious tilt and directed her few steps toward the gallery. She entered smiling, almost sure that she was about to encounter a refined collection of erotic paintings. The large room of the gallery was very faintly lighted. Janice saw several richly gilded frames on the walls, but couldn't distinguish any art on them. They were just rectangular black holes. It was as if the entire promising life expected to be seen in the frames has departed, taken away by the wand of a mad magician. A slight sound announced that the door through which they had just entered closed up. Janice turned inquisitively toward Armin.

"Is it a mausoleum in here?"

"Not really, unless you want to die of excitement."

"I advise you that I can withstand looking at anything except horror and brutality."

"We'll start with the first frame on the left. You may know the figure." With this, Armin pressed on his smart phone turned remote controller in front of that frame. As the light in the gallery became dimmer, the image of an older man started growing out from the frame until it reached its natural size, except that, being a painting from the middle up, it floated strangely in the mid-air. It was much more than a holographic image, it was actually an image in three dimensions, very realistic even in its truncated aspect. Armin spoke softly:

"Pietro d'Arezzo, also known as Aretino, writer and polemicist, poet and blackmailer of the 16th century, as painted by Tiziano, his close friend. Seen here, of course, with some modern enhancements.

"I appreciate Tiziano, or Titian, for his mastership, but what is special about Pietro Aretino?"

"Oh, he described paintings by Giulio Romano, who famously created a set of lovers' positions named 'I Modi'. With this, Armin clicked onto the second frame, which had the effect of making Aretino 's image disappear and a young man 's athletic nude jump out of the darkness. He looked very nonchalantly to the visitors, turned towards the frame and pulled out from there a female as athletic and as divested as he was. The three dimensionality of the video was such that you were attempted to move around the images to see them from different angles. Once together, the two nudes held hands first, then started gently stroking one another on the chest, on the nipples and on their hips, after which he directed her hand to his prick. Janice broke the silence with a casual sigh, then asked with some irritation in voice:

"How's this different from a porno movie, apart from it being in 3 D?"

"You'll find out. Pestina lente... rush slowly." The two protagonists were by now exploring intently at each other 's private parts and were kissing with voluptuous desire. As anatomically trained as Janice was by her medical school and practice, she couldn't escape the fact that the two beautifully endowed lovers in front of her provoked some ripples of desire in her own entrails. Was she going to continue her rigid masquerade of complete professional detachment from the skin rubbing and physiological responses of the brain concocting its own miscellanea of drugs, or she 'll succumb to the powerful stimuli coming not only from the images in front of her, but from her own imagination of what could maybe happen to her in the arms of the man that brought her there?

The two lovers, who let themselves down on their knees were about to lean onto a side, hugging, when the image started to become smaller and, through some editing trick, was sucked into the frame from where the acting protagonists had come out. Janice immediately experienced a painful pang of missing, as if it was her own desire that had been sucked away into the frame. She instinctively held onto Armin's arm in order to prevent herself from losing her balance. The contact with him felt reassuring. What was going to happen with her now? She couldn't be a novice in matters of sex, but was still expecting the first clear sign to come from him. Instead, he held himself straight and clicked again on his smart 'remote'. From the third frame came out a pair of lightly clad youngsters reminiscent in aspect to a Renaissance painting of two gods who started to undress one another while the male was kissing her neck. She bent her head backward in abandonment when he reached lower at her bosoms with his hungry lips. Janice felt that her brassiere was becoming too tight. Her clothes seemed entirely inappropriate on her in that moment. What was she waiting for? She slipped her arm down to grab onto Armin 's hand and put it on her bosom. Did he need more stimulation to act upon her? Was he trying to titillate her more in order to bring her to paroxysm before showing a definite interest in her, or was he a sadistic manipulator, exerting upon her a form of light, temporal torture?

As curious as I was, I felt tremendously shaken by what I was exposed to through my voyeurism. Alone in a house with so many couples benefiting from one another 's charms, I was spying on one of my own makers. I was not forgetting that I was an ape, but in human terms it was as if spying on my own mother 's, hmm, fertilization activities. I couldn't be too proud of this! Disgusted with myself, I threw my tablet, the accessory of intrusion for my voyeurism, on the bed. Whatever Janice and Armin were doing in the gallery or anywhere else, it wasn't my problem. If mankind was going ape with its propensity for most bare naked images, for raunchiness and variation of lewdness to the cubic power, it wasn't because their claim of inclination to return to the freedom of nature. It was mostly another form of manipulation on a grand scale, a special kind of trickle down manoeuvre: the super-rich could afford the real thing, while the relatively cheap images of the real thing were trickling down to the rest. It might also have something to do with the steady decline of the birth rate in the Western countries, as a very cheap compensatory form of cultural stimulus, a desperate attempt at raising this birth rate through encouragement of copulation. It might be true that a picture is worth a thousand words, but it could also be worth a thousand lost targets for the seeds of life. You think that I might be embarrassed at watching a good party of pleasure-seeking couples tangled into one another? Not on my little grown beard! Think about how care-free are my cousins, the bonobos, when going on with their frequent intimacies, and you'll understand that I do not have any opposition for such events. But however they occur, they need to preserve that special feature that gives them that name. Describe them, add details of more or less prurient character and you just loose that aspect of intimacy. Said differently, the penetration of words in lovers' travail may indeed in such deed disgorge the gorgeousness.

240

## CHAPTER 15

It looks like some nights are more restful than others, because even those who didn't sleep in their own beds appeared to be quite relaxed and overly merry the next morning at breakfast. Well, Paris might have a yet unclassified, but easily transmittable through unknown means, love virus in its atmosphere. You didn't have to have a degree in human psychology to notice that the average level of satisfaction in the entire group was putting a pinkish colour in everybody's cheeks and a shiny, but still tender light in their eyes. They tried to be not too garrulous in order to maintain the appearance of reserved people, but my senses did not cheat me at all. I could have pinched Janice wherever I wanted, she wouldn't have objected. As for Percy, he kept his face as close as he could to the plate from which he was eating, only to bring up his embarrassingly huge smile toward Valerie, who happened to be seated at the table right opposite him. Vania and Carlo were missing, early soldiers in the preparations for the hectic day that was about to start. As much as I wanted to maintain my discretion, I couldn't refrain from showing off just a bit, because I had felt somehow challenged by Jeanette's quip at her entrance yesterday. I had worked earlier in the dining room at a canvas on an easel and that painting was there for everybody to see. I had drawn myself in front of an easel on which rested a canvas with a good semblance of Jeanette as Maja desnuda. At the bottom I added, 'Ready to phaint', which I hoped wouldn't be taken as a writing error. Of course, the question remained obscure, if I was ready to paint, for what reason was I ready to faint? That's how great art goes, right? Obscure, prone to controversial, if not even with altogether quite opposite interpretations. Jeanette covered one cheek with her palm, then came to my place, took my hand and put it over one of her tits, saying:

"Maestro, make me as famous as Goya did that girl! I am ready to sit for eternity!" Her tit was warm, firm and so appealing, I closed my eyes with pleasure. But the grunt that came out from my throat was enough to make her step back, so I remained posing with the extended arm toward a tit that wasn't there any more. Janice, who was beside me, gave me a compensatory hug, saying:

"Adam Onkey, your wit is unquestionable, your talent is uncanny, your hand is genially unmistakable and your grunt is, hm, understandable. Just make us all happy and particularly Jeanette by not, mm, scare her off with your loudness." I smiled and started to applaud, because I really liked how Janice turned things around both with her gesture and with her little verbal effusion. With that, it appears that Jeanette didn't find me any more ferocious as when I grunted, and seeing that doctor Janice was so demonstrative with me, dared to approach me again to give me a hug herself. This time I was careful to stroke her back with utmost gentleness, using my backhand first, then the palm. She must have been still tense somehow, because I felt her body vibrating like, oh, such a lovable string! I moved her away from the soft embrace with care and with a slight smile on my face, added a slow, backhand rub to her shoulder, as if to tell her that she was safe with me. This time it was the breakfast party who applauded. The peace pact had been signed.

I found out later from Vania that he had gone directly to the police station in the morning in order to intervene for the ravishing Katya. He was sure that detective Pommier was going to put two and two together and realize that a connection between the two Russians couldn't be just a coincidence. Indeed, although Vania's French accent was almost exquisite, a trained listener like Pommier had noticed the still extra-long r 's in Vania's pronunciation, and together with Katya 's last name formed a non puzzle in the smart detective 's armoury. Neither of the two men were surprised when Vania appeared in front of Pommier, who greeted him with a smile and with an assured voice told him:

"I was about to send after you for some questions."

"And I knew you would, so here I am to tell you what you want to know, maybe what you know already."

"I spent some time with the girl last night. I confess that it was a hard job to question her, for the simple reason that she is so incredibly beautiful... It boggles the mind to look at her and wonder what the heck was she doing robbing a private art gallery in a chimp costume."

"I was shocked too when I unmasked her, but for an other reason. I recognized her as one of my recent acquaintances."

"From La Table Russe, I believe. At least that's what she told me," said Pommier.

" I hope that doesn't make me an accomplice to her in any way. This is what I came to clarify."

"Monsieur Weinberg, tell me your story about your relationship with Katya."

"It 's not much of a story, really. She is both a singer with the band and a waitress at the restaurant. With a group of Russian friends, I visit sometimes one, sometimes two Russian restaurants on week-ends. We maintain our language this way, we also enjoy the specific cuisine and we go nuts for our music. Two weeks ago it was La Table Russe that we visited. When we got in, she was already on the stage, singing. I guess that she was annoyed because we were a bit noisy when we came in. We didn't even notice her because of the fog machine on the stage and we were busy trying to seat ourselves comfortably. She stopped singing in the middle of a song, made a sign to the band to stop also, and after a good pause of several seconds, she told the audience to forgive her because she had started the song too early. She intended to sing it for us, but she had thought that we were in the room already. So she was going to start again, especially for us. Of course, that made us even noisier, as we already had a few glasses of vodka in an other local. But then we applauded her and settled to

244

listen. She sang a slow, sweet song about an Angora Orenburg shawl and an old mother. We couldn't resist. The song softened our hearts and brought tears in our eyes. We hardened Russians are like blind kittens when it comes to motherhood. So, when she brought us a round of vodka, we were able to see her from close up and we couldn't believe we had the fortune of encountering the silent splendour of her personality. She shook hands we all four of us, smiling like a million roubles. We knew it was a ploy to make us more permanent clients of the place, but we didn't care of anything, so mesmerized we were of her presence."

"The story is impressive, but can you get to the point? Did you become in anyway personal with her?"

"That's the thing! Nothing at all."

"But did she know anything about you, somehow?"

"Ah, there was an exchange between her and Kolia Jukov, one of my more garrulous friends, when she asked us what were we doing as occupations. He gladly presented us one by one. About me, he said that I worked for a big shot in the art trade. But that 's it, he didn't give her any name, any address, any phone number. At least not while we were all together there."

"Anything else about her? Did you mention her to somebody?"

"Sorry detective, this is not a mentionable girl. You have to live her presence to appreciate her. Even if you are not of our culture, hearing her shawl song and not understanding a word of it would put you into an emotional trance. I can only imagine it comparable with a fado sung by the great Amalia Rodrigues."

"But you agree that there must be a link between you and her, maybe something that escapes your present consideration."

"Well, I just mentioned fado, which makes me remember that our colleague Beatriz Solano, who is half Spanish, half Portuguese, asked me recently if I like fado. I told her I'm mad for it, then I mentioned the girl singing at La Table Russe. Can't think of anything else."

"Did you communicate with this girl when you discovered her in the costume of an ape?"

"Yes, I was so astonished seeing her there, the only thing I could muster was, in Russian, are you stupid?"

"And how did she react?"

"She just stood there and smiled. And I totally couldn't say anything else. I was dumbstruck!"

"OK, it's all for the moment. Keep me up to date if there is any other development."

"Speaking of this, I would like to intervene somehow in her favour, I don't know how. I guess this might sound dangerous for me, but could she be released if I vouch for her behaviour, whereabouts, something?"

"No need for that. She's been released already."

"Oh? I don't understand."

"Neither do I. A lawyer came in last night and assured us that Monsieur Offer has no interest to pursue the matter any further due to business considerations."

With this, Vania was dismissed and he told me that he left quite dizzy of the last turn of the events. How could I reproduce the entire discussion with the detective? Easy.

Not only Pommier had the conversation recorded, but Vania too, so it was a synch for me to get it from his smart phone. When he returned from other business that he had to do, he came straight at me to confess that he was much too emotional to think clearly. Could I, his new friend of another species, help him see the logic in what was going on? As if you can build logic out of air! There weren't enough details in the whole story to make it logical. Suppositions, yes, we could build several, but that could be dangerous, it might throw you onto a completely different plane. I thought that if Vania was so much interested, even after a torrid night with Jeanette, he should pick up the threads from the three ends that he had mentioned: Katya, Beatriz, and Armin, not to say anything of the fact that the other three robbers haven't been approached in any way yet. Who the hell were they? Maybe a visit to La Table Russe could help? At my suggestion, he arranged for Janice and Percy to be given a special lunch out, with me included, so we travelled not too far, between Jardin Botanique and Luxembourg Gardens, a stone throw from the Pantheon. The place was so small, it was hard to think it could accommodate a band and a singer, but the trick was in creating a warm, cozy atmosphere. The band  for lunch was replaced by an itinerant accordionist, playing for an hour here and an hour there, standing in the space between the kitchen and the serving room, behind the singer that doubled as waitress. Not all the tables were occupied, which made the work of the waitress a lighter one. Her gracious movements while bringing the hot borscht to our table were paired with a serious expression of her divine face when she noticed that Vania and I were among her new guests. It was after she had finished serving a second plate on the several tables and after some orders of vodka that the accordionist appeared to warm us up further with a few tunes from the most known repertory of folk songs. By this time Katya, because of course, she was the server, had appeared in front of the player ready to sing. She had  covered her apron with a red sarafan and her head with a head-dress called kokoshnik to bring an extra note of Russian authenticity into the room. Her voice was languorous, soft, sad, but velvety. You didn't have to understand the words to feel mollified by the melancholic tunes that so well suited her voice while her singing filled the small room. I followed Vania's eyes on staring at her and probably trying to understand how come this incredible talent has not yet been discovered by the right impresario. Maybe also what motive or stupidity has made her participate in the previous night robbery. When she finished her three songs, she took off her kokoshnik and used it as a collection recipient from the several customers that were happy to contribute above the cost of the food for the Russian musical moment that she had so masterly surrounded everybody with. When the accordionist made himself scarce through the door toward the kitchen, Vania excused himself and followed him. He wanted to ask the player a few questions, only to be told that he had to rush to another restaurant for another musical hour and he could be available at some later time. Anyway, what were the questions?

"Who was the leader of the break-in at the art gallery?"

"Like it or not, Katya. She convinced us all it was a no-risk, fabulous gain."

"What were her sources of information about the gallery?"

"That you have to ask her. We were stupid enough to follow her as if nothing else mattered. I 'm out now."

With this, the conversation ended. Vania returned to the table and waited for another moment to approach Katya. She had taken off her head-dress and the sarafan and returned to her less glamourous function. By now Percy was using a toothpick to get rid of the sturgeon meat that had been reluctant to follow the flow of the vodka. The few other customers had left the restaurant. Vania waited for Katya to clear the other tables, then called her to sit beside us. Janice took her hand and told her:

"You are a real artist. You deserve a much larger audience. What a heavy burden you must carry to be able to unleash the entire melancholy of the Russian soul!"

"Thank you, Madame. What do you know about the Russian soul? I guess you are American, aren't you?" The girl must have read enough about our arrival in Paris and the pictures of my chaperons had been extensively published in the press. One had to be blind and deaf not to be exposed one way or another to the gargantuan media brouhaha that our presence in Paris has created. It wasn't a daily occurrence to have a clever beyond comprehension painter ape visit the libertine capital.

I was tempted to answer Katya 's question with another question, but Janice was warm and pensive when said:

"Oh, dear, from Goncharov and Dostoyevsky and Gogol and Tolstoy, from Belinsky and Cekhov and Turgenev and Pushkin, how can we not know of the Russian soul?

"They are important writers, however, it is more direct through the folk music to feel what the Russian soul means."

Percy intervened with a tongue in cheek attitude:

"Look, I 'm really into rock and roll and bossa-nova, but if you put your hand over my chest, you 'd realize that my heart has melted listening to you and it's now just some gooey red paste with which you can make  a great borscht."

"Don 't listen to him, he actually liked your singing", tried Janice, and even I felt that Percy made a huge blunder. Vania made a gesture of dismissal toward Percy, saying:

"He just wants to attract your attention toward him, especially with the part where he hopes that you would actually touch him. Then he would catch your hand and claim that you have offered yourself to him."

"But the borscht would be excellent!" objected Percy, grinning almost like me.

"Katya, detective Pommier told me that you were let go with no case against you, but because I have met you before the last night unfortunate incident, I feel that I am under heavy scrutiny to explain myself to my boss. The accordionist told me that it was you who planned the botched ... mm... art lift. That makes it even worse for me. We all appreciate your musical talent. How did you end up a band leader of...well, the other kind?"

The young woman looked at us with a superior glance. The air of melancholy, of sad suffering and nostalgia that had been so pervasive in her entire demeanour while singing had been completely replaced by a strong sense of business–like matter of fact. She moved her lips to wet them slightly. She must have figured out that there was no need for her at this point to be afraid of anything, but speaking too much wasn't going to help either. She turned and looked at me with a whimsical air that might have intended to say, "I tried at least to get into your skin, so to speak." Looking at her from such a small distance one could breath in a certain aura that her beauty and personality was creating. I don't think that Janice could be indifferent to her. As for us males, we were somehow taken into an invisible vortex that seemed to make our conscience bend in various directions as if on a boat ravaged by strong waves.

"I guess that you didn't have time to look at the today's news yet." Katya said these words with a certain emphasis on the word today that made us wonder. She stood up and added with a soft whisper:

"You are all so smart! Ia, durak!" and with this, she left us. We looked at one another inquisitively, each one probably for a different reason. Vania explained:

"Ia durak means I am stupid. Let's get the news."

Lost Among ...

## CHAPTER 16

The newspapers were full of images from the break-in. It was clear that the police photographers made an extra income by passing those pictures that did not have strict police value to those newspapers that knew how to exploit such fodder. What was more shocking than the pictures themselves, in some of which I was shown beside the unmasked robbers – and I couldn't take my eyes off the ones where I was beside the unmasked Katya – was the incredibly stupid way in which the stories accompanying the pictures were trying to connect me with the robbers, Armin and Vania with the robbers, and how Janice and Percy, who had been presented to the detective last night, were themselves embroiled in the event. It appeared that the poor reporters didn't have enough meat for their stories, so they let the horses run freely out of the stables. Probably detective Pommier had been less than generous with the press about the entire affair, but he gave it a spin by saying that the whole thing had been a local exercise in preventing art robberies in his district. Why were the so called robbers dressed as apes, asked a reporter. Oh, somebody suggested an intrusion as animals, because who else could ravage an art gallery than such specimens, but from there it was suggested that only the ape costume could express my own intrusion onto the Parisian art scene. Was it a form of positive recognition or was it simply a media's detestable approach to my talent, the reporters didn't clarify the matter. Armin supposedly claimed that the entire exercise was expected to be totally secret, that is, the press was supposed to be kept away from it. Vania 's role was the most shocking revelation, as the press claimed he had been the recruiter of the so called robbing actors, when he actually knew mostly nothing about them. As for Janice and Percy, their role was presented as researchers into the efficiency of the break-in process based on the acting speed of the robbers-musicians, who had practised the entire event by using musical symbols and terminology written on staff for better understanding. Ah, such crap in the press? I wondered what exactly the population is given to reading on any other days while perusing the journalistic art.

It was clear that none of the mentioned individuals related to the arranged break-in came out from the journalistic scrimmage without some advantages: Katya and her bandits' had been paid for their services, became somewhere between notorious and famous as musicians, and Katya 's beauty was on an incredible photogenic display, overcoming even my pictures in number. Armin certainly became even more well known in the art milieu, reminding the readers that he was preparing a famous auction in which I was the main attraction. Although Janice and Percy appeared in the second row as personalities, there was an air of exoticism in their presentation as foreigners and quasi mad researchers, roles that might have insulted other types, but not my chaperons. Still, Vania remained confused by the fact that his role, although important, had been an invented one, until I found out from Beatriz that Armin and she had also visited La Table Russe one night on the basis of Vania 's indirect recommendation and had made all the necessary arrangements for the fake break-in with the musicians. When I pointed to him this last detail, his face brightened up suddenly and made him breath much easier about the whole affair. He cheerily concluded that Katya wasn't a durak after all.

Armin was convinced that the auction will be a major success. With such confidence, he arranged that the event will take place in two consecutive days, of which the first day was also the one that had been set aside for the surgical attempt to refresh his parents' memories. That meant of course that Janice couldn't be at the auction with me, so Percy took me over with an air of bonhomie. He told me tongue in cheek:

"Onkey, old boy, we are two geniuses with the same kind of ... hm... brushes. Behave like a saint while you paint, sonny, and make for us a mountain of money!" And he gave me a fiver with his clenched fist. That put me into a rub trying to figure out how to be at least as original as I was in Chicago and New-York. Going through my previous discussions with Vania and Beatriz, filtering and assessing the trends of the French market and those of its neighbours, guessing what tastes are valued higher at the moment was not a perfect science, maybe more like an art itself, but the more difficult task was to insert the surprising comical effect that had been so much appreciated in the previous auctions, to the extent that the buyers kind of lost their sense of size, that of the right perspective. Oh, yes, here was creeping an idea in my amalgamated mind, an idea worth considering. But I needed to have more than one trick up my sleeves, especially when considering that there were two days of trudging at the heavily loaded cart of the art. I stopped grinning. Whoever would have seen me in such moments, could have decidedly described me as quite pensive. Sitting alone on my double bed and rubbing my forehead with a slow motion might have been a good way of expressing my ruminating process, but I couldn't tell you anything of its efficiency. I just seemed to have, instead of a black hole in my head, a perfectly white hole. No wonder, my eyes kept fixing the bed sheets.

As for the auction itself, Armin was letting Carlo and Beatriz and another auction expert employee have a free hand or six. However, what actually was important at this expert was not the motor mouth typical for the usual auctioneers, but the prestige that was exuding from each pore of his skin, albeit that skin was perfectly covered by a very elegant suit. He had wanted to meet me before the auction itself in order to understand how to better adjust to the way I was going to present my bombastic artsy merchandise. These were exactly his words, but of course I wasn't offended. Strangely enough, he reminded me of the old auctioneer that made my day in Chicago, when he took his life in his hands to get up on the painting platform in order to hug me. The same class of men, old enough to have great-grand-children, wrinkled as veteran warriors and erect as first class ballet dancers, I thought. Men who needed to convey assured, total confidence when expressing the value of an object, no matter whether the object was the strand of hair from a recently dead celebrity or a Medieval chateau on the Loire valley. This auctioneer had an unusual story of his own and as he wanted to impress me and Percy when we visited him together with Beatriz, I couldn't resist to let you know some of his story too. Monsieur Savat, whose name sounds like the expression "it goes" in French, always used in public his full given names, because otherwise he would have just pronounced them as A. B. C., which sounded kind of silly and surprising, if you heard it before his last name as A.B.C. Savat. It was like saying, '1,2,3, it goes'. Instead, he was sure to present himself always with his rather pompous names of Auguste Bertrand Chartreux Savat, which wasn't much less silly, but there are certainly even worse sound names in any language. Anyway, the story he told us was about how he happened to become a famous auctioneer. It was, he said, a combination of luck and persistence. Luck, because he knew nothing about this profession, but when young, he happened to cut wood for a spinster in his town near the border with Belgium. It so happened that when it was time for her to pay him, she found herself with no money, so she asked if he would accept one of the several small paintings that she had on the walls of her living room. Savat figured that it's better to get something than nothing, especially that, for him, the lady seemed old enough to be on the brink of the ultimate disaster. He was thirteen at the time, already tall and well-built. With the painting wrapped into a piece of newspaper, Savat went directly to the town frame shop, where the old master framer asked him with a humorous air in his voice:

"What's your frame of mind, young man?"

"I cut wood for somebody and this is what I got, so I wonder who got framed, me or she?" and with this, Auguste unwrapped the little frame-less painting. The old man looked curiously at it and spoke with a coarse voice, almost imperceptibly:

"Young man, you are not frame-able, but this little croc would look more valuable with a proper frame around it."

"How valuable?" jumped Auguste with a strident voice.

"Oof, that's hard to say, it all depends..."

"Depends on what?" asked Auguste again, irritated this time, because he liked fast and straight answers.

"Now don't be so quick with me, young man, it all depends on many things. Do you want it framed or not?"

"But I have no money, and I don't even know if it is worth framing it!"

"Chop-chop, my friend, chop-chop."

"That is?"

"That is, you chop wood for me and I frame good

wood for you, my friend. This way we both work and increase the value of this croc."

"Why do you call it a croc? Is something crooked with it?" asked the boy.

"Oh, no, you see, this is a work of art, but the crooked thing is in how it gets valued. You may chop the wood really nice, I may make frames that give a painting a certain distinction, but this stretch of painted canvass gets its better value from a fight."

"From a fi-ight?" Auguste has prolonged the word as much as he could, then continued:

"I smell trouble, Monsieur, don't need no fight, me!"

"Don't you worry, what's your name, son?"

"Auguste!"

"Bertrand," said the old man.

"Chartreux!" added the boy.

"What do you mean, Chartreux?" asked the man.

"What do you mean Bertrand?" was his question.

"My name is Bertrand," said the man, huffing.

"Par bleu! Mine is Auguste Bertrand Chartreux!"

"Well, well, A.B.C.! It hurts my mouth to say more. The fight for the value of the painting shows up in an auction."

"What's that?"

"An auction is like a competition in a market. Say I hold an auction. I make known to people that I have paintings to sell in an auction. I ask them, say 20 francs for this croc of yours. 20 francs, 20 francs, who gives 25, who gives 25, 30, 30, who gives 35, 35 that gentleman in the grey suit, 35 once, 35 twice, now 40, who gives 45,

45, do I have 45, yes, 50, is someone with 50, 55, 55, who gives 55, 55 once, 55 twice, bang, 55. It goes to the lady with the red hat!"

"Oh, I see, you force them to buy it for more."

"No, no, they think it is worth more than I asked initially and they are ready to buy it for more. The one who offers or accepts the higher price gets it."

"Can we make an auction? I think I'd like to get 55 francs for this!"

"We could, but we might not have a good chance to sell it. For this you need other things too. Let's see first if you still want a frame for it."

"How much chopping for a frame?"

"If you chop heartily, one hour."

"Show me the wood, Monsieur Bertrand. I'll start right away!"

By the time Auguste had chopped wood for an hour at the back of Master Bertrand's shop, the painting received its unmistakably elegant, yet unobtrusive, frame. The boy kept looking at it as if it has seen it for the first time, but was still trying to figure out if his wood chopping at the old maid and the one at the master framer made it worth the trouble.

"So now we have a frame too, what else to make it more valuable?" asked the young owner of the painting.

"It would be good to have a known author, more like a famous painter who painted it, and a history."

"When you say history, what do you mean?"

"If you could show who and when painted it, who bought it and for how much, who else might have come in its possession through repeat selling and buying, that would give a new buyer the confidence that it is a valuable piece of art."

"I think it must be valuable, because the lady I work for has several that look kind of the same."

"Then you might consider it a collection from the same painter, and that might make it of greater interest to someone who likes the works of that specific painter."

"But I have only one painting!"

"So go chop more wood for the lady."

By the end of the harsh winter, Auguste became the owner of two more paintings possibly made by the same hand. It occurred to him that going to the local library and asking to get some help in identifying the possible author could put him on the right track, as he didn't want to make direct enquiries with the old lady, thinking that she might have become suspicious of him if questioning her. The library did help only in giving him the idea that the works were in the style of some old Dutch masters, but as there were so many of those painters, the librarian told him that they didn't have enough specialized books on the subject. When he returned to the old maid to ask her if she had anything that needed mending around the house or if she can provide him with other chores, Madame Huygens saw that he was turning his eyes from time to time to get a glance at her remaining two paintings on a wall in the living room.

"Auguste, mon cher, you kept my house warm with your wood cutting, now you could warm up my evenings with reading from whatever you fancy. As my eyes are tired, I have very little use of them with books. I promise that the paintings that you like will become yours with time. I have some papers showing how my father or my grand-father got them long time ago."

So the young wood cutter became a reader twice a week for the old lady, who had a small but good set of books in her possession.

At this point in the story I remember that Percy lost his patience and interrupted the old man:

"Monsieur Savat, what was written in those papers that the old lady mentioned?"

"You want to find out, eh? Can you read Dutch? I'll show them to you!" And with this, the prestigious auctioneer, who was at least a head taller than Percy, made a few moves that seemed to imitate those of a prestidigitator in front of an audience, ready to reveal a dove out of a hat. He then pulled out ostentatiously a plastic wrap from an interior pocket of his coat. He said with a serious and proud tone in his voice:

"I've carried them with me all these fifty-four years, because they are a part of what I have become. Actually, these are just the copies, as the originals went together with the five paintings that became my first auctioned art objects and launched me onto my career."

Percy had no idea how to read Dutch and neither had Beatriz, so I was starting to smile triumphantly, ready to use my tablet for the purpose, when Percy gave a click with his smart phone in front of the first paper, then asked the Google translator to do its job. This time Percy was faster than I. Probably because of my uncalled for and definitely too early triumphant smile.

"What does it say?" asked Beatriz, who otherwise could have guessed most of the important things from the paper by just glancing at the date and at the painter's name, if she could have recognized it from her truly encyclopedic knowledge of European artists.

"It's not a Rembrandt, and neither a Vermeer or a Frans Hals, if that's what you would have hoped, to make the whole discovery much more spicy," came Percy's answer. "But it's over three centuries old, which gives it some weight."

"And the name? Did you get a name there?" was Beatriz's frantic question.

"Yeah, only it doesn't sound Dutch... Not to me, it doesn't, Gabriel?"

"Metsu, isn't it? Gabriel Metsu, as Dutch as it can be. Poor Metsu, he died youngish, less then forty."

"Geez, you got that right. It is Metsu. Painting sold in 1662. The four others, let me see... Same guy, same time, these are the bills of sale with signatures that look like a Metsu at the bottom. Is he famous?"

"One of the best from the golden age of Flemish painting. Monsieur Savat, you had a treasure in your hands! Did you get rich with their auctioning?"

"Ho, ho! Rich, no, but on a path to a life full of rich encounters with art treasures, that I can declare!"

"Apart from those art treasures, have you had any experience with, hm... ape art?" Percy intended to be more flamboyant than usual, probably an effect of him being more relaxed after the previous night romp.

Anyhow, this way I was returned to the scope of the encounter with the auctioneer. What was he going to do about our presumed collaboration?

"To tell you the truth, I watched videos from the New York auction and I was slightly uncomfortable with Mister Onkey's garb there. An important painter like him, a personality of this kind from the animal world shouldn't be dressed in a clownish manner for an auction. I'd like to see him dressed more like me in order to underline a certain amount of gravity to the entire procedure. I am a lover of animal psychology and intend to make everybody aware of the excellence of our protagonist. What do you say about that, Mr. Onkey?"

Flattered as I was, I almost lost my composure at his dithyramb. What should I say? I couldn't say anything, I could only write! A pinhead parrot was superior to me from this point of view. I just smiled and gave him a sailor's salute, as I was still dressed with a mariner's suit.

"Obviously, he agrees with you, Monsieur Savat," said Percy to clarify the matter. "If you want a more detailed confirmation form him, he could write it for you on his tablet. Isn't it, Adam?"

Well, the animal psychology lover needed to be served right. His question could only be answered with another question. I wrote on my tablet:

"Do you know how much of the 1.6% of DNA difference between us is for speech and how much is for artistic painting?"

The big man watched my fingers run over the tablet with concentrated interest, then when he read the result, he started scratching his head with an embarrassed look on his face. I wrote again for him:

"I don't know either, but you can imagine that's a small but terribly important fraction. How do we work together to compensate for the difference?"

"Oh, that's easy!" answered the big man. "You paint fast for me and I'll speak fast for you!

"Yeah, but paint what? This is the question!"

"You could start with a hand holding Yorick's skull."

"Fine, but we are in France, not in Denmark!"

"Then make a croissant and write under it CECI N'EST PAS UN CROISSANT, as you did with the pipe."

"That wouldn't be too original. Maybe if I wrote just CROISSANTEST."

"Meaning what?"

"Meaning a lot: crois, croissant, santé , est, test.

"That's a bit confusing, better go just for one meaning."

"OK, I'll paint a nice cup of coffee, a croissant, and put 1914 beside it."

"And what would that do?" asked Monsieur Savat.

"For those who know their French history, a lot!"

"Touché, I heard that you are much more than an ambulant Encyclopedia. Can you enlighten me?"

"Café du Croisssant, Rue du Croissant, Paris 1914, the assassination of Jean Jaurès, the chief of the Socialist Party and the founder of the newspaper L'Humanité. As French as the croissant."

"Will that be painting or ideology?" asked Savat.

"You started me on the croissant, didn't you? I just gave it the proper meaning in a larger context."

"And what context would that be, Monsieur Onkey?"

"You cannot kill socialism, as it survived over a century from the assassination."

"The Nazis pretended to be socialists too. The Soviets and their acolytes, the same."

"People confuse terminology with ideology and its non-intended application through harsh methods. The Nazis and the Italian Fascists were war expansionists, racists and imperialists using the term socialism in order to attract confused masses to their inhuman ideology. The Soviets were using a wrong model of application for their brand of socialism."

"So, I see that you are a pinkey monkey, Onkey!" said Savat without refraining his disapproval at my short, but pertinent explanations. Beatriz felt necessary to intervene on my behalf:

"Monsieur Savat, you said that you are a student of animal psychology. In that case you should certainly know that we humans have many things to learn from the social organization of some animal societies, bees and termites among others. Our Onkey is just bringing a less partisan view upon ideologies that have been analyzed extensively from one and opposite perspective, to the obvious detriment of a deeper understanding of reality."

"You do have a socialist president here in France, don't you?" intervened Percy, as if to underline my attempt at presenting the continuity of socialist ideology in France.

"If it depended on me, I'd auction him off to the lowest bidder," said Savat.

That put an end to our zigzag conversation on art and ideologies, with firm conviction from the part of Savat about me being an irremediable pinkish lefty and from my part of him as being an extreme schmuck.

Lost Among ...

CHAPTER 17


Janice was too involved with the details of the double operation on the older Offers to be bothered with my "textiles", so Beatriz took me to a children 's fashion shop and bought me two suits and two shirts, in case I ruined one set, as most children probably do. We agreed that Savat might have a point with me getting properly attired for the performance–auction event, in spite of the fact that the French are less conformists than other societies in many walks of life. But Beatriz being who she was, not a milligram less practical, made sure that I also tried and was endowed with two overalls of the ubiquitous denim kind, which made me feel freer and much more "pinkish" in Savat 's interpretation. Still, the question remained on my mind, how should I better stun my buying fat cats audience with my artistic products. Approaching the matter from an ideological point of view might backfire and diminish the value of my not yet conceived paintings. There was no question that in my case, pricing depended in good measure by the amount of mass resonance created through the shocking message of the paintings, and the more pertinent to the locals, the better. Although paintings by non-French painters were among the highest valued in the world,

Lost Among ...

Cezanne 's and Gauguin 's works surpassed every others in recent auctions, reaching stratospheric prices in the hundreds of millions of dollars. Still, I was not a classical painter, not even a human one. My scribblings under the blotches of paint might have been recognized as a peculiar capacity to reason beyond what would be termed normal, overwhelming even the most sceptics. Well, it 's true, I did have at least a major purpose in skimming the fat cats off their mounds of cash. I had to play hard for my fellow innocent apes tucked somewhere in the heart of the African jungle.

Armin 's ruse with the gallery break-in worked its magic over the hungry-for-selling-excitement press. My auction had been so well advertised because of it that I was guaranteed full house without spending any press money. Dressed to the nines by the careful and loving Beatriz, who was behaving with me as I were her not quite fully grown up son, chaperoned by her and by Percy, I appeared ready to fabricate my magic with the brushes and paints awaiting on the stage of the famous Salle Pleyel, which is the main theatre of the Paris philharmonic orchestra. It looks like Armin was ready to beat any record sales from other auction houses by renting the fabulous Pleyel, with its almost two thousand seats. It was some kind of irony here. I, a voiceless or mute ape was going to perform my chromatic ballet with paints on canvass in one of the most musically renowned theatres.

It didn't matter that I already had a history of good

behaviour in other public places. A Kevlar chain attached to my left wrist had to be secured to the stage before the arrival of the curious and well to do art investors. Savat was there, animated both by my animal presence and by the gargantuan opportunity at which he was about to participate. As far as he could say, nobody has ever sold art in such a huge place as Salle Pleyel, if within art one wouldn't include the pop singers of recent times. To warm himself up for the occasion, Savat was rubbing his hands and was vocalizing like an opera primadona. Percy, who added a papillon, that is a bow tie, to his unusually formal dress, was holding both my hands while admiring my entire appearance and performing small whistles out of his mouth. From time to time, Beatriz, in a vaporous yellow and red silk gown and coiffed so that her large forehead was making an esthetic impression, would pass close by and caress me on the head. On one of these occasions, Percy anticipated her move and caught us in a shot with his smart phone. Fortunately for all of us, I was wearing the pants, as Beatriz 's repeated strokes caused me to have an erection. She was no mamma for me, no, she wasn't.

When the renovated huge amphitheatre got filled, a few workers moved the folding paravans that were hiding us from the audience, from the front of the stage to the back. Big as it was, the place wasn't oppressive in any way, embracing the stage with a number of seat rows that came close and seemed almost as if everybody was seating on a sofa around a coffee table. Beatriz stepped toward one of the microphones standing at the sides and introduced herself as the Offer art trade house representative and Dr. Percy Letabou as one of the closest persons to the performer of the day. That was a qualifier that made me show to the audience my entire set of teeth. My wonderful smile appeared large and promising on an enormous screen that hanged high somewhere at the back of the stage. As Percy 's name sounded so familiar for them, they applauded with such aplomb that he had to acknowledge their enthusiasm with several bows. Then Beatriz introduced Monsieur Savat as the auctioneer of the evening. He stepped in the middle front of the stage and moved his arms as if trying to embrace the entire room. Since many art customers knew him from his long years of trading with his booming, yet plastic voice against the multitude of art objects in several auction houses, they reacted rather placidly at his appearance. Of course, he knew how to change an audience 's mood, so, in spite of his personal reluctance toward my previous ideological imposition in front of him, he acted as if we were at least jungle brothers, if not more: he brought me to the front as much as the chain allowed and hanked me up, pirouetting me over his head before letting me down in front of his huge body. I might have looked insignificant in comparison with him, but the spectators didn't care. They have come for me, not for him. Although I did nothing yet, their prolonged ovation was a clear sign that they knew of my previous successful performances from the news. Ah, the news! They can paint an aureola around any villain, no matter how terrible that was. I bowed politely and applauded shortly with them, in order not to put the lie to the saying 'monkey see, monkey do'. Monsieur Savat grabbed the mic on the other side of the stage from where Beatriz had been talking and started a fervent eulogy to my address, using several times the same adjectives, adverbs and inflated words to describe my art work, like 'freshness', 'fresh', 'indubitably', 'profound', 'profoundness', 'deep', 'depth' and 'playful', 'jocular', 'meaningful' and 'double entendre'. Maybe he felt that he went too far with all this. He interrupted himself at one point, turned to me and said,

"Let's give the rascal the last word. Ah, no, the brush!"

That meant a bit too much for me, but hey, we were there for the collaborative fleecing of the snobs, weren't we? So I grabbed a crayon and started to draw the profile of a young woman in a whitish gown with an umbrella, took a brush and put enough light green paint on the canvass to give a springy air to the whole, and wrote in red at the bottom of the canvass, 'Eternel'. There were enough connoisseurs in the theatre to understand my reference to the word that I did not write. The applause came in waves, as the number of the experts was followed by the ones that got later from others the two key words to edify for them my intention, 'Spring' and 'Manet'. The effort seemed appreciated quite well, and even I was a bit surprised by the resemblance of my painting with one of the most highly priced works of the French painter. As I pushed the easel toward Savat, he understood that it was his turn. Without any modesty, he explained to the public that Edouard Manet 's 'Spring' has been sold recently for over sixty-five million dollars. He said that I am neither French, nor Manet, but he knows me well enough to say that he cannot start the auction lower than 6.5 million, which is one tenth of the value given to Manet 's work. He said that the word 'Eternel' written on the piece makes it an exceedingly rare object. Then he also mentioned the last price for which one of my works in New York was paid for: 5.9 million dollars.

"Who was going for 6.5 ? Yes, 6.6 ? 6.7? 6.7 one, twice, sold for 6.7 million to the representative holding the lucky number 213. I bet this furry genius will prepare some even more valuable surprises immediately."

He returned to face me and made a gesture that maybe not everybody noticed and even less understood, but for me it was like a slap over my head, if not more. He had jolted his arm as if having a horsewhip in his hand. Only I pretended not to see what he did, went to the back of the stage and took two blank canvasses, returned to my easel and put both of the canvasses on it, but of course, it was holding only one. The other canvass slid off it and it would have fallen to the ground of the stage if I didn't catch it with a fast swiping grab. I continued my arm move toward Savat and let the canvass fly into his shoulder. He was also able to save its fall with two or three attempts at catching it. Although the whole scene seemed spontaneous, the multitude of cynics in the theatre could have considered the entire manoeuvre a rehearsed act, necessary to variate the presentation and modify the rhythm of the performance. At that point, Percy stepped in from his retired position on the stage and bent slightly toward my right ear to tell me that I was much smarter than Savat, so I could avoid his provocations.

I gave Percy a fist bump approvingly, looking into his eyes with a smile, which he took as a clear sign that I was in control of myself. Of course I was. If I wanted, I could have made the canvass fly right in his boastful head. But it wasn't the moment to hurt him, and not that way. So I gave the audience a nice bow, then I concentrated on making my second piece. With Manet on my mind, I sketched a group of soldiers shooting into a mass of people over a barricade between two buildings. I kept everything black and brown, except for the soldiers' hats and some splotches of red flowing from the barricade. For the title I decided that a more precise reference was in order, since the French had so many barricades on their streets at different times. So I wrote at the bottom, 'Printemps 1871'. It could have been a definite challenge for some in the audience, if they did not learn their history, but their grave reaction said otherwise. Many stood up to applaud, somehow forcing others, more reluctant to do so, to follow them. After all, it was a matter of ideological reaction to a reactionary bloodbath toward the Paris people 's uprising, historically known as the 'Paris Commune'. I was pleased with myself, although I wondered about the exact reasons why they were applauding: a recognition of Manet 's favourable attitude toward the uprising in depicting the awful massacre of its crushing, an acceptance of the clever way in which I continued in one swoop both the theme of spring and the reference to the works of Manet, or the placing of themselves on one or the other side of the barricade, as sympathizers of the vanquished or of the vanquishers. Savat needed to cough a few times before he could get the proper tone in his voice for starting the second part of the auction.

"Your ape... ape... applause made me understand that indeed, you know how cleverly has Monsieur Onkey combined his talent for painting with his encyclopedic knowledge of both French history and French art. Obviously, he is also a... a... straight shooter. He brought us another Manet–like work to remind us of our turbulent and bloody history. As mm... mm... Manet made history with his paintings, it surely appears that mm... mm... ah... hmm... mister, mon... caugh... grrr... Monsieur Onkey makes ape... appreciated art history with his wro... renditions. Let's not be too pushy this time, who gives 5 mills for this shot, 5.1 yes? 5.2, what, 5.3, let's go 5.5, I see many hands, should we jump at 6 million, 6.2, 6.4, 6.6, Oh My God! I see double or what, 6.8. 7, 7.2, sss...leven, oh, oint, heaven, four... hea... ven.."

At this point, both Beatriz and Percy, who followed attentively the unmistakable unfolding of Savat 's stroke rambling, rushed toward him just in time to support his body from falling. Several custodians of the theatre intervened too and were able to seat him on an available chair. It was Beatriz who had the calm to call immediately an ambulance with her smart phone. She then asked everybody to wait quietly for the paramedics' intervention, promising that the event will continue shortly one way or another. Since someone in a tech room behind the last rows was probably manipulating the web cams taking the videos and placing them on the huge screen, the audience had been able to see in close–up many details of my previous working on the canvass. The screen was now inundated with several rectangles showing the stage protagonists and diverse reactions from the audience.

I decided to start another piece in the meantime, this way the spectators could keep themselves busy by following my skills. After all, they came to see me perform, so I had to make the show go on. What if I tried to stay on to the intertwining line of French history and art? Didn't I show my intention when Savat suggested to me the drawing of a croissant, an ubiquitous French pastry for all French breakfasts? But a word puzzle for an art auction wouldn't do, so I went on drawing the front of a café with some tables outside, a sign with the name of the establishment clearly visible and a seated man reading a newspaper while another man, standing, shoots him from behind. The tonality of the painting was predominantly light brown with lighter nuances for the seated man and darker for the shooter. The large windows of the café are somehow reflecting a few passers-by. I made the newspaper have its name partially visible, showing only L'HUMA. I worked directly with a brush for the background, but for the two men I first sketched their positions in pencil, then I added the paint. There was no need for me to rush this while we were waiting for the arrival of the paramedics. Even after they came, I kept myself busy with repeated touches to the basically finished work. After Savat 's removal, I turned to the audience, raised the brush high in the air and then applied the date in large, sanguine red digits at the bottom:1914. Beatriz stepped to the front of the stage again, this time giving a little speech that surprised even me:

"It is a great sign of appreciation that our artist is showing with this work, not to another artist, but to the one that has just left this podium, the respected auctioneer A.B.C. Savat who just had a stroke. Monsieur Savat has suggested in a previous encounter that Monsieur Onkey present to you a croissant in the style of Magritte 's painting titled "Ceci n'est pas une pipe". Our artist has gone much deeper into French history with this obvious reference to the inhuman ideological and physical violence by depicting the shooting of the famous Socialist founder of the newspaper L'Humanité by a man properly named for the action, Villain. It happened in the summer of 1914, just three days before France declared war. Permit me to mention that our artist has given a free interpretation to the scene, as the victim was seated inside of the café, and the assassin fired from the outside. However, as far as I know, such a depiction does not exist in the annals of French art and this makes the work a totally original piece. Most of his previous works were attempts to draw to your attention his knowledge and understanding of the great artists, in several variants of their outputs. This time here is something massively new. Adam Onkey, our cousin from the ape world that we also inhabit, has made history again in the world of human art with this last painting. His choice of nuances for the victim and perpetrator expresses his philosophical position of Good and Evil as light and dark, and his bloody red title is a reference to his disapproval of violence. Let's forget for the moment his previously painted work. I will change for this historic painting the rules of the auction. I ask you, what is your offer?"

The amphitheatre remained totally silent for a long and crucial moment. It was as if the mechanisms of reason in everybody 's mind needed to rewind in order to function within these new parameters. Here stood a gorgeous goddess well known in the rarefied world of high Parisian art trade opening for them a new door to a conceptually different moment in the history of art. The air became exceedingly heavy, pushing over everybody's heads and shoulders with unusual pressure. A hand went up, then a young man stood and shouted:

"My offer is ten euros!" Heads turned toward him.

"One hundred!" shouted another person. The crowd tried to catch a glimpse of the second offerer.

"Ten million euros," said clearly a woman's voice. It was almost immediately followed by another feminine voice, in a stentorian declaration:

"Twelve million euros!" The web cams of the theatre started searching through the audience, then focused on the person holding up her auction number. Her firm face appeared on the large screen in full detail. Well over fifty, with a strong air given by her pronounced wrinkles around the well cut, generous mouth, she exuded a particular dose of certainty, especially due to her large brown eyes. The slight opening of her dress under the chin allowed seeing a simple necklace of large pearls. The fist offerer stood up again and agitated his auction card up in the air, saying with an unconcealed ironical and joking tone:

"I raise my offer to fifteen euros!" A murmur of disapproval came out from several rows. Auctions weren't supposed to be places of jocular entertainment. Such discrepant and low biddings were practically banned. But it was not necessary to intervene otherwise than by a proper bidding. That came immediately:

"Fifteen million euros!" It was the same voice and face that offered twelve million. The spectators were wondering what was going on. She could have had her previous offer accepted if no one went higher. But no, she wanted to make something clear. My poor beastly work, at least in her view and that of a previous bidder, was indeed making history again. I was at a loss for words anyhow. A hot wave of emotion went up my throat.

CHAPTER 18

What Beatriz was able to do with the rest of the auction might become legendary. Of course, I say without false pride that I had a huge role with it too, but I must emphasize that the way she was able to goad the potential buyers for each of my other paintings seemed the outstanding mastery of mass manipulation. She stood there like a silent, overbearing oracle that only moved a few fingers in the air when necessary, allowing the bidders to know how much patience she had with a certain bid. With the left hand she just pointed higher and higher. Her exquisite sense found always the right moment when to clinch the bid. Apart from the employees routinely used for keeping track of the bids and of the bidders, Percy used his smart phone to make sure he knew exactly what was going on, adding the numbers and sending emailed notes to Carlo about the totals.

As not to stretch the things more than necessary, in view that the auction needed to be continued the next day, we stopped at only thirteen works. When I say we, I mean both Beatriz and I, with just an eye blink, understood each other. Actually, there were two eye blinks, mine first, hers next. The night brought in one hundred forty-eight million euros, an average of over eleven million per painting. I knew that my star was going to become even brighter overnight. The newspapers, the television networks and the internet were going to be full of my performance. The next day might be even more lucrative.

Beatriz took another forty minutes after the end of my show to check with exceptional attention each and every successful bidder's account, calculate the usual commission on top of the bids, make sure that nothing was improper with the immediate bank transfers from the buyers. She signed the acquisition certificates for each new owner, asked me to scribble my name on them too and on all the paintings, checked that each work had also attached a label with the Offer Trade House emblem and her signature, and gave dispositions to her helpers for the secure moving of the works to the owners' intended locations. To make my signature a bit more personal, I drew after my name a plus sign, the small letter m, a fraction line under them and a key under the line. As busy as she was, Beatriz noticed the play on my name and gave me, smiling, a friendly fist bump onto my left shoulder. I smiled back and delicately pulled her hand toward my lips to deposit a smooch. As cool as she had been on the stage just minutes ago, she couldn't retain a tear drop coming down on her face. Seeing that, I took her hand again, brought it closer and let her caress my face. It was good that Percy, with his back at us, kept himself busy with his smart phone, pestering the staff from the hospital where Savat had been taken and trying to find out if we could visit there right away. I am sure that seeing us, emotional as he is, Percy would have started crying, full of empathy at our sentimental effusion. Still, I was quite surprised that a practical woman like Beatriz was capable of such an intense feeling toward me. Could I have misinterpreted her tear? Was she just physically and mentally exhausted after her marathon intervention at taking care of the Offer house affairs? Maybe she was critical in her own interior about the work that she was doing, that of promoting the works of an ape painter that presumably was mocking the history of the country that welcomed her. How can you make the right supposition about what's on the mind of somebody, if that somebody is, to a certain degree, like a black box? Was she missing something in her life or she had just too much of it? When we had been resting on the steps of the staircase from the Sacrè–Coeur basilica she did open up to me quite directly. Telling me that Carlo had been her lover for a while was an act of courage, if one considered that she was talking to an ape that she had just recently met. Did she maybe have such wide liberal views that she could include me in her circle of trustworthy attenders of her confessions, or was there nobody else in such a circle?

Was I at the moment the only conductor through which she could unload her overcharged intellect, her overcharged Leyden jar, her dammed, ready to overflow accumulation of sentimental frustrations? There is no way for anybody to understand people unless there is a correspondence between their actions and their thoughts expressed in clearly defined sentences. She might like me, she might love me, although I wonder if she knows enough about my own motives for doing what I am doing.

Lost Among ...

And what, pray, was I doing? What were my actual motives for interfering with the proper flow of the capital from the hyper-enriched captains of a bubble economy toward the pale conceivers of the new directions in the esoteric world of art? I, a classless individual, not even a member of the same species as the utterly gorgeous that became my hosts, was syphoning oodles of money through my skilled artsy funnel to build an animal saving fund for those that should be considered my brethren, but still, decisively, aren't. This last thought put me into a quandary with respect to my position in the world. Didn't I have some kind of elitist vapours rising up into my head? Apart from Oldey, my cage comrade, whom among my brethren did I truly know? Directly, nobody. Indirectly, about all the apes that were planted into my memory chip. Which wasn't that much. Of course, I knew that I was different from them by way of the chip, but maybe by other ways too. Oh, I was quite different from my gorgeous fellows too, in spite of my smarts. After all, I was a beast, an ape, an unusual wandering furry jungle animal, but a beast nonetheless. Oh, it's true, my gorgeous companions here were beasts too, only a slightly different kind of beasts. Fur they had little, and brains, hm... Okay, they had more brains than I had, but their memory... just rotten. If they put too much into their brains, they'd slow down like a merry-go round at the end of its turns. Still, they developed their learning through verbal and written communication to compensate for the short span of their memory, and that made a huge difference. Increasing their power through more and more sophisticated tools, they remodelled parts of nature into nests of other calibre, spread over plains and forests and mountains and even water. In this partial separation from the mother that created them, they became sick with grandeur and started to lose sight of the proper size of things. 'More' and 'not enough' became almost identical concepts that turned some of these accumulators into megalomaniacs. Was I following their example by trying to increase the animal saving fund? Was I rising myself into a stratosphere of financial might just because I was a celebrity whose output was considered so many times pricier than gold? Mingling among all these berserk searchers of the ultimate investments could bring me to borrow, through some kind of social osmosis, their depraved hunger for what the old ones used to call the eye of the devil. It was a moral conundrum for me. I badly needed the money to put it to good use, yet the way it kept accumulating through my skills seemed too facile, or at least kind of impertinent. But then, it wasn't my game that I was playing, it was their game and I was just a player, surrounded by beastly scruples that were screwing my mind.

"We can go now," said Beatriz after a while, "let us see Monsieur Savat and find out how is he coping in his new state of mind. He might feel good if we tell him that his purse is assured and set aside for him."

"He is at the International Clinic of parc Monceau. Do you know how to get there?" asked Percy.

"It's quite close, I know the way. I'm better than a gps for Paris, trust me, " said Beatriz with total assurance in her voice. One of the few perks of her job was to have a reserved parking spot in the underground of the great theatre. She seemed at home in the halls and lifts of the place, asking us to follow her while showing us the way to her old, lanky Citroen. Outside, the traffic was relentless, and the grand boulevards were trying to show their grandeur through the exhibition of the multicoloured lights of the metropolis.

Savat was in better shape than when he left us on a stretcher, smiling crookedly with his big, slightly livid mouth. His double chin, together with the deeper wrinkles on his face were showing more than before that he was getting really old. He seemed almost comfortable in the hospital bed, with an iv jabbed in one of his forearms. Beatriz made him feel at ease when she told him:

"You lucky fighter, you did quite well showing them who was in charge there. Don't get too excited, but I'll tell you that you started them marvellously. We scraped them of a good chunk. Don't worry about anything, you are secure with your chunk of a chunk. I'm not telling you how much because you'd get too excited."

When he saw me, he brought up a bony finger and shook it toward me, saying half jokingly:

"You son of a gun, teaching us history, eh?"

Percy felt like saying something too, and it was about me again:

"He is the ultimate teacher, nobody dares to take his eyes away from him, so he gets total attention."

"Oh, he is a Goya, a Frans Hals and a Miro, all together. I'd want to have his grasp," said Savat with a tired voice.

"We'll see you again tomorrow and make whatever other arrangements are necessary. Rest well and get strong again," said Beatriz, and with this we left him.

It was midnight when we got back to the Offer mansion, where everybody was resting after a dramatic double brain surgery on Armin's parents. Everybody except the emergency nurse, who for this first shift was Sybil, the more senior among them. We found out the next morning that she reported to the doctors about a quiet, event-less night. Still, Armin, usually the epitome of coolness, looked tired, haggard, almost wasted. Janice and Seby visited their patients in the morning and declared themselves cautiously reserved with the prognostic, saying that it was a matter of healing time, hopeful connections without rejection at neuronal level and constant observation. Paulette had taken over from Sybil, then it would be Jeanette 's turn on the shift. The other nurses were let go for the day. The atmosphere in the mansion didn't actually change, but it seemed to hang heavier than before. And how could it have been otherwise, with such a delicate balance between recovery and possible slide into the total nothingness?
A nothingness that may come gradually or it may be abrupt, but still be a displacement of knowledge or an emptying of a previous dweller of a social network. Papa Offer and Mama Offer didn't have their own Facebook pages. Whatever their lives meant for others and especially for their unique son, whatever their

accomplishments have changed on the Earth that they might be leaving through that slide in nothingness, it would be without taking anything with them. If the ancients were trying to imagine that the soul separates itself from the body at death and carries itself high into another realm, they got it wrong. The soul is not the esoteric concept of the religions. The soul is what knowledge and acts and feelings a human spreads around him or her and leaves behind with those who survive him or her. And wait, not only a human. If I were to disappear right now, I would leave my own legacy, my own soul in the dozens of paintings that I created, in the animal saving fund that got amassed through my and others' efforts, and in the amazement of the people that learned one way or another about me and about my climb out of the anonymity of a cage and into the human jungle.

So, in a way I was lost among these gorgeous, but at least I wasn't a lost soul. At least not yet.


- THE END -

Laurian Taler

Lost Among ...

L OST
A MONG
U TTERLY
G ORGEOUS
H UMANS

BY LAURIAN TALER

© GONG PUBLISHING, 2015

www.gongnog.com

ISBN 978-0-9919867-7-4

www.ingramcontent.com/pod-product-compliance
Lightning Source LLC
Chambersburg PA
CBHW070217030726
47505CB00006B/1711